THE MATCHMAKING GHOST

"Don't swear," Lady Winifred said. "And I do wish you'd rid yourself of that exceedingly irritating and cocky way of speaking."

Lord Galveston stiffened, became very nearly as reserved as Lady Winifred, his voice quite as icy as she could sound. "Perhaps, my lady, *you* might loosen up a trifle and discover the delights in easy converse between a man and a woman."

"Not when such conversation leads to . . ." She cut off her sentence with a gasp. "There! You very nearly led me into making an improper comment myself. Now, do let me by."

As it crossed Lord Galveston's mind to wonder why he was acting in such a strange manner, he felt icy fingers walking up and down his spine. And, however strange it might be, it seemed he couldn't stop himself. "You'll have to pay a toll," he said, teasing her.

She eyed him. "Lord Galveston, have you been imbibing beyond your limit?"

"To be frank, not nearly enough. But where were we? Ah—" His eyes gleamed with a wicked twinkle. "The toll. A kiss I think," he mused, eyeing her lovely oval face. "Just a simple little kiss."

"You, my lord, are behaving in a totally objectionable fashion. Kiss you, indeed!"

Galveston blinked and shook his head slightly. "No, no," he said. "You misunderstood . . ." Another frisson ran up his spine and he finished his sentence. "I mean to kiss you . . ."

Books by Jeanne Savery

THE WIDOW AND THE RAKE

A REFORMED RAKE

A CHRISTMAS TREASURE

A LADY'S DECEPTION

CUPID'S CHALLENGE

LADY STEPHANIE

A TIMELESS LOVE

A LADY'S LESSON

LORD GALVESTON AND THE GHOST

Published by Zebra Books

Lord Galveston and the Ghost

Jeanne Savery

Zebra Books
Kensington Publishing Corp.
http://www.zebrabooks.com

ZEBRA BOOKS are published by

Kensington Publishing Corp.
850 Third Avenue
New York, NY 10022

First Printing: March, 1998
10 9 8 7 6 5 4 3 2 1

Printed in the United States of America

Prologue

Lady Gwenfrewi straightened her ghostly garments and nodded her nearly transparent chin. The time had come. Dear Freddy *must* be made to overcome her aversion to men—to say nothing of her feud with her father!

Oh, yes. Definitely. It was time and more than time.

Lady Gwenfrewi had, for centuries, had a hand in encouraging Alistaire lovers, setting like to like, and deftly separating those who should *not* wed. After careful thought, she'd concluded the moment was ripe for meddling in Lady Winifred's affairs.

Since her namesake's faults of character were much like her own had been when she'd walked the earth alive, Gwenfrewi had a certain fondness and a great deal of understanding of the stubborn child Lady Winifred had once been. Indeed, that stubbornness had led, in part, to the current situation. If only dear Winifred had not insisted on entering the storeroom from which Gwenfrewi had done her best to scare the nine-year-old away! But her very sensitive young ladyship *had* entered and at that particularly tender age had seen that from which she should have been protected.

The unfortunate result was that what she'd witnessed had set her mind firmly against the male of the species, an opinion Lady Winifred had repeated often in the years which followed. Gwenfrewi had listened to many conversations between the motherless Lady Winifred and her orphaned cousin, her father's ward, Miss Clare Tillingford. Conversations in which Freddy described the kitchen maid, her plump legs revealed to all the world, and the second footman's bare rump above his pushed-down trousers. Freddy, bless her, imitated the maid's groans and moans and the footman's grunts and snorts with uncanny accuracy.

Freddy had never understood why the maid hadn't screamed for help. Perhaps, she'd suggested after much cogitation, the footman knew something to the maid's disadvantage? But, whatever the case, if that was the way men treated women, then she was far too sensible to ever place herself where she, too, must suffer such attentions.

As they grew older, Clare scoffed at her cousin's deductions, saying it *must* be nonsense since a great number of women went happily to their weddings and appeared exceedingly content with their situations afterward.

Winifred, of course, retorted with the simple truth that many did *not* and *weren't*.

Setting aside memories, Gwenfrewi stretched and again straightened her veils. *Definitely* the time had come to settle Lady Winifred's future. Not only was the proper man, at long last, a guest in the castle, but Freddy's father's new wife as well. Or rather, the lady who would become his wife.

Unfortunately, Winifred's father was still more stubborn than Freddy. Lord Wickingham had sworn an oath to the effect he'd not rewed until he'd fulfilled the promise made his first wife on her deathbed. On that occasion he'd vowed to settle Freddy in a marriage as happy as theirs had been, but, some years back, Wickingham had lost all hope of obeying the happy-ever-after part. Now, he'd be content if only he could settle his daughter's affairs in any way at all.

However that might be, Lady Gwenfrewi had her own plans for Freddy. Lady Winifred *would* be happy. *In spite of herself,* she'd be happy! If she weren't, swore Gwenfrewi, she'd retire from her self-imposed avocation and fade away for all eternity!

Gwenfrewi floated along the castle corridor, a barely visible presence. She was *not* wrong. The love chosen for her latest Alistaire protegé would teach her ladyship what had *truly* happened in that storage room between maid and man, and dear Freddy would enjoy it very much indeed! For why else, Gwenfrewi thought complacently, had Lord Galveston become a much-practiced rake if not to gain the necessary skill to bemuse a reluctant bride into ecstasy!

Oh yes! Lady Winifred and Lord Galveston. It was perfect. And today they'd begin! Gwenfrewi twirled her substance into a spiral and sprang down the hall for simple joy because, if she'd not lost her talent for foresight, Winifred would approach this very place in just minutes. And, soon after, Marcus Galveston himself, the future Earl of Lymington, would appear around the very same corner on his way to the great hall to meet the subject of his current rakish interest, who would be returning from an early morning ride.

At least, grinned Gwenfrewi, the poor deluded man *thought* Lady Pelling was the reason he'd come to the castle!

That was nonsense, of course. Before Winifred or Marcus left this hallway Gwenfrewi would have assured herself that both experienced her ghostly presence. And that was all that was required to set two souls into harmony . . . or at least, thought Gwenfrewi, a trifle uncertain about *this* particular pair, in the *past* that was what always happened.

A sound behind her caused the ghost to spin on one toe. Or what would have been a toe if she weren't still partially in a spiral form.

Ah. Only Miss Tillingford. But perhaps that was for the best. Clare would make an excellent ally, if ally were needed, to convince dear Freddy where her best interests lay! Still elated, Lady Gwenfrewi played with her essence, thinning it, thickening it, forming it into this shape and that, a ghostly substitute for humming . . .

"Shh, you'll frighten her."

Gwenfrewi, hearing Miss Tillingford's voice, faded to very

nearly nothing. Over her disappearing shoulder, she glanced back up the hall. Her substance solidifying slightly, Gwenfrewi frowned. Now *here* was a bumble broth! She'd not divined that another *man* would arrive at just this moment, and certainly not poor Lord Grenville Somerwell! In actual fact, she'd been so interested in dear Freddy's situation she'd forgotten to check on anything else.

Ah well, there was nothing to be done about Somerwell now the poor fellow had seen her. Miss Tillingford, who had watched the castle ghosts from an early age, was an old acquaintance, of course. She'd check any interference on Grenville's part in the ghostly business about to occur.

That decided, Gwenfrewi put the pair from her mind, concentrating her essence carefully. She must be so completely *there* Lady Winifred could not, this time, deny her ghostly existence. And what a shock that would be to dear Freddy, thought Gwenfrewi, sadly.

She did so hate making anyone the least bit uncomfortable, but, because it was for Winifred's own good, it must be done. The young woman could not be allowed to continue in her present misconceptions. If it weren't for her father wishing to remarry, then perhaps one might delay the sad duty a bit longer, but he *did*—although he didn't yet know it. Besides, Lord Galveston was here now and, later, who knew where he might be . . .

Ah ha! thought Gwenfrewi, as she heard Lady Winifred's steps tripping along the side hall.

She put Lord Wickingham and his future wife from her mind and also Miss Tillingford and Lord Grenville. She'd work to do! Just as Lady Winifred came around the corner, and in less than a heartbeat's length of time, Gwenfrewi became *much* brighter and *far* more solid.

Lady Winifred *couldn't* avoid noticing. At the sight of Lady Gwenfrewi, Winifred abruptly halted, her eyes starting from her head. Under black hair coiled in an old-fashioned and rigid crown of braids, her normally pale face turned a chalky white.

"No!"

Actually, that wasn't what Lady Winifred said. One had to guess at the word because it had been no more than a squawked gargle of sound. Lady Winifred warded off the ghost with both hands.

Poor Freddy, thought Lady Gwenfrewi. *What a painful noise! And* just *as I feared. Oh dear, oh dear. You poor child!* she moaned softly. *If those distended eyes are any indication, you are very near a state of shock, are you not? Still, it must be done. One must keep in mind it's for your own good . . .*

"No, I say." This time Lady Winifred muttered her words, closing her eyes and squeezing them tight. "I don't see you. I refuse to see you!"

Both women, the one alive and the other long dead, moved. Lady Winifred backed a step; the ghost followed since she must be very close when the instant for action arrived.

"I've spent years avoiding you," wailed Lady Winifred. "I've sworn you don't exist. You *don't* exist. Do you hear me? *You don't exist!*" She peered through one partly opened eye. "I tell you I won't have it! *There are no such things as ghosts!*"

The ghost floated closer, fading as she heard the well-timed approach of her other quarry.

At that precise moment Lady Winifred took still another step back. Her last. She could go no farther because, behind her, strong hands steadied her shoulders. Shocked all over again by the unexpected touch, she twisted her head and looked up. Meeting the sardonic gaze turned down on her she blushed, her white skin turning a painful red.

Gwenfrewi, at the moment Winifred's gaze met Lord Galveston's, allowed the last of her substance to dissolve into nothingness. She engulfed the pair. The sensation of intense cold, the ghost knew, would remind dear Winifred that, once again, the castle's most famous ghost had fulfilled her traditional role of pairing off another Alistaire with her own true love.

Lord Galveston, too, would learn what the cold meant . . . although not until later. *Much* later if Lady Gwenfrewi had anything to say about it.

Perhaps it would be best if he learned nothing until after the two were wed . . . ?

One

So! The ghostly Gwenfrewi had once again achieved her traditional, if mischievous, role of choosing lovers—whether the couple would or no!

Lady Winifred, horrified at the notion she might be forced to endure a notorious rake's attentions, took the only road open to her. Her eyes rolled up and she sank gracefully to the floor in a dead faint. But even unconscious, her classically perfect features and lovely figure were incapable of presenting themselves in anything but the most advantageous of fashions.

Perhaps it wasn't to be wondered at that Lord Galveston, shuddering in a chill draught which seemed to come from nowhere, stared down at her and felt nothing more than mild surprise that *this* particular lady would try such a trick. One eyebrow slightly lifted, he waited, anticipating the usual dramatic moans or, alternately, mournful sighs. After all, such behavior was common in his colorful past and, in his experience, always the same.

But was it? *This* woman didn't make a sound. She didn't move, didn't even flicker so much as an eyelid to discover why he hadn't reacted in typical male fashion. Faintly perplexed, Galveston knelt on one knee, but even though slightly bewildered by her behavior, he was as yet unperturbed by either her beauty or her condition.

"Well done, Lady Winifred," his lordship said, with mocking approval. "I don't believe I've ever witnessed a better swoon."

Lady Winifred still didn't shift so much as a finger and Galveston's mockery faded. He frowned slightly. When, after a rather long silence, she still hadn't so much as twitched her lashes, he lifted her hand, shifted his fingers to her wrist, and searched for a pulse. Once he ascertained there was one, he chafed it.

"I suppose we'd better help," said Miss Tillingford softly. She looked up and smiled at Grenville Somerwell. "You saw what happened, did you not?"

His head slightly turned to the side, Somerwell eyed the young woman's lightly freckled face. "I don't know," he said, wary and wishing to be certain. "What did *you* see?"

"Lady Gwenfrewi, of course," responded Clare cheerfully. "She's the best of the castle ghosts. Some of them rather frighten me although I know they cannot truly harm anyone, but Lady Gwenfrewi is a different kettle of fish, don't you agree?"

"Never heard of her."

Which was true. Somerwell did his best to ignore the existence of ghosts and wished such phantasmagoria would be equally polite and leave him in peace. Instead, they seemed to delight in plaguing him at every turn. They'd been particularly bothersome here at Castle Alistaire and he'd had to admit it was his own fault. He should have known a place which had endured so long as this castle had would be infested with the dratted things. He should never have accepted Lord Wickingham's invitation.

If he hadn't desperately needed an excuse to refuse his overbearing but rich aunt, Lady Baggins-Keyton, when she demanded his presence in Bath, he'd not have been pushed into grabbing the only means available to say her nay and far more aware of the dangers!

"*Should* I have heard of her?" he asked when Miss Tillingford gave him another of her pert looks.

"Most know, but if you have not heard, then I'll tell you her history later," promised Miss Tillingford, a soft laugh in her voice and her eyes twinkling merrily.

The sound of voices brought them to the attention of Lord Galveston who called, "Miss Tillingford, your friend appears to have swooned. She could use a woman's help, I think."

"Yes, my lord," responded Miss Tillingford promptly. "At once." She hurried forward. "Can you lift her? Perhaps if Lord Somerwell were to help?" Miss Tillingford shared a conspiratorial smile between the men. Lady Winifred was slim, but she was overly tall, carrying the solid muscle of an active woman and no light weight!

"I will carry her if it isn't far," said Galveston, eying Somerwell's willowy build a trifle disparagingly.

"Then, if you will follow me, my lord, her rooms aren't far."

Lord Galveston carried her ladyship with seeming ease. As he trailed along behind, Grenville Somerwell fought jealousy of the man's well-muscled body. Wistfully, he wished his own slender frame were neither so stringy nor quite so lacking in inches. Then he shifted his gaze to the woman with whom he'd watched the ghost harass someone other than himself.

For a change.

A sense of wonder filled him as he watched Miss Tillingford's straight back and pleasantly rounded little figure scamper on ahead of Galveston. Miss Tillingford spoke of seeing ghosts as if she did so often. More surprising still, she acted as if they were merely another bit of furniture leftover from another age and tucked away like the armor or an ancient tapestry, rediscovered only when one wandered into some odd corner of the old pile!

Could Miss Tillingford truly be that nonchalant about such things? An intriguing thought! Grenville Somerwell decided he wanted nothing more in the world than to discover if it were true. Besides, he'd just discovered freckles were not nasty things, as he'd always thought. At least, not when sprinkled across a cute little nose and joined to a dimple-ridden smile! Why, it was possible for them to be a most attractive adjunct to a young lady's complexion! Especially when lovely blue eyes sparkled and twinkled and begged one to laugh with them.

Since it would never occur to Somerwell to intrude on a lady's bed chamber he stopped just inside the door to her ladyship's private sitting room. He watched Lord Galveston and Miss Tillingford disappear through a door on the far side. Galveston immediately reappeared, crossing the neat but not particularly well-furnished room with strides that appeared to Grenville just a trifle hurried.

Actually, Galveston *was* moving more quickly than normal. He was so wishful of escaping the danger of a young unmarried woman's chamber, he'd not thought to close the bedroom door. And he'd not quite reached Somerwell—and the hall door to safety!—when Miss Tillingford's light clear voice drifted out to them.

"Open your eyes, Freddy," they heard Miss Tillingford say. "If you don't instantly open your eyes I'll slap you."

Somerwell's gaze met Galveston's. Simultaneously and silently they mouthed, "Freddy?"

Galveston repeated it. *"Freddy!"* he whispered softly but emphatically. "Someone has the nerve to call that icicle by a pet name and *such* a pet name?" His startled gaze revealed astonishment.

Somerwell, remembering how unaffected Miss Tillingford had been while watching a ghost, responded, "Miss Tillingford, I think, would dare most anything."

"Would she?" Galveston stared at the bedroom. When the men heard the distinctive sound of a sharp slap he winced. "Yes, I guess she would."

"I warned you," said Miss Tillingford, her voice softer.

"Oh, Moonbeam! Whatever shall I do?"

Again the two men eyed each other. This time it was Somerwell who, head tipped to one side, spoke softly: "Moonbeam?" A stranglehold on his cane, he nodded several quick nods. It was an apt name for a lady with pale blond hair and a rounded face which beamed up at one in a friendly fashion.

Her voice, answering a repetition of Lady Winifred's question, brought his attention back to the bedroom door: "Do? Why, what *can* you do? Lady Gwenfrewi is never wrong."

"This time she is." Lady Winifred's voice sounded stronger. *"Ghosts do not exist.* Therefore there cannot possibly have been a ghost in the hall and therefore the whole thing is nonsense. And, therefore, there's nothing to concern me!" With each phrase the voice's timbre reverted, more and more, to Lady Winifred's normal clipped tones. "Get out of my way, Moonbeam. I was on my way to do up my weekly accounts and that's exactly what I mean to do."

Galveston and Somerwell realized they were eavesdropping. In silent agreement, they stepped into the hall and strode toward the nearest corner, Grenville needing three steps to Marcus's two. They rounded the corner and, from the sound of voices behind them, none too soon.

Once out of sight, however, Galveston put a hand on Somerwell's shoulder and guided him into an alcove in the outer wall into which, through glassed-in arrow slits, sunlight poured.

"Somerwell," asked Galveston, "what did Lady Winifred mean? What was that she said about a ghost?"

"You want to know," asked Grenville cautiously, "about a ghost? What ghost?"

"The ghost," said Galveston patiently, "which is never wrong, according to one young lady, but does not, of course, exist, as the other firmly asserted. What were they talking about?"

"Don't exist, hmmm?" Somerwell gave Galveston the

sideways look which was, all too often, his mode of eying someone. "Didn't see anything, then?"

"See anything? In the hall before Lady Winifred swooned? Of course not. Besides, she wasn't looking at some nonexistent ghost but at *me."* Galveston was a trifle put out that his features could cause a female, even *that* particular female, to swoon. To honestly and truly swoon, that is. Such experiences couldn't be avoided by a man of his nature, but the maiden involved had never before fainted in earnest!

As his lordship mused about feminine foibles, Grenville remembered how the phantom had floated right through the couple. "Didn't *feel* anything either?" Somerwell asked. "A chill?"

Galveston blinked. "Chill?"

"A . . . hmm . . . draft, maybe?" Somerwell asked cautiously and tucked his cane up under the point of his chin.

Galveston's eyes widened slightly. "Now that you remind me, I *did*. Damn odd that." He rubbed his forehead. "Someone must have opened a roof door for such an icy blast to come down on us that way." He glanced at the blazing sun and remembered, from his earlier ride, the warmth of the day. "In fact, given the weather, I don't see *where* it came from. Not such cold, bone-chilling air . . ."

"Couldn't have been a ghost, hmm?"

Lord Galveston grabbed at his straying thoughts and hauled them back to rationality. "Somerwell," he chided, "surely you don't believe in the existence of ghosts!"

"Who me?" Grenville Somerwell opened his eyes wide. "Now do I look like the sort who believes in ghosts?"

Lord Galveston's eyes narrowed. "Now that you ask . . ."

"Well, I don't." Grenville stared out an arrow slit, then swung back. "Yes I do," he admitted. He sighed. "I've seen them. When they come too near I've *felt* them, that bitter cold that comes from the inside out." He paused, biting his lip in thought. "I even *smelled* one," he remembered. "That was the worst."

"And do they tell you bedtime stories?" sneered Galveston, eying Somerwell a trifle sardonically.

Somerwell's eyes narrowed, his mind busy. "Don't think one's ever actually *said* anything to me," he admitted after a moment. His eyes grew blank, his vision returning to some inward scene. After a moment he muttered, "I wonder. Do you suppose the things *can't* speak?"

"Gudgeon! Something which, by definition, does not exist, couldn't possibly speak."

Somerwell snapped to attention as he realized that, once again, he'd confessed his weakness to someone who would tease him unmercifully. If not worse. Rather belligerently, he said, "Miss Tillingford saw it, too."

"Since she seems the sensible sort, she must have been coddling your delusion."

"No. Wasn't that." Somerwell shook his head, his mouth set in a stubborn line. "That wasn't the way of it at all! She was already watching the ghost before either Lady Winifred or I arrived." He brightened, his eyes widening in sudden wonder. "I'm *not* the only one who sees ghosts!"

The completely conscious realization he was no longer alone in his oddity filled Somerwell with such joy, such exultation, that he simply wandered off down the corridor, forgetting to say goodbye and wondering where Miss Tillingford was to be found. As he wandered, Somerwell peered left and right, as if the lady might be hiding behind one of the chests or under the table which stood against the wall.

Shaking his head, Galveston watched the younger man gradually disappear into the distant gloom of the badly lit hall and gave concerned but brief thought to the problems of inbreeding. Grenville Somerwell was, he feared, a prime example! But the thought faded as his memory returned to Lady Winifred lying on the floor at his feet. Absolutely boneless, she'd simply slid from under his hands and collapsed. And how very lovely she'd looked, too. He wondered that he'd never before noticed that she had perfect features, a perfect body . . .

Galveston instantly pushed that totally improper thought from his mind!

At first, of course, he'd thought Lady Winifred was employing an old trick often used to gain his attention. Not that it ever worked. Galveston was awake on every suit and up to every rig and row in town and wasn't about to be caught in a compromising situation with a conniving woman in his arms—him thinking he was doing her a service when she only wished to lure him into parson's mousetrap! But Lady Winifred . . .

Galveston frowned. Lady Winifred had *not* been shamming it. Or at least, if she had, she hadn't done so to gain his attention. More a desire to avoid him, he decided, remembering how, the instant he'd laid her on her bed, she'd turned her head away.

By then she'd come to her senses, of course. Sometime between the moment he lifted her and when he reached her rooms she'd realized she was being carried and had, at that instant, no longer been a child's rag doll but something far more rigid. The task had been easier when she was still merely a dead weight and not . . . embarrassed, perhaps?

But was that it? He recalled how a flicker of something he could only call distaste passed over her face when she'd awakened in his arms and realized where she was. Her expression then settled into the smooth mask habitual to her. Actually, her countenance was lovelier when she was unconscious and all the hard planes of her perfect features relaxed, softer.

He shook himself. Why was he even thinking about her? It wasn't, certainly, that he cared whether or not she were the ugliest creature in the castle rather than the most beautiful. *He* hadn't come to the house party to pursue Wickingham's heiress, although he'd a friend or two among the guests who were so desperate they meant to have a touch at her dowry.

He'd come in pursuit of other game entirely.

Galveston settled his forearms on the stone of the thick wall and gazed through the arrow slit which, except for being closed in by glass, was just as it was when first constructed. He looked across the ancient walls and across a narrow meadow. Beyond the lea was an ancient forest through which rides had been cut. Galveston caught a glimpse of movement in the one he could see and was soon rewarded by the appearance of several equestrians—including the black-clad figure of the spirited young widow who was his latest interest.

He frowned. Did she have to look up in just that particular way at the man riding beside her? Galveston watched Lord Ramsbarrow reach for her reins and pull both his own and her horse to a stop. Then his lordship called out and the other riders paused, turned, trotted back. Several joined the first two, forming a straggling line. Finally, sitting a fine black gelding off to one side, their host, Lord Wickingham, raised his arm, let it fall—and the horses were off.

They'd reach the courtyard in minutes!

Galveston took off, too. He'd a long corridor, two flights of stairs—one a circular staircase, on which he'd break his neck if he weren't careful—and the ancient main hall of the castle to cross if he wished to reach the courtyard in time to lift Lady Pelling from her saddle. Such a tiny little woman she was, he thought, with the most perfect figure he'd seen in years. He'd enjoy holding her between his hands as she slid to her feet, lightly touching her, perhaps, with his body, giving her a hint of his hopes?

No, not today. She hadn't yet, so far as he knew, taken a lover. He'd have to go cautiously with her. For reasons he'd never understood, deciding to take one's first lover was always a trifle difficult for a new widow. But he *could* lift her down.

Galveston didn't actually break into a run, but the ground-covering stride with which he moved was not only graceful, it was also exceedingly effective. But Ramsbarrow! Blast it, his old friend and rival had caught him on the blind side, riding off with the widow this morning. Now that he, too, knew the lady had no objection to the exercise, Nigel would not get in first again! Far too often he and Nigel Ramsbarrow had vied for some woman's sweet favors. Honors, however, were pretty much equal between them.

The men, not-too-distant cousins, had become friends in childhood and, even with the rivalry, that friendship had continued unabated. It would be much less strained, however, if they didn't find the same sort of women appealing! Still, it wasn't as if either of them were hurting for female attention.

Although recently . . .

Galveston sighed. Recently he'd discovered he was rather tired of the struggle between them when involved in the same chase, where once he'd been stimulated by the competition. Just yesterday he'd caught himself wishing Lord Ramsbarrow had taken himself elsewhere, that he had the little widow all to himself. There was less pressure that way. It was much more . . . peaceful?

Galveston reached the main hall and crossed it, approaching the massive double doors. They were opened for him, each by its own footman. He smiled his thanks but didn't pause or break stride. The horses were clattering across the drawbridge and would appear through the sallyport in half a second. He took a position at the top of the stairs, waited, and caught the widow's eye as she appeared.

He strolled down onto the cobbles just as several grooms raced around the corner from the stables. Lady Pelling pulled to a halt right beside him, obviously exultant, and smiled down at him.

"That was glorious," she said, laughing.

"And you won." He reached for her, slowly lifted her down, never taking his gaze from hers. They were both a trifle breathless when she put her hands on his forearms and steadied herself on her feet. "Congratulations," he said softly, caressingly.

She blushed, looking away. "Thank you."

Nigel Ramsbarrow approached. "Well done, Lady Pelling," he said, smiling broadly.

"I was congratulating her myself," said Galveston.

"That's what I thought you were doing," said Ramsbarrow.

Lady Pelling glanced from one to the other, her face expressionless. Several other ladies had been helped to dismount and she turned to Lady Westerwood, a somewhat older guest and also a widow. "I must go up and change now, my lady. Do you, too, go to your room?"

"Oh, yes, I must, I fear," said Lady Westerwood, smiling. "I'm sure I'm much in need of my maid. I haven't raced in ages and I'd forgotten what it does to one's coiffure." She nodded pleasantly at the men and, linking arms with Lady Pelling, climbed the steps, disappearing within the castle's entrance.

Galveston sighed.

Ramsbarrow sighed.

They looked at each other, grinned at how deftly the widow had avoided the both of them, and, understanding each other tolerably well, they too went, arm in arm, up the steps and through the doorway where the footmen stood as stiff and as unaware of anything that happened as was the armor standing around the ancient hall—or so one was expected to believe.

That afternoon Lord Wickingham organized a trip to nearby ruins for the enjoyment of whichever guests might like such things. Nearly all the young ladies took sketchbooks, of course, and, equally to be expected, required the help of a gentleman to decide exactly what view and what exact angle would make the most efficacious composition. The older couples strolled among the fallen stones or beside the broken walls where every cranny had a tiny flower to add a spot of color to the ancient gray stone or dirty-yellowish lichen.

A stream drifted over rounded stones along one edge of the grounds, disappearing among trees old when the Hanoverians had been offered the English throne. A path following the water's edge also disappeared into the woods and a few people set off in that direction. Lady Pelling and her cousin-by-marriage were the first to disappear down it.

Lord Galveston and Lord Ramsbarrow followed, each determined the lady would return on *his* arm instead of the new and diffident Lord Pelling's. A very distant cousin of Lady Pelling's dead husband, the man had never expected to inherit. It was said he actually hadn't known he was in line to inherit. He was, or so he appeared, very much a fish out of water and should be easily removed from Lady Pelling's side. In fact, no competition at all!

The third pair to take the path were Lady Winifred and Miss Tillingford. Lady Winifred carried a basket which she meant to fill with a particular herb, common artemisia, which grew nowhere near the castle except in a small glade some distance up the stream. Clare, knowing her cousin should not wander alone as she so often did, went along to play propriety in the eyes of their guests. But it was her intention that, once they were well beyond prying eyes, she'd go to her own favorite spot, an equally tiny glade, but in the woods some distance down a side path.

The young women separated, agreeing to meet again in not more than half an hour at the same spot. Lady Winifred continued on, her long stride eating up the distance to where the stream curved and, long ago, a tree having fallen, there was a nicely damp area where the herb grew thickly.

Lady Winifred had picked perhaps half the stems she meant to harvest when Lord Galveston strolled around the curve and into view. He stopped, startled, at the sight of his hostess, her sleeves rolled well up and her hat dangling down her back, her skirts kilted up so that her bare feet and even a bit of one calf were revealed.

"Lady Winifred! Good heavens, what are you about?"

Winifred straightened, holding a handful of greenery. "What a ridiculous question when it must be perfectly obvious what I'm doing." She glared.

Lord Galveston chuckled. "Yes, I suppose it was rather ridiculous at that. I shall, instead, ask *why* you do it." Raising his quizzing glass, he eyed her ankles. Very nice ankles they were too. Winifred didn't respond and finally he dropped the glass, looking up at her. His brows rose at the scorn he read in her expression.

"If you are interested, which I think you are *not*—" Her voice dripped ice. "—I am harvesting common artemisia or, as some call it, mugwort, which I will dry and which I will use as a febrifuge this winter. Every sign says it will be harsh. I can foresee needing several different herbs which help drive off fevers since sometimes one will not work where another does."

"Do you nurse your tenants then?"

Hearing a truer interest in that question, Winifred frowned. After a moment she remembered to respond. "Yes."

"My mother does a great deal of that. She even bullied all of them into letting her inoculate them for smallpox."

"How did she manage that?" asked Winifred, suddenly interested. "I have tried and, for the most part, failed to induce ours to allow it."

Galveston gave a wry chuckle. "Her biggest argument was that she meant to inoculate *me* and she made a big production of it too, inviting the most important of our tenants to observe. Which meant I didn't dare cry, and I still remember how much I wished to do so. But the future Earl of Lymington mustn't show fear—" He shrugged. "—so I didn't."

"You must have been very young."

"I wasn't very old. Have you suffered in the same way?"

"Yes. Unfortunately it is too late to use myself as an example. Your mother must be a very intelligent lady."

"She is. Also determined. An excellent match for my father!" Galveston studied the glade. "Have you much more to do? Can I help?"

Winifred realized she was talking quite rationally with a man. She eyed him again, giving him another sharp look as his words reminded her that the castle's ghostly matchmaker insisted this man was *her* match.

"I promise to do exactly as you say," he said meekly when she didn't immediately respond.

Winifred gave in. Silently and only to herself, she was willing to admit she'd enjoyed talking to him. "I will hold you to that, my lord," she said, warningly.

Galveston didn't pretend to misunderstand her. He caught and held her gaze. "You need not fear me, Lady Winifred."

Again she hesitated, uncertain whether or not she should allow the response rippling on the end of her tongue the freedom she wished to give it. Unfortunately, like Lord Galveston, she did not allow herself to show fear and the words trembling there might give him insight into her greatest dread. So instead of telling him that any woman of sense would fear any man, she merely said, her words clipped, "Good. Now, if you will be so kind as to find and cut only the stems which have . . ."

While Lady Winifred went on to gather her herbs, Lady Clare approached her private glade—only to discover it occupied. Lord Somerwell sat on the log, her usual perch, well hunched forward, his cane set before him, both hands on top of it, and his chin on his knuckles. He stared at the wildflowers which starred the long grass with white.

"My lord?" she asked, gently. "Is something wrong?"

Grenville started, his hands slipped, his chin jounced on

the ivory top of his cane, and then cane and man fell to the ground.

"Oh, dear," said Miss Tillingford, running forward, "I didn't mean to alarm you so. Are you hurt?" She helped him up and brushed him down. "There, now. As good as new." And then noting a bit of grass stain on one knee, added, "Or, almost."

"Miss Tillingford." Grenville's eyes bugged out. "Is it really you?"

"I *think* so," she retorted, smiling. "At least," she said with her most mischievous look, "it was the last I looked in my mirror."

Grenville smiled. "You're jesting."

"Well, yes," she responded, smiling back. "It is a great failing on my part. I cannot seem to stop myself even though I've been told again and again it is unbecoming in me."

"I like it."

After a moment, when he said no more, she rather awkwardly, even perhaps a trifle shyly, said, "Thank you." Miss Clare Tillingford was used to being *liked,* but she was *not* used to compliments.

"Miss Tillingford, may I ask you something?"

"Of course."

"This morning . . ."

"In the hall?"

"Yes. Did you . . . ?" He gulped.

"Did I see a ghost? Is that what you wish to ask?"

"Did you?"

"Don't pretend," she scolded softly. "You too saw Lady Gwenfrewi just as clearly as I did. Have you seen any other castle ghosts?"

"They won't leave me alone," fumed Somerwell, and then realizing he'd once again admitted to the impossible, cast her a look reminiscent of a startled rabbit. He stuffed the head of his cane in his mouth, waiting for the worst.

But Miss Tillingford didn't react with scorn, as most people did. "I think ghosts are much like cats," she mused. "They like to tease people who dislike them. Have you always seen ghosts?"

"I don't know. Don't remember any before I was a boy at Eton." He shuddered. "For a lark the bigger boys tied me to a tree near Windsor Castle. Herne The Hunter appeared." He shivered. "Forester to Richard II, you know? He hung himself from the tree they tied me to."

"And you've been seeing them ever since," said Clare softly, "but no one will believe you. I know just how it is!" Miss Tillingford patted his arm. Then she smiled. "I've an idea. Since we both had long experience of ghostly behavior, why don't we sit down and exchange tales?"

Grenville smiled back, his eyes glowing brightly. "Could we?"

"I don't see why not." Clare seated herself and motioned for him to take his place beside her just as if they were in a formal salon and it was a sofa rather than a mossy log in a forest glade. "Do you want to go first or shall I?" she asked.

Two

That evening Lord Wickingham entered the salon in which the company was gathered, testily telling anyone who would listen that his daughter would not be down for dinner, that the chit had the headache. In a far more gracious tone, a bow accompanying his words, he asked if Lady Westerwood would deign to act as his hostess at dinner.

Lady Westerwood was not at all averse to acting as Lord Wickingham's hostess. In actual fact, she had vaguely defined hopes she might eventually have the right to do so on a permanent basis. And not merely because her jointure was small and her son all too often in need of funds, but because she'd discovered she actually *liked* Lord Wickingham. Of course, Lord Wickingham treated her no differently from his other female guests. It was just that, for quite some time now, she was *always* on his guest list where others came and went.

It had occurred to her more than once that Lord Wickingham hadn't *allowed* himself to know he'd a partiality for her company. She had tried, in suitably modest ways, to hint to him this might be the case but, so far, she'd had no luck.

Well . . . *some,* perhaps. He'd play piquet with her and seem to enjoy it. And he allowed her to read to him once in awhile while he half dozed beside the fire. So, although she'd been nowhere near to giving up hope, she'd never allowed herself to become overly optimistic. His selecting her to take the foot of the table that evening raised hope to new, if still reasonably modest, heights.

Galveston and Ramsbarrow, converging from different directions on the other widow in the room, were chagrined to discover she was, once again, smiling up at her husband's cousin, the new Lord Pelling.

She laid her hand on Lord Pelling's wrist just as the rakes reached her. "Good evening, my lords," she said to them. "Did you enjoy your stroll this afternoon?" She looked from one to the other. "Did you go far? I know you didn't arrive back at the ruins before most of us left for the castle."

Galveston looked at Ramsbarrow, from whom he'd parted not long after they'd independently arrived at the conclusion Lord Pelling might have been routed from Lady Pelling's side if only she'd allowed it. But she hadn't. They'd made their bows and Galveston had strolled on while Ramsbarrow returned toward the ruins.

Lord Ramsbarrow chuckled softly. "I would admit it to no one but you, my lady, but, since it was all your fault, I think you should know. I was thinking about your loveliness and lost my way! I didn't think I'd ever find it again, but then I stumbled—almost literally, I'll have you know—onto the stream, and followed it back to where we'd left the horses. You'd gone by then, had you not, Marcus?"

"Yes."

Galveston didn't elaborate, not wanting to reveal he'd been alone with Lady Winifred whose sun-touched cheeks still made him want to touch them . . . ah, but that was ridiculous. The cheeks might have looked warm, but Galveston was willing to bet they'd feel icy if he'd tried to lay his lips against them.

"But, Lady Pelling, that was this afternoon! It is now evening and I thought," he invented, "we'd agreed I was to take you into dinner."

"No, no, Galveston. Quite otherwise," said Lord Ramsbarrow, giving the lie with a completely straight face. "The lady agreed to make use of my arm. Pelling, take yourself off like a good lad," added Ramsbarrow, glaring at the younger, although not *that* much younger, peer. Certainly it was an exaggeration to call him a lad!

Lord Pelling, an agreeable soul, glanced inquiringly at the widow, who blushed furiously. Her eyes flashed and her fingers closed tightly around the arm of her cousin-by-marriage.

"My lords," she said in icy tones she might have learned from Lady Winifred, "I made no such agreement with either of you. I have," she said, a gleam in her eye, "far too much care for my reputation." The butler looked into the room just then, checking to see if the guests were ready for dinner and decided they were not, but Lady Pelling used his appearance as an excuse to add, "Lord Pelling? Shall we make ready to take our places?"

Ramsbarrow scratched his smooth chin in a thoughtful manner. "Bet you we neither one get that one." He glanced at his cousin. "A monkey? Straight up? Instead of our usual bet?"

"Sorry, I never bet against a sure thing." Galveston stared regretfully after the woman who had most recently inflamed his senses. Flames he'd just realized he'd not be allowed to quench in the usual manner. He sighed. "Just remembered a bit of gossip, you see."

"Gossip *I've* not heard?" Ramsbarrow's brow's arched. "Come now! That must be nonsense."

"No, no. *Old* gossip."

"Old gossip . . ." Ramsbarrow half closed his eyes, concentrating. Indulging a habit that indicated to those in the know that his curiosity was roused, he rubbed his nose, but he couldn't recall anything specific to Lady Pelling. "Concerning our widow? You're certain?"

Galveston nodded.

"Give me a hint."

"We haven't, my friend," said Galveston, his voice as dry

as gunpowder, "what one needs in order to attract her. Give it up, Nigel. She's not for either of us."

"Haven't what will attract . . . ?" This time Ramsbarrow's brows climbed toward his neatly arranged Brutus hairstyle. "Now, Marcus," he said, pretending outrage, "maybe *you've* lost it, but I'm quite sure *I—*" He ceased roasting his cousin when Galveston waved an impatient hand. "I don't recall," he said, abruptly. "Remind me."

"The reason she married *old* Pelling," hinted Galveston. "The *same* reason she'll marry the new and much younger Lord Pelling."

Ramsbarrow froze, his eyes on some distant point. Remembering, he glanced at Galveston. "Pelling Hall," he said.

"Exactly."

"They said," elaborated Nigel, "that she wed old Pelling because she's obsessed by the Hall."

"And we, neither one, will ever own Pelling Hall. Lord Pelling does. By fair means or foul, she'll bring him to the point."

"I see. Well—" Ramsbarrow rubbed his chin. "—that's that then." He brightened. "For *now.* Once she's trapped his lordship I'll try my luck again." He stared sorrowfully at the charming little widow and, when she happened to glance his way, he held her gaze and sighed in a deep, if unbelievable, soulful manner. "If I remember correctly, and despite the evidence of our immediate conversation I believe there is as yet nothing wrong with my memory, they do a very good goose pie down at the Wickingham Arms."

"Nice evening for a walk, too," said Galveston just as thoughtfully. He watched the other guests pairing off, making ready to leave for the dining room. Abruptly he turned his back on a mousy-haired chit, who cast him lovelorn looks, obviously hoping he might choose to lead her in to dinner.

"Suppose we dare?" asked Ramsbarrow, turning as well, but away from another husband-hungry girl who had her eye on him, this one with a sharply pointed chin. "It'll upset the table, two men not coming in."

"Only one short. Remember? Lady Winifred won't be there."

"Ah! Only *one*."

They stared at each other.

"Do you care?"

"Not a jot!"

Making an about-face, they strolled toward the door, reaching it just as the butler arrived to check the room for the second time. Galveston caught the man's eye, saluted, pointed to himself and then Ramsbarrow, and shook his head. The butler sighed, nodded, and disappeared back into the hall to remove two places from the table before he could return and, finally, announce that dinner was served.

Ramsbarrow, who had been to the castle before, said they'd a choice of two paths. They could reach the village by going through the park, out the gates by way of the gate house wicket gate, and then a long stroll around the park's walls until one finally came to the village. Or they could go through the garden to a stile, take a short walk between a pair of hedges leading to the village church. And just beyond the church, according to Ramsbarrow, one turned a corner and, after a few more steps, entered the inn yard. Galveston chose the shorter route and they set off.

"Given we're stymied in the chase, the fox going to earth, so to speak, I'd like to leave," said Ramsbarrow a trifle pettishly. He strolled with his fingers in his pockets, his shoulders slightly hunched. "I would too, if I could think where to go."

"I've places I could go," responded Marcus, "but I was foolish enough to promise Wickingham I'd stay a few weeks."

Ramsbarrow stopped short. When Galveston looked back, his friend shook his head. "Don't do it. Leave! Run! At once!"

"Nigel, I promised."

"You don't understand. He'll throw the icicle at you."

"His daughter?" Galveston laughed. "At *me?* He must have reached the bottom of the barrel if he's the notion in his cockloft I'd wed her!"

"He's desperate all right. He wants her married off. Anyone would do." Nigel Ramsbarrow grinned, a wry self-deriding look. "As, for my sins, *I know.*"

Galveston was never slow to catch a man's drift, but this boggled his mind. "Wickingham thought he could lure you into parson's mousetrap?"

"I don't have a notion what *he* thought, but I was told in no uncertain terms what *she* thought. She blistered me up one side and down the other for not leaving as she'd asked me to do, preventing her father from carrying out his plans."

"So?"

"So, since by then I'd had an example of her father's machinations, I obliged her and left."

"What example?"

"Perhaps I'll let you find out for yourself." Ramsbarrow cast a look at Galveston and chuckled. "Just don't drink any wine a solicitous Wickingham brings to your room late in the evening!"

"Drugged, I suppose?" Galveston grimaced. "And his daughter, as well? I see."

"She knew better than to drink it. But he is desperate," said Nigel. "Promised his wife or some such thing. Babbled on and on about it when I insisted I must leave. I admit I didn't listen too closely. His daughter doesn't see why she must help him to the peace of mind he wants. Says he very likely deserves to suffer, or so Lady Winifred told me in that Arctic tone that makes one's skin crawl."

But, for some reason, Galveston was remembering the horror in Lady Winifred's face before she'd dropped into that swoon. And only because he'd touched her lightly, steadying her when she'd backed into him. Was that a completely normal reaction?

It was not!

"You think," he asked cautiously, "it is merely perversity on her part? The fact she doesn't want a husband?"

Ramsbarrow shrugged. "Does it make a jot of difference *why?* I just thank heaven she's no intention of obliging him. Or I'd very likely have been trapped!"

"I admit," mused Galveston, "that I can't imagine the woman as a wife. She's the coldest woman, her voice *dripping* ice—"

Galveston's words stopped abruptly as he overheard a voice. Lady Winifred's voice. It drifted to them from beyond the hedge protecting the churchyard. *And there was no ice!*

How was it possible for Lady Winifred to speak so gently, so kindly? Ramsbarrow, equally astonished by what they heard, stopped.

"That's right," said the unexpectedly warm, but quite recognizable voice encouragingly. "Easy now. You need worry no more. We're here and we'll help you . . ."

"Icicles don't have such warm voices," whispered Ramsbarrow. *"Can't* be her."

"Easy now," said the gentle voice. "Bite the strap and don't fear you'll squeeze my hand too hard—" The next words were in a much firmer tone. *"—Now* Jed."

There was a sudden gasp and a muffled groan in the deep tones of a male trying hard not to reveal pain.

"See?" said Lady Winifred gently. "Just as I warned you. But it hurt for only a moment, did it not? Now we've only to strap it up." After another short silence her voice again sharpened: "Gently, Jed! Don't undo your good work!"

"Thankee, Lady Winifred, Jed," said the quavering voice of an obviously elderly man. "I don't know what I'd a' done if you hadn't come by. Laid here all night, I s'pose."

"Hush now. All is well with you. *Now,"* she said, very

slightly more astringently, "all we need do is find help and a gate and get you off this hard path and into bed."

"I'll be off to get help," said a so far unheard voice, a slow deep-chested baritone.

"Very good, Jed. And while you get him settled, I'll return home for laudanum so he can sleep tonight. There'll be someone in the tap room willing to give aid, I'm sure."

Ramsbarrow and Galveston looked at each other and, not wishing to be discovered eavesdropping, they strode around the corner, through the coach entrance to the inn yard, and on inside—where they met a giant, youngish man, entering by the back way.

The man started to speak, took a second look, and, recognizing castle guests, merely said, "Evening, m'lords." Lackadaisically, he reached to tug a nonexistent forelock. He slid by them and into the tap room where he could be heard asking for volunteers.

Galveston felt a trifle chagrined the man hadn't bothered to ask them.

Several men, including the innkeeper, followed the giant back into the hall. ". . . and you just get him up to the small back room, Jed," the man was saying. "He can't be left to fend for himself all alone in that sma' cottage of his until he's back on his feet. My Manda and I will see to him." The man noticed his new guests. "Ah! Gentlemen!" he said with a start. "What can I do for you, then?"

"When the excitement is over," drawled Ramsbarrow, "and you've a moment to spare, we'll have a private parlor and our dinner. Including a nice slice of your goodwife's fine goose pie, if you will."

"No goose tonight," said the innkeeper regretfully, "but there's a meat pie that's nearly as good, or a venison stew if you'd prefer, to say nothing of slices from the haunch roasting in the kitchen or—Jed," he interrupted himself, turning toward the rear. "Do be careful!" he cautioned, and, when the man on the hurdle groaned, added, "Don't tumble him about so!"

He turned to his guests. "Harry'll be feeling that for a day or two, I think," he said ruefully. "Broke cleanly Jed said, but broke is broke and takes time to mend . . . Ah! You'll not be interested in old Harry's problems." He gestured. "Right this way, please."

They were led to a very pleasant private parlor and the innkeeper disappeared. He returned with two bumpers of good nut brown home-brew, and Galveston asked, leadingly, "I was surprised to hear Lady Winifred's voice when we passed the churchyard."

"She were come to check the altar likely," said the man indulgently. "She or Miss Clare does that, regular like. Jed says she actually stepped on old Harry. A-lying in the path, he were, which were as far as he could crawl, poor man."

"Crawl?"

"Silly ol' fool fell into Renfew's empty grave, him who'll be buried on the morrow," explained the landlord. "Got hisself out of the hole and to the path, but then passed out. From the pain likely. Now her ladyship's off, he's a swearing a blue streak for being such a guy. Complains he never come off a nag at a gate when he were a groom, so why stumble over a gravestone?"

"How do you know what he's doing?"

"I've got very good ears, I do!" The landlord grinned. "I can *hear* him." He pointed over his head. "Can't you?"

Actually, when he listened, Galveston could hear. "A gentleman then? That he'd not swear in Lady Winifred's presence?"

The landlord looked shocked. "Swear where Lady Winifred might hear? Ain't none of us brave enough to do that!" He shook his head as if pushing away such a notion and then bowed a quick bobbing bow. "Well, then, I'll just be off to the kitchen and order you up a meal."

"Interesting," said Galveston, idly turning his mug around and around, one finger pushing at the handle. "Our hostess appears to have been cured of her headache very quickly, does she not?"

"It's too soon for her father to have begun his scheming," mused Nigel, "so it can't be that . . ."

Galveston expressed an idle interest and Nigel obliged.

"After I was almost caught that way," he said, "I talked to others Wickingham thought might suit. Each one says he takes a few days to make up his mind which of his guests to maneuver. Since we arrived only day before yesterday, we haven't been here quite long enough for him to have made a choice. Not if he holds to form."

But perhaps, thought Galveston, his lordship had concluded his daughter wasn't quite right in the head and had chosen more quickly this time? Galveston remembered Lady Winifred's raving just before she'd backed into him. Something about not believing in ghosts. Something about ghosts not existing, that—whatever it was—couldn't possibly exist.

But there'd been nothing there.

Or was there? The cold, for instance. Such an intense, freezing sensation which came from the inside out. A shiver went up his spine at the memory. His mind still on Lady Winifred, Galveston accepted the new mug brought him by a buxom maid and let his thoughts run on. At some extreme edge of his consciousness, he realized Ramsbarrow was teasing the jade. With intent. He found he not only didn't care, but wished Ramsbarrow every success.

For himself, well, the chit didn't appeal at all.

Which was a notion to pull him up short and, putting aside thoughts of Lady Winifred, Galveston really looked at the wench. He concluded her plump figure and merry laugh truly were not of interest, which was strange since—he was quite certain of this—only a day or two earlier he'd have set himself into competition with Ramsbarrow for her favors.

More especially since Lady Pelling had made it very clear she'd have neither of them!

Ah, well. So what? So, for once, he and his old friend did

not want the same woman. Given he had no interest himself, Galveston wished to give Ramsbarrow every opportunity for success. He realized he needed to attend to a personal problem which involved excusing himself.

Lord Galveston made his way out the back door just as Lady Winifred approached from the churchyard.

"You!"

He blinked. "I assume it is. I mean, it was the last time I looked."

"Don't play the fool!"

His left eyebrow arched and he nodded. Then, blandly, he said, "We were informed you have the headache. I hope it has eased?"

Her ladyship bit her lip. "Why aren't you at dinner like everyone else?"

"Like you, for instance?"

"I have my reasons."

"So did we."

Her look sharpened. *"We?"*

"Ramsbarrow promised me the best goose pie in creation, but, sadly, we were informed by the innkeeper that we must make do with another sort of pie or stew or roast meat."

"Mitcham didn't mention the ham? Try it. You'll find it nearly as good as the goose—but why am I bothering to tell you anything at all?" She frowned. "If you'll excuse me, I must see to my patient. You did know a man was brought here with a broken leg?"

"Yes. We overheard you helping to set it. If we'd come a moment earlier, I'd have volunteered to help, but we were too late."

"Oh yes. I'm sure." She cast him a scornful look and eased by him carefully so that, even on such a narrow path, she didn't touch him with more than her skirt's hem. "I'll bid you good evening, then," she said and whisked herself into the inn.

"Cynical wench," he muttered, but her slim form and

graceful movement wouldn't leave his mind as he continued on to the convenience sited, as usual, at the far end of the garden and well away from the inn. He was returning when he once again met her ladyship.

"You!"

"Now how do I answer that when you've forbidden me the sort of flippant response it calls for?" Was that a smile she hid so quickly?

"Never mind," she scolded. "Just let me pass." As an obvious afterthought she added, "Please."

Galveston shivered in a sudden draft, "I've a suggestion," he said. "Instead of leaving us to our lonely meal, why don't you come enjoy a slice of that ham you recommend?"

"You and who else?"

"Ramsbarrow. Only my old friend Nigel Ramsbarrow."

"Only Lord Ramsbarrow?"

The frown Galveston was coming to believe approached a permanent fixture on her otherwise lovely face appeared once again.

"I'm quite certain," she continued, "you are aware an unmarried woman would never dine alone in an inn with two men unrelated to her. Especially men of your stamp! You know better than to suggest such totally improper behavior on my part, so why did you do so?"

He *did* know, of course! It was his turn to frown. "My lady, I'm damned if I know."

"Don't swear. And I do wish you'd rid yourself of that exceedingly irritating and cocky way of speaking."

He stiffened, becoming very nearly as reserved as Lady Winifred, his voice quite as icy as she could sound. "Perhaps, my lady, *you* might loosen up a trifle and discover the delights in easy converse between a man and woman."

"Not when such conversation leads to—" She cut off her sentence with a gasp. "There! You see? You very nearly led me into making an improper comment myself. Now, do let me by."

As it crossed his mind to wonder why he was acting in such a perverse manner he felt icy fingers walking up and down his spine. And, however perverse it might be, it seemed he couldn't stop himself. "You'll have to pay a toll," he said, teasing her.

She eyed him. "Lord Galveston, have you been imbibing beyond your limit?"

"To be frank, not nearly enough. I left my second tankard in the parlor now I think of it. But where were we? Ah—" His eyes gleamed with a wicked twinkle. "—the toll."

"Move aside," said Winifred coldly, "or I'll call for help."

"A kiss, I think," he mused, eying her lovely oval face. "Just a simple little kiss."

"You, my lord, are behaving in a totally objectionable fashion. Kiss you, indeed!"

Galveston blinked and shook his head slightly. Had he actually asked for a kiss? "No, no," he said. "You misunderstood . . ."

She tipped her head, watching him warily.

Another frisson ran up his spine and he finished: ". . . I mean to kiss you."

Had he actually said that? From the shocked expression on her face, it appeared he had! Galveston felt a trifle stunned himself. What in heaven's name had gotten into him?

From somewhere not far away came the soft rumbling voice of the man called Jed. "Lady Winifred? Where be you, then?" he asked, and, approaching at an ambling stroll, added, "Ready for me to escort you home, then?"

"The church, Jed. I've not yet checked the flowers."

Galveston watched the tension drain from the woman standing before him. Her back straightened and her features fell into their usual blank expression.

"Saved," he breathed in a dramatic tone. He stepped aside and she passed him. "This time," he added.

She swung around, but, accepting that the better part of valor could be summed up in the old adage that one retreat in order to fight another day, Galveston had already turned away and headed for the inn.

"You!"

"Good night, Lady Winifred," he called, not turning back. "Sleep well."

"Bah!"

He chuckled but didn't allow himself to pause or look around.

"I defy Lady Gwenfrewi!" called Lady Winifred. "She is *wrong,* Lord Galveston. We'll *not* wed."

That stopped him. He turned. *"Wed!"*

"Isn't that why you're flirting with me?"

He stared. Coming back a few steps, he said, "I haven't a notion of what you speak."

"Why, that you've decided to wed me, of course."

He blinked. "It never crossed my mind. Wherever did you get the notion it might? Not," he added quickly, "that you aren't a very attractive lady, because you are, but I've no desire to marry just yet."

"But Lady Gwenfrewi, she . . ." Lady Winifred bit her lip. "But, if *not* that, then what . . . Why . . . ?"

The ghostly fingers which had walked Galveston's spine earlier did so again. And then, so quickly he couldn't help but notice, a faint chill seeped out of his body, leaving behind a web of confusion in its place. The feeling so startled him, he blurted, "Lady Winifred, will you believe I haven't the least notion?" Eying her, he frowned and then, more thoughtfully, added, "Perhaps it was a sudden and, I admit, despicable desire to put a dent in that icy veneer you wear like a shield."

"Icy?" It was Winifred's turn to blink. "Me?"

"You."

"You jest, surely."

"Glacial as an ice-chilled wet compress," he said promptly.

"Surely not," she insisted. "I've never thought myself particularly cold."

"Just watch yourself, Lady Winifred. Especially when speaking to men of a marriageable age!"

". . . the shield part I understand," she continued, ignoring him and speaking as if to herself. "Any sensible woman . . ." Suddenly she looked up, startled. "Good night, Lord Galveston," she said, speaking in her usual passionless manner. "I must go now."

"*That,* my dear Lady Winifred, is *exactly* the frigid tone I mean!" he said softly.

Either Lady Winifred didn't hear his low-spoken comment or she ignored him. In either case she quickly disappeared into the churchyard, the silent Jed in close attendance.

Galveston wasn't sure he believed his own eyes, but he was *almost* certain he'd seen the big man wink just before falling into step behind her ladyship. Maybe, thought Galveston, getting to know the lady's giant-in-waiting would be of use.

And then he wondered why that particular notion had crossed his mind. Why in heaven's name would he want to do that—unless he wished to know the lady herself far better than he'd be likely to manage on his own?

But he didn't want to know her better . . . did he?

Three

Thoroughly bemused, Galveston wandered back into the inn. He entered the room to which he and Nigel Ramsbarrow had been shown earlier only to spin on his heel and exit. Instantly. Ramsbarrow and the serving maid were occupied in a manner that precluded the need for company.

The tap room had filled to capacity since they'd arrived. Galveston's appearance there led to such a wave of silence as to make a less sensitive man than Marcus aware he wasn't wanted. He nodded, smiled, and strolled back into the hall, wondering what he should do next.

He was, he decided, deuced hungry and he wasn't about to starve just because Nigel was satisfying a different appetite. Sniffing, he let his nose lead him to the kitchen. A well-scrubbed round table took up much of the middle of the comfortably warm room, a woman standing at one end, her arms up to the elbows in a mound of dough.

"Please don't stop," Galveston urged the cook, charming the woman with a smile. "I haven't watched anyone make bread since I was a nipperkin. What's your name?"

"Amanda Longfellow." The overly plump middle-aged woman hesitated only a moment, then continued the rhythmic motions necessary to proper kneading.

Galveston headed for the ham which stood on the sideboard, a carving knife laid beside it. There was a loaf as well. He cut a thick slice of ham, a couple of slices of bread and, putting the ham between the bread slices, he took a seat at the table where he munched as he watched the cook.

"I don't suppose it'll be ready for the oven anytime soon," he said, ruefully aware of a wistful note creeping into his voice. "I was a dab hand at making knot rolls, years and years ago."

Manda grinned, never ceasing her mixing. "Go on with you! Quality-make don't bake their own bread."

"I don't suppose my mother would know where to begin and she'd find it a dead bore long before the dough was properly ready, but I liked it." He chewed and swallowed. "There's something very satisfying about kneading bread."

"Satisfying?" The cook eyed him indulgently. "What sort of satisfaction to a man like you?"

Galveston settled back. "That's a very good question . . . and I haven't a notion. I just remember I felt good after it was divided into the pans or made into fancy rolls or rolled out to make buns. If I'd been good, Cook would make those lovely ones with chopped nuts and currants plumped up in a bit of rum." He finished his bread and ham. "I wonder," he said, truly wondering, "why I ever stopped visiting the kitchen on bread-making day."

"Most likely sent off to school and too big for your britches when you were come home again," said Manda dryly.

"You suggest I conveniently managed to forget what I considered a childish pastime." He grinned appreciatively. "Sounds as if you once worked in a big house."

"Knowing one, ain't you? Well, I did then. Back afore I met up with my Mr. Longfellow. Learned all sorts of fancy cooking." She watched Galveston pick up a crumb and put it in his mouth. "Still hungry are you?"

"I believe I am," said Galveston. "What I'd really enjoy are eggs, more of that ham, and maybe a bit of good aged cheese?"

"A Frenchified omelet, then?" She nodded smugly. "I'm a dab hand at that, I am."

Marcus hadn't actually thought of putting the eggs, ham, and cheese together, but now the notion had been put into his mind, he liked it. "That would be excellent. Now, a good sharp cheese, mind!"

"As if I'd use anything else," she said scornfully. "And proper herbs fresh from my garden, too." A drift of flour wafted upwards, making her sneeze. "Won't be long now afore I set this to rising and then I'll make you the lightest, loveliest omelet you ever ate."

It actually did come close to the best Galveston could recall. "You're wasted here," he said fervently, and mopped up his last bite just as Nigel strolled in. "I don't suppose you'd leave your man and come work for me?"

The cook chuckled, her whole body shaking. "That'd be the day! Yes, sir," she asked, turning to Nigel. "What can I do for you?"

"I merely wondered where my friend had got to. He disappeared and now I see why. Never knew such a man for finding out all the best things in life. If you won't work for him, I don't suppose *I* could tempt you instead?" Nigel lifted the lid off a good-sized pot snugged into the ashes and sniffed. "Hmm. What's this?"

"Potage. *Soup,* I mean! Now see what you've done?" she scolded Galveston. "You set me to using those fancy words I learned when I worked for Lady Gravesend. My poor Mitch struggled long and hard, getting me to speak proper English again!"

"I don't suppose I could have a bowl of potage?" Galveston asked, still a trifle hungry. "And then a bite of that fruit tart on the sideboard to finish?"

"Now then," teased the cook, "didn't you have anything to eat today?"

"Well—" He flashed a grin. "—not for hours."

"But Molly was to—" Her gaze tipped toward Nigel and

widened. "You!" She plopped soup into a bowl. "I remember you!" she said, as she pointed her dripping ladle directly at Nigel. "You leave that girl alone, now! Haven't the time, now, to train new maids and that's the truth. Not like the *last* time you visited the castle. So no more of your fooling with them, you hear me?" She glowered. "Haven't the patience to set another breeding female to rights!"

Nigel's ears turned red. "What makes you think I'd a hand in it?"

"As if it were your *hand* in it! And, if'n I'd only gone and made a guess, your pretty color would prove me right, wou'dn't it? I mean it!" she warned. "Don't you go putting a pudding in any more ovens. I'm the only one supposed to do any cookin' at this inn!"

Nigel, not about to lose access to the rosy-cheeked maid who had just given good value for his money, set himself to turning the cook up sweet and, by promising a small annuity for the love-child he'd only just learned existed, pretty well succeeded.

Marcus, ignoring their bickering and bargaining, finished eating and, ready to leave, rose to his feet. "If you think of any way I could tempt you into my kitchens, Mrs. Longfellow, you tell me!" said Marcus. "That was the best soup I've had in ages. And the tart!" He bunched his fingers and thumb, kissing them in the way he'd once seen his mother's French chef do when a sauce had turned out especially well.

Nigel, as was his way, gave Amanda a goodbye hug and a loud smack on the cheek which left her blushing rosily.

The cook slapped at him. "Go on with you! Between the two of you, you'll set my head in such a whirl I won't know the salt from the sugar!"

The men took the longer route to the castle's front gates. Neither had any particular desire to hurry. A saunter by way of the road and up through the park would keep them from what each secretly feared would be an utterly insipid evening of traditional house party entertainment in which the younger guests, including themselves, would be expected to take part.

At least, Marcus recalled seeing a harp in the drawing room which he was certain hadn't been there earlier and Nigel was equally sure a violin case had rested on the closed piano. If there were harp, violin, and piano, there were likely flutes and guitars and, *far worse,* sopranos ready to torture the ears of a captive audience with a long repertoire.

"Cards are kept in a cabinet in the games room," said Nigel, casting his friend a sideways glance.

"Piquet?" asked Marcus, brightening. "Now you mention it, I remember it's my turn to win our great-great-grandfather's watch."

Nigel grinned. "You just try it. *I've* been taking lessons, *I* have. Our esteemed progenitor's watch is quite safe." He patted his pocket.

The friends had traded the watch, which hadn't worked for decades, back and forth at the end of an evening's gaming for as long as either remembered. How it began neither could have told, but it was now the standard bet between them. The watch was laid on the table and, when their play ended and scores were toted up, one or the other would have possession of it.

The gaming room was empty, dimly lit by one lamp turned low. Ramsbarrow lit the ready-laid fire and moved the lamp to the baize-covered card table. The cards were exactly where he'd thought they'd be.

As Ramsbarrow arranged everything Marcus paced, picking up a cue stick, putting it down, rolling a ball from one end of the billiards table to the other as he passed, poking the fire which didn't need poking and, finally, he approached the table where his cousin sat shuffling the cards.

"What's the matter, Marcus?" asked Nigel.

"I haven't a notion. I just feel . . . unsettled? Maybe I'm coming down with something?"

Nigel's brow creased. "Ain't got a fever, do you?"

"More like an ague. I've experienced the oddest chills. Off and on all day. Like cold fingers on my spine. Otherwise, I don't feel at all sick."

Nigel dealt. "In that case . . ." He tipped his head, queryingly.

"Yes, in that case." Marcus seated himself and picked up his cards. "Hmmm. You have learned a thing or two, have you not?" he said, looking at his hand. "I haven't held cards this bad since the last time I wandered into a Spitalfields Hell."

Nigel froze. "If you're accusing—"

"Pax, friend," interrupted Marcus. "I'm not suggesting you cheated. I'm merely commenting on this hand."

Lady Gwenfrewi allowed a broad smile enough substance it could have been seen if either man had looked. It was quite true Lord Ramsbarrow hadn't cheated. *She* had. And she'd continue to see the cards fell badly. Marcus Galveston would find the game so frustrating he'd willingly give it up and go to the drawing room.

Where he belonged.

Where he'd be near Lady Winifred.

Where Lady Gwenfrewi could *and would* work her wiles on one or the other of them.

While listening to Miss Smythe sing, Miss Tillingford smiled across the salon at Grenville Somerwell. Their talk that afternoon had been interesting, but hadn't included Lady Gwenfrewi's history. And Clare hadn't had a moment to herself since, during which they might have managed a few words.

Actually, it might take quite a few words, because sometime, about halfway through dressing for dinner, it had occurred to Clare that, not only Freddy and Lord Galveston had experienced the matchmaking ghost while *together and aware of each other,* but so too had she and Grenville. Ex-

cited little shivers ran up and down her spine every time she
thought of it. She had waited forever, it seemed, for Lady
Gwenfrewi to choose for her her own true love.

But *was* Somerwell the one? As she eyed his overly slender
figure she admitted he wasn't exactly what she'd dreamed
of in the way of a lover. But what could she, with her freckles
and less than romantic nature, expect? She'd no special tal-
ents or anything else for one to brag about! So *he'd* be getting
a bit of a Smithfield bargain as well, would he not?

Besides, the way the poor man looked at her, that hopeful
puppy-dog sort of expectant look, was rather endearing, really. So, well, why not make an effort and see what came of
it? He was certainly a better prospect than the nonagenarian
who pestered her after church each Sunday!

Miss Smythe finished the Italian aria she'd rendered with
a great deal of ill-placed expression. While the young woman
took her bows, Clare moved to Grenville's side. She was
forced to give only two or three hints before he followed her
to a oddly-shaped alcove tucked between the anteroom which
led to the hall and the castle wall. There they could speak
quietly without anyone thinking a thing about it—except perhaps that they were a trifle rude to ignore the entertainment!

"I promised to tell you about Lady Gwenfrewi," said Clare
the instant they were seated.

"You *did* see her, did you not?" asked Grenville anxiously.
"You weren't just . . . just being nice to me? This afternoon
when we talked, I mean? It's *true* I'm not the only one who
sees ghosts?"

"Have you thought you were?" Clare asked kindly. She
put her hand on his arm and squeezed gently—and, for some
reason, the surprisingly hard muscle under her hand had her
suddenly and unexpectedly feeling quite shy about explaining Gwenfrewi's role in the lives of the Alistaire family.

Somerwell nodded his head several times. "Certain of it."

Clare forced her mind back to her question. "But I certainly do, so you are not, are you? I've suspected a lot more

people experience them than are willing to admit it. However *that* may be, some of us are more sensitive to them than others are. You and I, for instance. Lady Gwenfrewi is actually a very nice ghost. She was Welsh and said to be very beautiful and was stolen away from her father's house by the then lord of this castle on the very eve of her wedding to another. That particular Lord Wickingham must have been a wicked man, I think," mused Clare, "although surely it turned out well or Lady Gwenfrewi would *not* be so nice? Perhaps?"

Enthralled, Grenville gripped his cane in a strangle hold. "But what happened?"

"What happened? Oh. To Lady Gwenfrewi, you mean?"

Again Grenville nodded several times. He brought the head of his cane up, tucking the ivory head just under his chin, his eyes fixed on her face.

"Well, that wicked Lord Wickingham married her. I wonder if he actually meant to when he stole her away?" Clare tipped her head and stared thoughtfully into space. "Although perhaps that's not important since he *did?* Lady Gwenfrewi lived a long and happy life. Still, or so the story goes, she never entirely forgot her first love and how she was, almost literally, torn from his arms. The legend has it that she swore that, if she'd anything to say to it, her children would wed for love and their children, too, and she wished it were possible that *no one anywhere* should ever wed the wrong person ever again."

"But why is she a ghost? I thought only those who died a bad death or were desperately unhappy became ghosts. Why does *she* still walk the world—" Grenville glanced about, warily, as if fearing she'd appear. "—instead of resting in peace?"

Clare had never asked herself that question. Now, hesitantly, she suggested, "Her oath, perhaps? Ever since she died, she's attended to the matching up of Alistaires with their own true loves, assuring they never make a wrong marriage. That's what she was doing today. Lady Winifred and Lord Galveston." She cast Lord Somerwell a quick sideways glance, her color high. "Occasionally, according to family history, she's matched up others as well." She chanced another quick look, saw he didn't catch her meaning and added, "Someone not in the *direct* family line, I mean."

Always obtuse, Grenville didn't catch this hint either. He was far too curious about the tale to notice he'd been given one. "But how?" he asked. Grenville eyed Clare expectantly and she gave him a questioning look. "I mean, is there some special thing she does? Some trick?" he explained.

"The stories suggest she does no more than come upon a couple when they are aware of each other, and then she makes certain they both have some experience of her existence."

Again Clare cast a sideways glance at the man with whom *she'd* experienced the ghost's existence. *Was* he the one for her? Or had their particular experience been an accident, merely a happenstance, a coincidence—and not a match ordained by Lady Gwenfrewi at all?

"So far as anyone knows," Clare continued, casting him still another quick look, "that is *all* that is necessary. You'll have to admit Lady Winifred and Lord Galveston were each treated to an experience of her existence! Why, she passed right through the two of them just as Freddy, I mean Winifred, stared up over her shoulder and straight into Lord Galveston's eyes!"

Grenville's eyes bulged. "Is Lady Gwenfrewi *never* wrong?"

Clare chuckled. "You are thinking that Freddy and Lord Galveston make an odd couple, are you not?"

"Well—" For half a second he hesitated. "—*yes*. I mean he's a rake and she . . . she's an icicle wrapped up in a snowstorm!"

Clare sobered. "Freddy isn't a cold uncaring woman, my lord. Not at all. She *pretends* to be in order to frighten off any man who thinks to wed her. *She* says she'll never wed, but—" Clare beamed. "—Lady Gwenfrewi has said differently, has she not?"

A confused Grenville ignored that last bit, his undisciplined thoughts caught on another notion. He blurted, "I thought that *all* women wished to marry and have children and that sort of thing."

Very gently Clare suggested, "I wonder if that isn't something men have made up because they *prefer* to think women are that way."

Grenville frowned, bumping the knob of his cane against his chin, trying to decipher Clare's meaning. "You mean there *are* other things women wish to do?"

"Oh, yes, although they mostly know they'll never be allowed to reach for their dreams. I am acquainted with a woman who aches to be a doctor of all things and another who would like to explore the world. That particular friend reads every book she can discover about odd places and other peoples. Travelers' tales, you know? And I know one who is very good at mathematics. She dares show no one her work because no one would believe a mere woman capable of it. At least," added Clare a trifle doubtfully, "what she *says* she does. *I* don't understand a bit of it so I wouldn't know, would I?" Clare grinned conspiratorially, quite certain Grenville wouldn't understand either. "Then there is Miss Smythe, who was singing just a bit ago? She paints."

"But—" Somerwell blinked. He blinked again. "—most women do that, don't they?"

"I don't mean watercolors." Clare leaned toward him and he leaned closer. Lowering her voice, she whispered, "Miss Smythe *paints in oils*. And very well, too. I've seen some of them."

A touch of anxiety whispered over and around Grenville and he eyed his companion. "Do *you* have a secret wish?" He elaborated to his exact concern. "Do you *not* want to marry?"

"Me?" Clare chuckled. "I'm a simple creature, really. The only thing I want is to love a man who loves me and we'd marry and I'd take care of him and our children. I suppose that makes me boring and lacking in dash, but it's the way I am. One shouldn't, I think, fight the way one is made, which—" She sighed. "—is what Freddy, I mean Lady Winifred, does."

Grenville, for whom, since Waterloo, only a single idea at a time could find headroom, ignored the reference to Lady Winifred. "I don't think you're lacking in dash, Miss Tillingford," he said earnestly. "Why, you didn't even flinch while watching that ghost! And you were very brave when . . ." Grenville blushed, remembering just in time that it wouldn't be tactful to admit that he and Galveston had overheard Clare slap Lady Winifred!

"Brave? Because I accept that there are ghosts? Nonsense," Clare scoffed. "I am not at all brave. There are *two* castle ghosts I run from. They are quite frightening, I think, even though I'm convinced they'd never hurt me in any way. Well, how could they? They are only *ghosts* after all!"

"One frightened me into *hurting myself,*" admitted Grenville, once again coloring up. "Once. One of the first I ever saw."

"I can see how that might happen," said Clare slowly. "If a specter jumped out at one and startled one badly, then one might fall downstairs, for instance. A timid soul might actually be hurt at second hand, so to speak."

"But not *you,*" he insisted. "I'm sure you are the bravest woman I've ever met."

She turned a mischievous smile his way. "Is that a compliment, my lord?"

"I guess it is." Raising his cane, he sucked on the knob as he gave her one of his sideways looks. "I suppose," he said after a moment, "that what I *should* say is, what beautiful eyes you have and what lovely pale hair which is just like moonbeams."

Her tinkling laugh turned eyes their way. "No, that is rather trite, is it not? I much prefer to be thought brave! I only wish it were true. *You* are the brave one. I mean, you must have seen lots of ghosts since coming here and you haven't complained or . . . or *gone away,* which you might have done."

Grenville's blush deepened. "Well. Er . . . no. I . . . er . . . haven't, have I?" He cast her a quick look and, guiltily, lifted his cane to his mouth again.

Clare made a guess. "You *wouldn't* leave even though you *want* to?"

"Have to go to Bath," he admitted, glancing around with a hunted look. "Don't *want* to go to Bath."

"Why Bath?"

"M'great aunt. Lady Baggins-Keyton. Ordered me there. A tartar, she is. *Always* ordering me to do this. Do that." Pouting slightly, he added, "Don't like it."

"So why put up with it?"

Grenville sighed and this time twisted around to look her in the eyes. "It's her money," he admitted, making a clean breast of his situation. "Haven't much more than an easy competence myself and she says I'm her heir. Or will be if I behave. Thing is, get so tired of being poked in the ribs!"

"She pokes you?"

"With her cane. When I'm not paying proper attention. When I'm thinking? I do think about things," he said defensively. "Now and again." He slid his eyes sideways to see if he'd given her a disgust of him by admitting such a thing and was relieved when she reached out and patted his hand where it rested on top of his cane.

"She sounds spoiled and demanding and not very nice. I think you should get money somewhere else."

The notion appealed and Grenville brightened. He'd not have to visit his aunt ever again! But the good feeling faded as he tried to think of how he'd manage it. "Gambling, you mean?" he asked, his voice sounding as tentative as the notion felt.

"Oh no! *Not* gambling." Clare looked horrified at the notion. "Please. I don't like gamblers very much."

Clare thought, unfondly, of her father whose gambling would have left her destitute when he and her mother were killed in a carriage accident. Then she reminded herself, as she always did when bothered by thoughts of her father, that her great aunt had left her a fortune tied up in such a way no man *could* gamble it away. Not the *principal,* at least. And then there was her grandfather. Oh yes, definitely. Her very special grandfather!

While Clare thought of family, Grenville had confused memories of intrepid gamblers who, losing everything, proceeded to hang themselves from lamp posts or, if wishing privacy, had gone home and shot their brains out. He was certain to find himself in the same position.

"Have to hang myself from the lamp post," mumbled Grenville, having, in imagination, already lost his little fortune.

"Oh no! Please don't. Think of those who depend on you."

"Hadn't thought about those depending on me," admitted Grenville. "Won't do it, then."

But he wouldn't anyway, would he? Find himself in such a position?

"Can't," he added. "Don't *have* money to throw away!"

"Would you if you did?" Clare asked a trifle anxiously.

Grenville remembered Miss Tillingford didn't like gamblers and shook his head. "Don't think it's likely," he said.

"Good."

She beamed at him and he felt the glow of her approval warming him inside and once again glanced sideways at her. A comfortable little woman, he decided. Nice. He *liked* her.

"I like you," he said.

"That's nice. I think I rather like you, too." She patted his hand again, and as she did so, noticed a commotion near the fireplace. "I believe they've brought in the tea tray, my lord. Will you join me in a cup?

Grenville jumped up. "I'll get it for you," he said and was

off before she could deny him. He *wanted* to get her tea. He wanted to do something, anything, which would have her making him feel good like that, deep down inside, all over again!

As Grenville returned from the tea table holding Clare's cup and saucer with great care, Galveston and Ramsbarrow strolled into the room. Ramsbarrow was tossing a fob watch and catching it, grinning at his friend. Galveston wore a look of resignation.

Then Galveston saw Grenville and stepped forward more briskly. "You! I need to talk to you."

"What? You want to *talk* to me?" Grenville carefully steadied the tea but not before some slopped over into the saucer. He scowled. "See what you made me do!"

"That isn't important. Come along now, do," Galveston coaxed.

"Don't *want* to talk to you. Want to take this to Miss Tillingford." He glared at Galveston and added, "Before it gets *cold.*"

Galveston had seen that stubborn look on Grenville's face before and knew he'd get no satisfaction until the younger man did whatever it was he wished to do. He sighed. "Do so then, and come back here."

"Some other time," grumbled Grenville, made brave by his desire to spend more time with Clare. He eyed Galveston. "Tomorrow, maybe."

Galveston scowled, but let him go.

"What can you possibly have to say to that one?" asked Ramsbarrow, astounded.

Thinking of his experience in the hall with Lady Winifred, Galveston said, "You wouldn't believe it." Galveston heard the bitterness in his voice and decided that perhaps it was just as well that Grenville had escaped his clutches. He'd no desire to discuss ghostly fingers walking up and down up his spine when anywhere near Nigel. And certainly not ghostly fingers attached to what might be a real ghost! Nigel would never let him hear the last of it—And there they were again! Those icy fingers, which were becoming familiar to him, trailing up his back. Eerily cold fingers . . .

. . . and Galveston discovered he was thirsty.

He moved on to the table where he looked down into Lady Winifred's face. "No sugar. Just tea, please," he said softly, edging the commonplace words with danger.

With mild satisfaction, Galveston watched Lady Winifred's hands tremble as she poured, then lifted the cup and saucer toward him. If she trembled, he thought, then she was aware of him and that was good. Was it not?

Half a moment's confusion on that point faded as that ridiculous desire to flirt with her came over him again, along with more of the funny tingling along his spine! So he took great care to run his fingers along hers as he removed the saucer from her hands.

Lady Winifred glanced up at him, blushed, frowned, and turned a questioning glance toward Ramsbarrow. She turned a sharp look back toward Galveston, nodded a sly nod, and then favored Ramsbarrow with a broad smile. "Tea? *You*, my lord?" asked Lady Winifred. She continued in an unusually lilting tone. "I wouldn't have guessed *you* drank anything so innocuous as tea. Ever."

Galveston tipped his head. Was Winifred flirting with Nigel? And if so, why? According to his friend, she had, on another occasion, made it clear she'd not marry him for all the tea in China. So . . . ?

"Tea has a certain cachet this time of the evening, my lady," responded Ramsbarrow, his mouth quirked at one side, his eyes twinkling. "More especially when served by someone as lovely as yourself."

And he was flirting back? That, of course, was easily explained. Nigel was such a consummate flirt *he* responded that way to any woman. But, *Lady Winifred?*

"What a bouncer, my lord."

She actually batted her lashes at him! His Winifred was

behaving like a common minx, which was *wrong*. The last thing in the world Winifred was was a minx! So why . . . ?

"Not at all," teased Ramsbarrow. "You must take a closer look in your mirror, my dear! It will prove me right."

And why did Ramsbarrow . . . ?

And, wondered Galveston as the odd sensation along his spine disappeared, *why am I wondering any such thing?*

It couldn't possibly be *jealousy.* Not when a lady he didn't want himself jested lightly with his friend! Even when the cousins vied for the same woman's favors, he'd never felt jealous of Nigel's successes. So that notion was absolutely ridiculous.

Besides, he assured himself, this particular woman was nothing to him. She was completely different from those he'd had an interest in in the past. She was cold and revealed not the slightest hint of the compassion, the warmth, he desired in a woman. She hadn't the intelligence, the liveliness, the happy nature, the—

From some paces away he turned and stared back at Winifred: He'd just remembered how warmly, how gently, she'd spoken to old Harry when helping set his leg, how perfectly rational she'd sounded when telling Miss Tillingford she meant to get on with her accounts, which was *not* a task set a featherbrained scattergood! If Lady Winifred kept the castle's housekeeping accounts then she couldn't possibly be the dull, mentally inadequate soul she managed to make herself seem.

And how *did* she manage that particular trick? Galveston studied her surreptitiously, secretly watching the way she dealt with the people who came for tea and discovered her secret was nothing more complicated than the adoption of totally expressionless features and blankly staring eyes devoid of the intelligence he knew her to have!

Galveston finished his tea in a gulp and returned to the table. He presented his empty cup and waited for Lady Winifred to notice him. Except that she didn't. Or, more likely, she ignored him. She spoke briskly and in a lively fashion with Miss Smythe, making suggestions about entertainments the young woman might enjoy and places she might wish to visit while staying in the region.

He waited patiently until, running out of ideas, Lady Winifred had to turn to him. Obviously reluctant, she lifted her face, that blank look back, a look which would never again fool him as it had before their several odd encounters.

"Yes, my lord?"

"More . . . tea, my dear?"

"Tea. Of course."

And more tea was what he got. Nothing else. Not even a final glance when he thanked her for it. He emptied his cup into a convenient planter and got himself one more cupful with exactly the same non-result. Tritely concluding that tomorrow was another day, he took himself off to bed.

He was almost asleep when it occurred to him to wonder, "Another day for *what?*"

The question bothered him and he sorted through his mind for an answer. He didn't find one and that bothered him still more, keeping him unreasonably wide awake.

Worse, when he finally gave up, sat up in bed, and relit his lamp, he got the odd feeling he wasn't alone. A glance revealed his room was occupied only by himself, so he'd another mystery to add to the first: *Why was he utterly convinced someone was laughing at him?*

Half a dozen pages into a treatise on deaths and injuries in Welsh coal mines Galveston yawned widely. Good. He was sleepy. He lay the pamphlet aside, blew out his lamp and, lying back, his gaze drifted lazily around the dark room until caught by a cloud of misty white, a soft curtain blowing at an open window in a gentle breeze. It was a peaceful thing, that gently wafted curtain. Very gradually, feeling strangely comforted, Galveston fell asleep.

When he woke the next morning, it occurred to him that there was no light-colored curtain in his room and that, even if there were, the window was tightly closed and, *worse,* it was on the far side of the room. *There couldn't have been anything blowing, just there, in a nonexistent breeze!* A shiver slid up his back—but it was a different sort of shiver from the one he'd felt, off and on, the day before.

Thinking about that difference, he couldn't decide which was worse! He managed to put the question aside during the delicate process of shaving and dressing and finally forgot it completely, as he took a secondary set of stairs toward—according to a footman polishing brass door handles in the hall—his quickest route to the stables. What he needed was a long hard ride which would shake away the cobwebs.

It was early and the morning activity in the barns was just beginning, so it was a rather sleepy-eyed groom who led out his Princeling. The gelding was the only living thing in sight which seemed full of energy and a willingness to use it.

Galveston eyed the prancing horse. Perhaps *too* willing? After all, he himself wasn't exactly a ball of fire! But, having ordered the animal tacked up it would be inconsiderate to then order him back to his stall.

Besides, another gelding was just then led forth. This time by the giant who had aided Lady Winifred the evening before when setting the old man's leg.

"Good morning," said Galveston. He walked around the horse. "Your name is Jed?" he asked the man.

"That it is and a very good morning to you, too. I like that animal," the groom added, thrusting his chin toward Princeling while his hands gently checked and tightened the girth on the horse he had in charge.

"That's a very good specimen, as well. Good lineage, I'd say. Is he Lady Winifred's, by chance?"

Jed nodded. "Much More Likely out of Rampager by Steal My Groats. Lady Winifred'll be coming for her morning ride any minute now."

The young groom dropped the animal's reins and moved back into the stable. Very soon he returned leading a much larger horse, a strengthy beast such as, given his size, he'd need, but not, thought Galveston, a particularly fast animal.

"Which way will she ride?" asked his lordship.

A knowing smirk crossed Jed's face, then disappeared. "Nearly every morning she takes the narrow path through those woods—" He pointed. "—and a canter along the lane the far side. Then up over Old Cross Hill and back by way of the village." Jed looked disappointed when Galveston merely nodded.

Belatedly Marcus realized the groom had expected a coin or two for the information and, although he didn't mean to make use of it in the way Jed anticipated, he was happy to have it. He dug out a sixpence and tossed it up in the air. "What," he asked, "would I find in that direction?" He pointed away from the route Lady Winifred would be using.

"Old Tower's not too far. You go about three miles toward Stretton and then a mile or so up a path off to the right soon after you pass the crossroads. It's marked by a tall black stone."

Marcus tossed Jed the coin. Although not at all interested in something called an old tower, he rode off without a moment's hesitation toward Stretton.

Jed watched him go and scratched his head, perplexed. Why hadn't the proper-looking lord gone off where Lady Winifred was likely to be found? Why wasn't he intending to meet up with the lady somewhere along her route, accidental-like? That's what other men did, hoping for half an hour's ride with the heiress during which they might pursue their suit.

"Jed?" Lady Winifred took the groom by surprise. "Are we ready?"

"Yes, my lady," he said, a trifle subdued.

"There's a change today. I must ride into Stretton and complain to the butcher that the side of beef he sent out yesterday is already gone off and he's to bring out another immediately if our guests are to have their dinner."

"Stretton, hmm?"

"Have you any objection?" she asked.

"Oh, no," said the startled groom. "None at all."

Nevertheless, wonderingly, Jed glanced around. Lady Winifred had, the evening before, denied that Lady Gwenfrewi was up to her tricks, which meant the old matchmaker *was*, of course. But was *this* one of them? *Could* a ghost spoil a haunch of beef so that Lady Winifred was forced to ride in a direction she almost never went? The direction already taken by Lord Galveston, the other half of the castle's favorite ghost's current project?

And, most important of all, should he or should he not tell her ladyship what he knew? Jed very sensibly decided to keep out of it. He'd heard tales of people who interfered with Lady Gwenfrewi's plans and, from what he'd heard, he'd no desire to make that one-time lady-of-the-castle the least little bit angry! Not at all. She could, it was said, make life very unpleasant for one—itchy skin the least of her tricks!

He cast one more wary look around the yard, wondering if the ghost were there. Mounting, he followed Lady Winifred, who had already trotted off along the route over which Lord Galveston had cantered not more than twenty minutes previously.

Unseen, Lady Gwenfrewi waved like a flag from the weather vane atop the stable and smiled happily. Then spiraling high into the air she too made her way, but at a far speedier rate than any horse could manage, into Stretton.

Four

The Stretton Arms supplied Galveston with a totally inadequate and nearly inedible breakfast which he nevertheless wolfed down. After he'd eaten, he sauntered down the street, idly looking into shop windows as he went.

The milliner was so far out of tune with current styles he wondered to whom she sold her wares. The bootmaker's window, however, displayed a pair of white-topped riding boots over which a London dandy might drool. Next door, the hosier's window held several pair of stockings with delightfully different clocks up the side. In fact, if the shop had been open, Galveston thought he might have been tempted to buy a pair.

He stared at them for a long time, not having anything else in mind to do and not yet ready to return to the castle where he'd be expected to play the proper guest.

Usually that was no particular chore. In fact, he usually enjoyed every aspect of a house party. Except for participating in, or even listening to, the amateur music, of course! So, why not this one?

Why, he wondered, was he so restless? With a sigh, he turned and picked his way across the unswept accumulation of dirt—and worse—that littered the cobbled street. Having crossed safely, he started up the other side. The grocer's shop was open and a number of women stood outside it gossiping. Galveston stepped back into the dirty street and around them.

He tipped his hat to one impudent maid who, catching his eye, curtsied to him. Next to the grocer's a tiny bakery had propped open its door and the aroma wafting into the street very nearly teased him into entering, even if he *had* just eaten. He drifted on, approaching the butcher's shop . . .

. . . just as Lady Winifred stepped out. Her ladyship stopped short. "You."

"I think we've had this conversation," he said, chuckling, his lethargy instantly evaporating. "But what is this? I was assured you rode the *other* way—" Two spots of color touched his cheeks as he realized the implicit insult in admitting he'd asked about her and then *not* gone where he'd been told to expect her.

Winifred, on the other hand, relaxed the instant she realized he'd not followed her. In fact, that he'd *made an effort* so that he'd *not* follow her. Only then did she realize that, in actual fact, it was an insult. She felt the tension flowing back and had to tell herself she was a fool before she could, once again, relax.

"Are you all right?" asked Lord Galveston, as he watched the subtle changes in her expression.

"Of course. Now, if you'll excuse me?"

"Are you returning to the castle?" he asked abruptly.

"What else? I only came into town on an errand."

Was there impatience in that? And something else? An excuse, perhaps? An assurance *she'd* not followed *him?*

"I inadvertently admitted I didn't expect the, uh, boon of your company this morning, my lady, but—" He spoke quickly since she showed signs of walking away from him. "—since we both go that direction, will you allow me to ride with you?"

Lady Winifred eyed Galveston. His awkward speech earlier had held truth in it. He *had* meant to ride where she did *not* and had *not* followed her. This was *not* a trick on his part of the sort her would-be suitors played on her.

"It would," she admitted, "be ridiculous of us to ride along the same road some few yards apart if you, too, are going that way."

"Shall I order our mounts tacked up then?"

"I believe Jed has already taken care of that." Winifred gestured across the street where the groom held the reins of three horses. "I wonder," she added, casting Galveston a look of rampant suspicion, "who ordered him to do *yours*."

"Not I," retorted Galveston instantly. "I'd no notion you were in town until you stepped from the butcher's door."

"That rings true . . ."

"Perhaps—" Galveston, speaking haughtily, scowled down his nose at Lady Winifred. "—because it is true?"

She smiled. "Climb down off your high horse, my lord," she scolded. "If you'd ever been pursued by nearly every fortune hunter in existence along with other men who merely believe a large dower should not go to waste, you too might be wary of dealing with still another one."

He ignored the fact she implied *he* might be such a fortune hunter and asked, *"Has* it been so *very* difficult?"

There was a great deal of sympathy in his voice—much to Winifred's surprise.

"I've never thought—" He stared off at nothing at all "—about how a woman feels when she believes she's pursued for the wealth she will bring rather than for herself, her person, and her importance in a man's life . . ."

Lady Winifred's eyes widened. "How could you possibly understand something so femin—" She broke off, turned on her heel, lifted her habit skirts a tiny bit higher, and began crossing the street before Galveston knew she meant to. He hurried after her and had very nearly reached her side when, beyond them, her gelding whinnied shrilly, reared, and very nearly tore his reins from Jed's grip.

"Whoa there, Likely!" said the surprised groom. But the horse whinnied again, a panicked sound which made Galveston's high-strung Princeling act up as well, which set the third to sidling. Jed couldn't possibly control all three horses, especially not with one behaving in the oddest fashion.

Galveston, fearing that Lady Winifred was about to try to catch her mount's reins, rushed in and jumped to catch the animal's halter. Jed instantly released Much More Likely. Galveston was pulled off his feet again and again as Lady Winifred's mount backed, reared, backed, and reared, moving down the street.

Gradually the animal settled and, talking soothingly, Marcus managed, after only a bit more rumpus, to calm the shivering beast. "Now, boy," he said, running his hand over the trembling horse's shoulders and down his legs, "what's got into you?"

"Let me, m'lord," said Jed.

Galveston let the groom take the gelding and glanced around to find Lady Winifred holding the other two horses, her free hand covering her mouth which was opened in an "oh" of concern. He moved toward her. "Are you all right, my lady?" he asked. "You weren't hurt?"

"I'm not hurt, but you, my lord, *you* might have been killed!"

"Little chance of that, I think. It is a matter of timing, you see," he soothed. "One is reasonably safe so long as the halter is well made. If it were to break, then one would be in danger, yes, but I much doubt a weak piece of tack is allowed in *your* stables, my lady."

"Certainly not, but you make too little of it, my lord."

"Certainly not," he mimicked her stern tone then grinned. "If anything we make too much of it. Jed would have handled the situation if he'd not been burdened with an extra horse." He removed his Princeling's reins from her hand and discovered she trembled. "You are *not* all right," he accused.

"I will be. In a moment," she admitted.

"Allow me to get you a glass of wine."

"Please, no. I am already better." She drew in a deep steadying breath. "In fact I am perfectly fine. Shall we go?"

Galveston hesitated. "Do you think you should ride—did Jed call him Likely?—before it is discovered what happened?"

Lady Winifred glanced at Jed, who shrugged. She turned back to Galveston. "It must have been a bee sting or some such thing. Much More Likely seems quite himself now."

"If you are certain?"

"I'm quite certain," she said a trifle shyly.

Never before had Winifred felt a man was truly concerned about her as a person. Even her father rarely revealed more than irascible irritation now she'd grown beyond childhood. To him she'd become little more than a quantity of stubborn humanity to whom he must do his duty in a certain way, a daughter who balked at all his attempts to fulfill his duty!

But Lord Galveston was different. He'd been worried about the *person* and not the *heiress,* had he not?

Or had he? How did one know?

For certain?

She watched him talk to Jed about the gelding, asking about the animal. But the groom had found nothing which would explain why the creature had acted that way. A notion crossed Lady Winifred's mind and she tensed, looking around and about and seeing . . . nothing, of course.

But, blast and bedamned to Lady Gwenfrewi for . . . ! Lady Winifred forced the partially conceived thought from her mind. *I will not believe in ghosts. I will not.* Winifred was so distracted by the effort required, refusing to believe, that she actually allowed Galveston to help her mount . . . and discovered, when she realized he'd done so, that she hadn't minded his touch at all.

Which, all in itself, was upsetting.

"You are very quiet," he said, picking up the pace just beyond town.

"I was thinking about . . . something." Winifred threw off her preoccupation with the nonexistent Lady Gwenfrewi and said the first thing to pop into her mind. "Did you sleep well last night?"

The trite question brought her a studied look, but then Galveston shrugged. "When I finally slept, yes. It was rather strange actually . . ." He cast her a second, sideways, glance.

"Yes?"

"I had the oddest feeling someone was in my room. At one point I'd have sworn someone was *laughing* at me. But there was no one there, of course—" He decided not to mention the nonexistent curtain wafting in an equally unavailable breeze. "—No one at all."

Winifred's mouth firmed into a tightly bunched rosebud. "Drat that . . . the . . ." She scowled, her chin thrusting forward. "No! There is no such thing as a ghost. I'll *not* believe."

"Ghost?" he asked softly.

Winifred struggled with her emotions. "Ghosts do not exist, my lord," she said primly, when she'd recovered her poise.

"Do they not?" he asked blandly. Even twenty-four hours previously he'd have agreed without giving it a thought, but now there was that nonexistent "curtain" which needed explaining, to say nothing of Somerwell's assertion both he and Miss Tillingford had seen a ghost when—

Lady Winifred forced a chuckle, interrupting his thoughts. "You know they do not." The chuckle faded when it was not answered by one from him.

"But *do* I know it?" he asked.

"A belief in ghosts is just so much nonsense," she said sharply. "This is nothing but superstition."

"*What* is superstition?"

Lady Winifred compressed her lips.

He added, "In this particular case, I mean?"

She turned a quick glance his way, looked back at the lane. "That old story about Lady Gwenfrewi, of course."

"Lady Gwenfrewi?" he asked.

Lady Winifred sighed. "An ancestress. Welsh. I was

named after her. Winifred is a modern form of the name, you see."

"Ah! But a story about her?"

"Story?" Why oh *why* had she mentioned the castle's most famous ghost!

"You said there is an old story about the lady. I do not know this story." He glanced her way and, when she didn't go on, back between his horse's ears. "Perhaps you will tell me?" he coaxed.

Lady Winifred bit her lip, casting him, in her turn, a sideways glance. She'd assumed he knew. Actually, the story was so common, she'd assumed everyone knew. "It is a bore, my lord—" How could she distract him? Make him forget about Lady Gwenfrewi? A Lady Gwenfrewi who no longer existed! "Are you in a hurry to reach the castle?"

"Not at all," he said, glancing at her.

"We'll go by way of Old Tower," she decided. "The view is excellent and beyond it there is a pleasant ride which takes one through the village." Lady Winifred turned her gelding into a side lane which soon rose at a rather steep angle up and around the highest hill in the region. They'd gone only a little way up when Jed, riding some yards behind, called to them.

"My lady!"

She pulled up and turned slightly in her saddle. "Yes, Jed?"

"Old Sal's cast a shoe," he said, his disgust clear. "I must lead her." Jed looked from Galveston to Lady Winifred and back to Galveston, a frown creasing his young brow. Jed hadn't a notion what to do for the beast.

Winifred bit her lip. Of all times for something like this to happen. The problem would leave her alone with Galveston. With a rake! If it were discovered she'd ridden, *unchaperoned,* with Galveston, propriety-loving gossips would be chortling behind their fans and into their teacups!

So *now* what did she do? She glanced at Galveston just as he cast her a look. Their gazes crossed, held.

Galveston read something in Winifred's eyes that appeared very like fear. He sighed and, turning, said to Jed, "I'll lead Sal to the farrier's if you'd like."

His words interrupted Winifred's unsettling thoughts and she stared at his broad shoulders.

"You," he continued to the groom, "can run by her stirrup and escort Lady Winifred home, which is your duty, I believe?"

The frisson of fear chilling Winifred faded. His suggestion was the perfect solution to leaving her unchaperoned, but somehow, although it left her no longer afraid of him or the situation, Winifred could not feel particularly satisfied by the generous offer.

"It is not your place to do a groom's work, my lord," she objected. "Jed should have checked the shoe—"

"I did," Jed interrupted, biting off the words and not hiding his irritation. "Just before I saddled her, just as I always do every animal I saddle. Oh!" His ruddy features reddened still more. "I ask your pardon, my lady, but it is more than a man can bear to be accused unjustly!" He scowled fiercely.

"Perhaps, my lady," suggested Galveston smoothly, "you will agree to show me the tower tomorrow?" He didn't wait to see if she'd deny him, but continued, "I'll take Sal, Jed. To the village smithy? Or does Lord Wickingham have his own?"

"The village," Winifred answered, reluctantly giving in to propriety's demands rather than, as was usual, wrapping herself into its protection. "The castle has first call on his work, but when he has nothing to do for us, he's free to do any which comes his way. Just leave the mare."

She watched Galveston ride slowly back down the trail to the main road, leading Jed's limping mare behind him. She'd not have admitted it to anyone, not even herself, but there was the faintest bit of wistfulness in the expression in her eyes.

Jed watched his mistress stare after the handsome Lord

Galveston and hid a grin he knew would be unappreciated. It seemed that Lady Gwenfrewi *was* up to her tricks! Assuming the ghost had something to do with the lost shoe, that is. Except, this particular ruse hadn't worked—not if Lady Gwenfrewi hoped to get Lord Galveston and Lady Winifred alone together! And if the ghost was *not* at work, then Lady Winifred was acting in the most perverse way possible, actually sending a longing look after a mere *man*.

Although Jed hadn't a notion why, he knew his mistress had sworn she'd never wed, never have anything to do with the male of the species. He knew she'd sent more men than he could count to the right-about. Knew that she scorned them as fortune hunters and opportunists. And knew he agreed . . .

For the most part.

On the other hand, this Lord Galveston seemed a trifle different, so perhaps Lady Gwenfrewi knew what she was about? Jed loped alongside Winifred's mount as they continued around the hill to where a right-of-way leading to the village crossed this one. Yes, he decided, Lady Gwenfrewi definitely knew something about which mere mortal man could only guess: *Jed's* guess was that at long last Lady Winifred had met her match.

After the luncheon provided for those guests who ate at midday, a croquet match was organized. Those who didn't wish to play sat around the green on cushioned benches or on chairs set around small tables.

Galveston stood, his mallet over his shoulder, and watched Lady Winifred knock one impudent gallant's ball nearly under a hedge. She'd enjoyed doing that, he thought. It was a revenge the impertinent young idiot deserved. Galveston marveled at how easily she handled the various approaches, from the obviously flirtatious to those of a more subtle sort. Not that *that* idiot's manner had been at all subtle!

Winifred looked across the court and realized Galveston had seen her latest maneuver. He grinned at her and tipped her a salute. She felt a bit of heat in her throat and was very glad of the high neck to the dress she'd changed into when she'd returned from her aborted ride with his lordship.

"You still have a shot," reminded Clare.

Winifred glanced at her cousin, who, for some reason, had chosen to partner that dimwit, Grenville Somerwell. How could Clare bear to have the slowtop stare at her with those big puppy eyes?

"Freddy?" Clare called and gestured toward her cousin's ball.

Winifred glanced down and reacted with the startled second glance one gives when realizing one's forgotten something. This time she blushed furiously as she set herself to her ball. She lined up the shot with far less care than usual. Luckily it was an easy one and went through the wicket. That minor success settled her and she took her next shot with more confidence.

The ball stopped rolling right where she wanted it. Assuming no one knocked her out, she was placed perfectly for her next turn. She walked to the side to await it and discovered that, thoughtlessly, she'd strolled to within a yard or so of Galveston.

"I saw what you did to that whelp's ball. Masterfully done, my lady."

"I've been told I've no business being so cruel, that it is merely a game . . ." Her voice trailed off in a sigh.

"Ah, but that's it exactly, is it not? We are certainly playing *one* game here, merely an entertaining way to pass the afternoon, but on *other levels* we all play a hundred other games, and the game that young wastrel plays is not one in which you need take part!"

"Well said, my lord. In fact, that is exactly what I have tried, many times, to explain to my cousin, but have never found the words which meant what I felt inside."

"She's the one who tells you you are cruel?"

"Yes. Clare has an overly soft heart." Winifred grimaced as her cousin gently turned her partner's mallet head so it would hit the ball in the proper direction. "As you see! Where does she find the patience to deal with Somerwell otherwise?" She glanced at him and saw that he frowned slightly. "Could *you,* then?"

"He was a much different man before Waterloo," mused Galveston, his brows knotted together. "I'd rather forgotten that. Not that he was ever the greatest intelligence I've known, but he seems much more the fool these days. Before, he was a conscientious officer and his men liked him."

"He was in the army?"

"For several years."

"Were you?"

He grinned as he repeated, "For several years."

"Waterloo . . ."

He sobered instantly. "I don't want to talk about it, if you don't mind. You cannot imagine the carnage, the pain, the horror . . ." His eyes lost focus and he stared at nothing another could see. Finally he felt a hand on his clenched fist and looked down.

Lady Winifred patted his hand and drew away, wondering at herself for voluntarily touching a male creature. "It is your turn, my lord," she said softly.

"Turn?" He glanced around. "Oh. My turn." He strode onto the playing ground, made two brilliant shots and returned to her side. "I'm sorry. What were we saying?"

"I was being overly scornful about Somerwell and you had chided me."

"I *did?* " He cast her a startled look and was still more startled by the mischief he saw in her face.

"I should remember," she said, sobering, "that often there are reasons for a person's disabilities. That last battle affected him deeply, as, I think, it did every man who survived it. I'll try to have more patience . . . although I fear I can never match my cousin in that respect!" She walked back out to her ball which, luckily, lay exactly where she'd left it.

Galveston watched her first play and then turned his attention to where Miss Tillingford stood beside Somerwell. He'd not yet managed to speak with the man and, after Lady Winifred's insistence that ghosts didn't exist, he was more interested than ever in hearing about the ghost Grenville claimed to have seen.

Especially he was interested in the story about—what had Lady Winifred called her?—Lady Gwen-something?

An appreciative murmur went up from among the spectators and Galveston wondered what he'd missed, but then dismissed the question and returned to the more important one. Now, obviously, was not the time to question Somerwell, but perhaps he could go to his lordship's room when the dressing bell rang. Surely it wouldn't take long to discover . . .

. . . Except that *everything* took forever when dealing with poor Grenville.

Marcus sighed softly. Later? When everyone went to bed? Then he could spend as much time as he needed to dig what he wished to know from the man's Waterloo-disordered mind. Marcus stared at Grenville; it had been something over a year since the battle. Was it possible the poor fellow would never get back to being himself?

Galveston frowned at that notion too. As he'd told Lady Winifred, Somerwell had never been the sharpest of men, even when himself. On the other hand, before Waterloo, he hadn't jumped at shadows and he could concentrate on whatever was under discussion.

But why was he thinking about Somerwell? Marcus let his gaze drift back to Lady Winifred. She was talking to Miss Smythe, making the tall, overly serious young woman smile. He watched her drift on to where Sir John and Lady Smythe sat in the shade. She soon had them laughing. What could she be saying? One of the young male guests joined the trio and Marcus watched the transformation as Lady Winifred adopted her 'I'm a nothing' mask.

It was enlightening, seeing that withering of emotion, the blanking of all thought from her eyes. But *why* did she do it? Lady Winifred was capable of turning away an unwanted suitor in a trice merely by using her tongue on him. Instead, she'd chosen to pretend she was so stupid she hadn't a notion what was going forward. Lady Winifred was, he decided, something of an enigma.

Which was fine. Galveston had always enjoyed puzzles. He'd spend his weeks at Wickingham Castle unraveling this particular mystery. He heard his name called. Realizing it was again his turn, he looked around for his ball, discovered it was well off the court, and sighed. Who, he wondered, had managed that nasty trick? He'd have to discover the villain so he could return the favor!

Late that evening Marcus yawned widely and tightened the belt to his dressing gown. He was determined to have his little chat with Grenville. Somewhere along the hall intersecting this one, toward the far end, one would find Somerwell's bedroom. Now exactly which room had the butler said? The third door from the end and on the right, was it not?

"Or was it not," murmured Marcus, frowning. "Did he, instead, say the left . . . ?"

He paused, the frown deepening. Right? Or left? Before he could make up his mind, something at the far end of the corridor caught his attention. Something white, fluttering and dancing and waving in a draft.

Except there was no draft, dammit!

All the talk about ghosts! *Someone* was playing games with him. He wouldn't have it!

Marcus strode out, determined to catch the culprit and give him a good bop on the bone-box. As he approached the turn, the thing disappeared around the corner. He hurried and there, again at the far end, it flirted tatters of white at him. The devil! How had his tormentor moved so quickly? Or was there a conspiracy and more than one idiot wishing to drive him mad?

Marcus, deciding they wouldn't have their way, broke into a light-footed run, reaching the end of the hall just as the . . . *thing* . . . whisked itself down a set of circular stairs.

On and on it led him. Down endless halls; up and down stairs he hadn't known existed. Around and around and around again . . . until, very nearly ready to collapse, Marcus stopped.

"You win," he called softly.

The fluttery thing paused.

"I give up."

Very slowly the thing approached him.

"I can't catch you, but I'd like to understand. I want to know who plays such a Maygame with me."

The thing paused again. And this time it began to assume a form. A woman's form. Gradually it brightened, becoming more and more opaque as it did so.

Marcus put a hand to the wall to steady himself. "A ghost? Really truly, a *ghost?* But there are no such things as ghosts . . . ?"

And then it disappeared. Nothing was there. No one answered.

"I imagined that."

Still nothing.

"I must have."

Somehow the *nothingness* seemed to taunt him.

"Bah! I'm going to bed.," Marcus turned on his heel and started back down the long hall . . . only to stop before he was well started; he stared at the little name plate screwed to the door beside him and realized that, somehow, in all his running around, he'd managed to end up right back at his room.

It crossed his mind to go on and have his talk with Somerwell. But then he yawned a huge jaw-cracking yawn. A feeling of exhaustion fell over him like a blanket enveloping him
and, opening his door, it was all he could do to drape his
robe over the back of a chair before falling into his bed and
into the deepest sleep he'd experienced in years.

The next morning, very early, he was once again at the
stables. As he awaited Lady Winifred's arrival he questioned
Jed about the lost horseshoe.

"Nay, never that!" Jed objected to the jesting suggestion
he'd done it himself. "I know my place far better than *that!*"

"But if none of the shoes were loose when you saddled
up, how did Sal there manage to lose one so quickly?"

Jed cast his lordship a quick look and returned to rubbing
oil into the harness he'd laid across his lap.

"A village lad perhaps? A prank?" suggested Galveston.
"When you were working on one of the other horses?"

Jed's hands stilled and he looked blankly at nothing at all,
a startled expression fleetingly crossing his features. "Hadn't
thought of that, had I?" There was a great deal of relief mixed
with satisfaction in that.

Marcus's brows snapped together. "What else could it
be?" When the young man didn't respond, he demanded,
"What *had* you thought?"

"Well, my lord—" Jed was still slow to reply. "—it's this
way . . ."

"You!"

As Galveston rose to his feet and turned to face Lady
Winifred, he heard the groom's relieved sigh that he didn't
have to finish his explanation. For half a moment he wondered at it. But Winifred was striding toward him and the
sight of her pushed thoughts of lost shoes and ghosts from
his mind.

"I believe I must change my name," he said, teasing. Lady

Winifred, he decided, was lovely when anger animated her features. What would she look like when enjoying another sort of passion?

"But why aren't you long gone?" she asked.

Marcus deliberately widened his eyes. "Surely you remember we are to ride to Old Tower this morning?"

"I did not say I'd go!"

"Ah!" Marcus felt his body tighten with the laughter he dare not release. "But, my lady, you didn't say you would *not* and, with you, that is as good as a yes!"

She eyed him and then sighed. "I *cannot* go." She turned. "Jed, have you heard that Luke fell from the barn roof?"

"That lad!" exclaimed Jed, looking up with a frown. "What will he be a'doing next?"

"I don't know about next, but this time he was attempting to fly and broke an arm," said Lady Winifred, obviously not knowing whether to laugh or frown.

"Fly?" asked Marcus, curious.

"It seems he heard the story of Icarus—" Lady Winifred wouldn't meet his eyes. "—and all about wings of wax and feathers. He tried it. Thank goodness he'd enough sense he didn't climb so high as the roof tree before jumping!"

"You must see him this morning?"

"He's my godson."

"I wonder if he's heard the story of the Minotaur."

"He has. And many of the other old Greek tales as well. Why?"

Marcus looked at his fingernails as he admitted, "I'm a dab hand at telling stories."

"You?"

"I hear disbelief in that, my lady. I'm insulted by your lack of faith and now I must prove my mettle." He caught her surprised gaze and held it, adding, "I'll go with you. Jed? Mount your mistress." He turned away to retrieve Princeling.

Winifred stared after him.

When Jed, politely waiting to put her up on her mount, asked, "My lady?" the stare changed to a glare which she turned on him. "Afraid, my lady?" Jed asked softly, his eyes glinting mischievously.

"Are you daring me to do something?" she whispered back, reminded by his expression of the days long past when, children together, she, Clare, and Jed had roamed the countryside.

"I dare you to prove Lady Gwenfrewi wrong," he whispered, grinning. "Go along with her tricks and, in the end, show her you'll have none of him."

"Lady Winifred?" called Galveston from near the stable yard gate. "Are you ready?"

One long last glare at Jed and, her chin thrust out, Winifred ordered, "Put me up."

She didn't see Jed silently chuckling as he mounted his huge mare. Nor did she see him turn and salute the wispy flag that didn't really fly from the weather vane. And no one, not even Jed, noticed that same "flag" turn into the merest outline of a cannon and fire off a silent nine-round salute to Jed's quick thinking!

While Winifred fussed over her godson, Galveston drew Farmer Rawlins aside. As he watched Lady Winifred with the boy, the lad's exasperated father told him that his son was always wanting to know how things worked.

"Enough to drive a man to downing a blue ruin or two, my lord," finished the farmer, finding he'd a sympathetic ear in which to confide. " 'Tain't enough, you see, that we do something the way we do it because that's the way we always *have* done it. No sir. He wants to know *why*. More than half the time I don't know *why*. What's a man to do?"

Galveston watched the boy lean over Lady Winifred's shoulder, eagerly pointing at a picture in the book in her lap. He felt something inside soften at the way she reached up and patted the boy's cheek. With an effort he drew himself back to the conversation and found the farmer waiting patiently for his reply. "Mr. Rawlins, I suspect your boy is a very bright lad. Only the ones with quick and questing minds ask why, you know."

"Don't need to be that bright to be a good farmer," grumbled the father.

"I doubt that very much," objected Galveston, laughing. "There's more to farming than following your grandfather's calendar! It takes good judgment to farm well. And judgment requires intelligence—such as *you* have."

Farmer Rawlins's ears turned bright red at the compliment. He grinned an embarrassed grin.

Galveston sobered. "But if the lad has started experimenting with feathers and wax . . . !" For another long moment he looked searchingly at the boy. Then, almost sharply, he asked, "Mr. Rawlins, would you be willing to enroll him in a school of which I know?"

"School?" asked Rawlins cautiously, his eyes narrowing. "Boy already reads and writes and ciphers a little." A touch of scorn colored his tone when he added, "He won't be needing Latin and like that."

"No Latin or Greek. Men who have built bridges and others that work in laboratories with minerals and electricity and such things are the tutors. Men who want to learn why the world works as it does. Practical men, some of them, alongside a few dreamers who think up new things for practical men to play with and make useful. Some of the boys at the school turn into the one sort and some turn into the other. We let them find their own way in that."

"Sounds like foolishness to me," growled Rawlins. "Don't think I want a son of mine doing silly things like going up in balloons." He gave Galveston a sharp look. *"That's* the sort of man you have in mind, hmm?"

"That's the *one* kind," responded Galveston with a grin. "The kind *I* prefer builds canals and learns how to make mines less dangerous for miners and hopes to discover ways to cure people sick of things we don't know how to cure . . ."

He glanced at the broken arm which, if the boy had any sense at all, and didn't break it again before times, would heal properly.

"An engineer, you mean?" asked the lad's father, frowning. "Or an apothecary . . . or even a *surgeon?*"

"You've other sons who will help with the work." Galveston nodded toward an older lad and one slightly younger than Luke who, just then, came from the barn carrying steaming pails of mash for the pig. "Besides," added Galveston a trifle slyly, "if Luke were at school you wouldn't have to find answers to all those whys!"

"I'm not a poor man, my lord," said Mr. Rawlins a trifle grimly, "but I don't know that I've the money to send Luke away to school."

"This school is free. You'd need to spend nothing much except for his uniforms and perhaps a bit of pocket money. And very much of *that* is strongly discouraged. Besides, they've discovered that the sort of boy who makes a success of this school is far too interested in getting the answer to 'why' to go running off to the bun shop very often!"

Galveston noted that Lady Winifred had pulled the lad around and down beside her, hugging him. At her gesture, that warm softness, deep inside him where it could be felt only by himself, heated up another little bit. Her ladyship was *not* cold and unfeeling. She *didn't* have a heart bound up in ice. This tenderness toward her godson proved it beyond a doubt.

So . . . was it possible she could be warmed up to cuddling a larger, much more mature male of the species?

Galveston brought himself up short. "Sorry. You asked . . . ?"

"My lord," repeated Rawlins, patiently, "I wondered if I could ask a question?"

"Certainly. All you want."

"How do *you* know about this school?"

Galveston started to speak, stopped. His ears heated up.

"I must ask that you not repeat what I say," he said firmly, and with a glance toward Lady Winifred.

He looked back at Rawlins who, with a quick look at her ladyship and a quick grin, nodded. Galveston hid a sigh at what the grin indicated was going through Rawlins's mind. After all, keeping Lady Winifred in the dark was only part of his reason; he wished *everyone* kept in ignorance!

"My father helped found the school and I've since become a trustee," he explained. "It isn't a large school and only a decade old. It takes in very few new students each year. In fact, it is less a school than a place where a man comes to talk to men like himself about things which interest them, to find help if he's got a problem. We've six teachers. They are responsible for the boys' education, but any man who drops by may be asked to teach his theory or supervise a more practical lesson." Galveston grinned. "For instance, we've a river near the school which has six bridges over it, some going from nowhere to nowhere else. Each is different. Each group of boys is determined to find a better way of doing it than the last managed."

"And who cares for the lads?" asked Rawlins. "Luke's mum is rather partial to the boy, you see, and wouldn't let him go off where he wouldn't eat right or have clean clothes . . ."

"There are two women, both widows, who run the house in which the boys live. They were chosen with great care." He watched Lady Winifred and Luke and wondered if she, if she'd needed a place, might not have enjoyed such a position. "Both women are excellent plain cooks and both love children." He could see that Rawlins wavered. "It isn't too far away. Just a little west of Chester. You could take Mrs. Rawlins and go see for yourself, if you'd like. There's no need, after all, to decide this instant."

Just then Jed came from the barn leading a magnificent team of work horses. He tied them to a fence and returned to the barn, coming back with a pair of brushes. Jed was still grooming the horses when the younger lads took brooms to the stable yard. Only then did Galveston realize there was a pronounced likeness.

"Jed your boy, too?" he asked.

"Jed's the oldest," said Rawlins on a sigh, "but from the first, he were only interested in horses. He hopes to be head groom up t'the castle one day. His next brother, Mark—" The man's chin jutted toward the lad. "—will be a farmer. Comes natural-like to him. Then comes Luke, and who knows where that boy will end." Grumbling under his breath the farmer added, "If'n he don't kill himself with his nonsense before he lives long enough to be anything at all. And the last?" Mr. Rawlins sighed. "Well, little Ben's too young, yet, to know . . ."

"You think about the school for Luke, Mr. Rawlins. I'll give Jed the directions for reaching it and a letter of introduction in case you decide to look it over. I'll include a second letter concerning Luke and my support of his admission which you may give the school's head—just on the off chance you decide to let the lad enroll."

Lady Winifred cast his lordship a look over her shoulder. He responded by excusing himself to the farmer and strolling closer. "See, Luke," she said, as he approached. "I told you his lordship meant to tell you a story!" The look she turned on Galveston was a silent dare that he prove himself.

Galveston didn't hesitate. He turned over a large wooden bucket and sat on it, which put him down at the boy's level. "Once upon a time," began Marcus promptly, "there was a horrid old dragon harassing a kingdom in which lived the most beautiful young lady in all the world . . ."

The story went on for some time and included the heroic young woman's decision to sacrifice herself, at the demand of the dragon, for the greater good of her neighbors, an equally heroic prince who was determined to save the brave and beautiful girl, and a magician who provided the means whereby the prince could defeat the dragon and win the girl—to say nothing of winning for himself the dragon's hoard of gold and jewels with which he built a castle in which they lived happily ever after, including the good magician, of course, whom they rewarded by giving him his very own tower high on a nearby hill . . .

Galveston wasn't at all surprised to look up and find the other Rawlinses clustered round, listening avidly. People made their own entertainments, after all, and a new story was a rarity.

"Well, now," said Mrs. Rawlins, "if that wasn't a right treat. If they aren't burnt black, what with me forgetting all about them 'til just now, will you come in for a fairy cake and mug of ale?" she asked.

"We'd be glad to," said a subdued Lady Winifred, a look of confusion in the gaze she rested on his lordship. When she realized he stared back, her gaze sharpened. "I've questions, my lord," she whispered as they followed the others into the farmhouse's gleaming clean kitchen.

"Do you? I'll answer what I can," he said. "After all, what have I to hide?" he added insouciantly, thinking of his association with the school, which he'd managed to hide from all but one: *Nigel* had discovered his secret.

What business, after all, did a man of rakish tendencies have with an interest in educating the young? Especially the young found, as these were, in the oddest places, the only requirement being that the child have an inquiring mind. The ton, if it knew, would instantly put together his lordship's reputation and boys' lack of background and make rash assumptions about their fathering! Galveston had no desire to endure the teasing he'd receive as a result.

They hadn't gone far from the farm when Lady Winifred's inquisition began. "According to my sources, my lord, *you* are a confirmed rake," she said, sternly. "What business has a rake knowing stories with which to beguile the young?"

"Even confirmed rakes are allowed nieces and nephews, I believe," he responded meekly.

"You've both?"

"I've six sisters, five of whom are married and four of those have children. I visit them often."

"Then why are you considered a rake?"

"I suppose," he mused with a sideways glance her way, "because I've earned the title?"

"But . . ." Winifred stared straight ahead between her horse's ears. "But, I thought . . ." She gave it up and sighed.

"But you thought a rake must be a care-for-naught?" he asked gently.

Winifred nodded, wondering once again at the sensitivity, the degree of intuition, he displayed.

"My dear, a man would hardly be a successful rake if he didn't like women. And understand their sensibilities. It is another sort of man you've in mind, one who never thinks of a woman as a human creature with feelings and needs and thoughts of her own. I've never, I hope, bedded a woman I didn't like," he said gently, "or one who didn't like me. The pleasure should be mutual. I cannot see the . . . the *entertainment* . . . in forcing myself on another, which that other sort of man *is* willing to do."

This was plain speaking indeed. In fact, having said so much Galveston was shocked at himself and wondered what had led him to say any of it. *One did not speak of such things to gently bred unwed women!* Shivering with a sudden chill, he turned a faintly horrified and questioning look Lady Winifred's way, wondering if she'd faint or have the vapors or fall into hysterics.

Winifred did none of those things. The concept of "mutual pleasure" was a new one. One that did not fit into her beliefs on the subject of couples doing "that." Could Lord Galveston have been fooled into believing women enjoyed "it?"

But . . . so many women?

"I don't understand," she muttered, still staring straight ahead.

"What don't you understand?"

His voice brought her head around and she must have realized they were discussing something never discussed between men and women. Her complexion turned a rosy red and her head snapped back.

"Lady Winifred?"

She responded with only the barest of nods.

"I should not have said those things to you. I don't know what got into me to do so. It certainly isn't that I don't know better. Will you please accept my abject apology?"

"I'll . . . think about it . . ."

"Have you other, *safer* questions?" he asked, relieved and determined to make her forget her obvious turmoil.

"Other safer questions?" She forced herself to relax. "Of course," she said primly. *"How many* nieces and nephews, my lord?"

He responded and the rest of their ride allowed Lady Winifred to learn a great deal she hadn't been aware she wanted to know about his family and his life when he wasn't playing a rakish role.

"So you were next to the youngest?" she asked.

"Hmm. My father says it will be a great relief to have the last off his hands after her season next spring. But I think Alice may fool him and he'll be free of her somewhat sooner. I've noticed, for a couple of years now, that she and a neighbor boy have been growing closer and I think they may, before the new year, take their courage in hand and, hand in hand, ask my father's permission to wed."

"It would be a misalliance?"

"Oh no. Perhaps not so good a prospect as she'd achieve if she put her mind to it during a London Season, but not so unequal as all that. He's his father's heir, a barony. And despite my father's words, which would make one think he wished to be rid of her, it's my opinion he'd like her living nearby. She's his favorite. By far the youngest, you know, and coming quite a few years after my parents thought there'd be no more children . . ."

"Hmm." She cast him a quick look and a little color rose up her throat again.

Galveston could have kicked himself. He'd inadvertently reminded her of the fact that children are not found under a cabbage leaf, that it takes both a man and a woman to achieve a child.

"Tomorrow," he said quickly. *"Tomorrow* you will show me Old Tower, will you not?"

She eyed him. But something made her want to discover more about this man who was such an impossible mix of contradictory traits. "Perhaps," she decided.

Besides, Jed had laid a dare on her just as he'd done when they were children. She'd never turned down a dare. When she was young, anyway. Now, fully adult, she should have more sense . . . but it seemed she did not.

"I'll look forward to it," he said, approaching to help her dismount, only to notice how she stiffened as he neared. He motioned to Jed, who instantly helped his mistress to her feet while Marcus merely held Much More Likely's reins.

"I did not say I'd go," she warned when she was safely on her feet.

"But you said perhaps," Galveston teased. "I'd call that a yes, where *you* are concerned!" He offered his arm. "May I escort you back to the house?"

Lady Winifred hesitated only a moment before, shyly, placing her fingers on his arm.

And then wished she hadn't. Even through his coat she could feel hard muscle and the warmth of his flesh. But she was an Alistaire and she wouldn't back down.

Besides, she reminded herself yet again, Jed had dared her to discover more about this man and she couldn't if she were to totally reject him and his perfectly normal, formal, and natural help, which was all the offered arm represented. She should, for instance, have allowed him to help her from Likely's back. And she must never forget, she thought darkly, reminded of his perceptiveness in calling Jed to do the job, just how clever the man was, how *noticing*. It was disconcerting, that sensitivity he had to her every feeling. Most, she was certain, would *not* have noticed she didn't wish his help. Or, if they had, would have ignored it!

Once inside the castle, however, she was relieved that she could be free of him. Too much had happened. Too much been said. Too much to think about . . .

"You will come to the breakfast room when you've changed?" he asked, his gloved hand resting on the newel post.

She stopped on the fifth step, looking down at him. "Breakfast?" Suddenly she wanted to come back down for breakfast. She wanted to spend more time with him . . . It was a thought which frightened her half to death and she backed up a step higher before answering.

"No," she said determinedly, her mouth momentarily forming a prim line. "I always spend the hour after my ride with the housekeeper," she continued less coldly. "It would be unfair to change her plans with no warning." With that quite reasonable and, what was better, perfectly *true* excuse, she turned and hurried up the stairs, disappearing down the hall toward her room.

Galveston was not unhappy, however. He'd noticed that moment's wavering when she'd almost said yes. It was a beginning . . .

. . . A beginning? *For what?*

He pushed the question aside as several men, including Ramsbarrow, approached, obviously on their way to the stables.

"Slug-a-beds," said Galveston, smugly. "I've already been for a ride."

"Well, come for another," suggested Nigel. "We're off to Stretton."

"I've already been into the town. I'll pass. Besides," he added, untruthfully, "I haven't breakfasted and I'm hungry." Fairy cakes were not enough!

"See you later, then," said Nigel and sauntered after the others.

Marcus looked after his friend and wondered just how much longer he'd get away with his secret pursuit of the daughter of the house. Nigel had the nose of a bloodhound when it came to ferreting out secrets.

For instance, there was Nigel's discovery of Marcus's involvement in the Longbarn Laboratory and Experimental School. Luckily, Nigel had no more than a deep need to discover secrets for his own satisfaction and no desire to blather his findings around the world. Another sort of man and the secret experiment in education would be no secret at all, but very likely ridiculed in every publisher's rag and held up to mockery in the printmakers' windows where he, the other trustees, and the school itself would be lampooned.

Still, having been reminded of it, he mustn't again forget Nigel's curiosity. He'd have to be very careful if he weren't to rouse it once more and this time to a lady's detriment. Nigel must never know of his current interest. Lady Winifred must not become a source of gossip. She would hate it. She shouldn't be required to suffer from even *Nigel's* knowing!

They were going into dinner that evening when Marcus saw Grenville Somerwell with Miss Tillingford on his arm. He was reminded he'd not yet quizzed Somerwell about that ghost the man claimed to have seen. Exactly why he'd not done so slipped his mind, but he made a mental note to corner Somerwell sometime soon . . .

The very young woman on Galveston's arm blushed rosily every time he glanced at her. Why, Marcus wondered, had the chit put herself where he'd no choice but to escort her into dinner if she didn't truly want him to do so?

Galveston sighed and tried once again to start a conversation with the inarticulate girl. "I think I've met your oldest brother, Miss Moorhead-White. He went to Oxford, did he not?"

"Our Jemmy . . ." she said so softly he couldn't hear her

without leaning toward her. Once again her face flushed an unbecoming red.

"He *was* in Oxford, was he not?"

"Yes, my lord."

"I believe he became a vicar?"

"Up north."

"Far north?"

"Near York."

Her skin color had faded to merely a rose pink from the rose red and Galveston persevered. "He was a few years behind me, so I didn't know him well, but I'd guess he was a very nice brother?"

"Yes."

He tried again. "You must miss him . . . ?"

"Yes."

They reached the dining room none too soon to suit Marcus. He found the young lady's seat easily enough but had to search for his own which was, he thanked the lord, nowhere near the tongue-tied chit's! It was, instead, next to Lady Winifred's and he wondered how that had happened. Usually he was placed more nearly in the middle of the table . . .

"My lord?" said Winifred frostily.

"My lady?" he responded, emulating her tone. Then, more softly, he added, "But it *is* an improvement, is it not, over your usual greeting?"

"My usual . . . ?"

"It seems that every time we meet—" He cast a comical look her way. "—you exclaim "you" in tones of such utter disgust I haven't a notion how I'm to respond."

Winifred bit back an unexpected chuckle. She reminded herself she was angry that he'd had the gall to rearrange the table so that he was seated beside her. "I don't know how you could think I'd appreciate your moving the place cards around . . ."

"Move . . ." His head snapped up. Turned. He stared at her. "Lady Winifred, I did no such thing!"

She stared back at him and realized his expression was a mixture of both faint outrage at her accusation and confusion that she'd made it.

"Actually," he continued, "I was surprised to find myself seated here and very pleased. After attempting, manfully, for the whole of the time it took to walk from the drawing room to the dining room, to make Miss Moorhead-White respond with something beyond conversation-killing monosyllables, I was happy to find my seatmate was one who spoke her mind freely. Then, of course, you *did.*"

"Did what?"

"Spoke freely." He glanced at her. "Lady Winifred, I did *not* move the place cards."

She sighed. "I believe you." She cast a wary glance around the dining room. "Never mind."

"Never mind that someone is playing tricks on us?"

"Not someone, my lord . . ." Winifred glanced at him sideways from under lashes he only then realized were exceedingly lush and long. "No, my lord. Not a someone."

He heard her sigh softly, but she refused to explain further and rather than tease her he changed the subject to the history of the castle.

Five

Still another morning dawned bright and clear, a delightful day for an early ride. As Marcus approached the stables, he saw that, this time, Lady Winifred awaited him. He hurried. "My lady. I'm sorry," he said. "Am I very late?"

"I don't believe a time was set," she responded shortly. She'd been berating herself ever since she'd arrived because of the disappointment she'd felt that Lord Galveston wasn't already there. "Jed?"

The groom lay aside a harness and an oily rag and, after scrubbing his hands on the seat of his trousers, moved to lift Lady Winifred to her horse. She pushed him away.

"Your hands, Jed!"

He looked down at them. Even after scrubbing them, he could see oil gleaming on his skin. A flush rose up his neck and he turned toward a pump.

Lady Winifred glared after him, her crop tapping the side of her habit in quick little taps.

"May I help you?" asked Galveston.

She hesitated, then nodded.

Knowing she'd not appreciate being lifted into her saddle as Jed had been about to do, Galveston bent and cupped his hands, ready for her foot.

Winifred placed her heel and was surprised at how deftly she was tossed up. His lordship judged her weight very nicely and neither made her feel as if she'd go over her mount's back, nor that she'd slip back down into his arms—a trick more than one suitor had played on her. She hooked her knee, found her balance, and reached for her skirts only to find he'd already arranged them for her.

Galveston had turned away, so she stared at his back, avidly watching the play of muscle in his thigh as he rose into his own saddle, and then admired the way he easily settled his gelding, which was overly frisky that morning.

They turned toward the gate, and took a lane leading between high hedges that would cut across the ancient right of way between the village and Old Tower Hill.

"It is a beautiful day," said Lady Winifred after a long silent moment. "I cannot remember seeing the sky so blue."

"Like your eyes," said Marcus without thinking. When she stiffened he forced a chuckle. "Ah me," he said self-deprecatingly. "Once a rake, always a rake, it seems. You must forgive me the personal comment, my lady, but you gave me the perfect opening, you see, and, without thinking, I took it. It is only natural, of course, to do so."

"Opening?"

"You mentioned how blue the sky was. How could I not compare it to your azure eyes which are, by the way, an almost perfect match to today's sky? You cannot see them, of course, so you wouldn't know, but they are such an intense deep perfect blue . . ."

She glared at him.

"I'm sorry?"

"So you should be! First you ask me to forgive you for making personal remarks and then you make *more.*"

Marcus opened his mouth to reply in a saucy and flirtatious manner—and shut it. "So I did." He frowned slightly. "I didn't mean to . . ." Again her body exhibited that taut line suggesting she felt insulted, and he turned, his frown deepening. "My lady?"

She relaxed and quite suddenly, laughed. "I am behaving with an absurdity I do not understand. I was upset with you for commenting on my eyes. Then I become upset when you claim you'd no intention of complimenting me! Such contradictory behavior is quite out of character and, as I said, absurd."

"Now," said Galveston, reverting to his mildly caressing tone, "I didn't say I didn't mean to compliment you. You are very easy to compliment, my lady. What I didn't mean to do was anything which would upset you or make you the least bit uncomfortable. And then almost the first thing out of my mouth does exactly that. I do, most sincerely, apologize."

"And I forgive you," she said sharply. "Now that is finished—" And from her tone she meant *finished*. "—I'll tell you the history of Old Tower?"

"Please do," he said, stifling a sigh. He wondered why he hadn't the least interest in such history, but a great deal of interest in flirting with this woman who must be the only female creature in the world who wouldn't—or didn't know how—to flirt!

". . . So you see, Old Tower has a rather bloody history. And there it is," she finished, as they turned the last curve up the hill and came off the trail onto the grassy area surrounding the tower.

"It *looks* like it should have a bloody history! What a gloomy, glowering old place!"

"The sort of place the magician in your story might have lived?"

"Oh, no. He had a brand new tower, remember? I picture it made of golden Cotswold stone with vines climbing up the side. A wisteria, perhaps, magicked to grow quickly, and covered with sumptuous purple blooms?"

He smiled and Lady Winifred chuckled.

"Well," she suggested, "perhaps before he had his *new* tower he lived in this sort of place. I brought the key if you'd like to climb to the top. The view is truly spectacular."

"A temptation not to be refused!"

He dismounted and came to help her down—and realized they were alone.

"Where is . . . ?" he asked just as Winifred looked around in a puzzled way, saying, "Jed will . . ."

They stared at each other blankly.

"Oh, dear," said Winifred softly, her eyes turning from his, and darting hither and yon as if the missing groom would appear from behind a bush or fly down from a branch of one of the three trees triangulating the tower.

"I'm sure he was ready to leave with us, was he not?" asked Marcus.

"Old Sal was saddled," she responded slowly. "I'm certain of it."

"Could something have happened? Should we return and see if—"

"He'd have called out. We'd have heard something."

"But where is he, then?"

"I don't know . . . but it is surely nothing to worry us." Uncharacteristically she shrugged away her concern and turned toward the tower. "I will discover what happened when we return, but for now, my lord, since I'm certain you wish to see the view, I'll unlock the door."

Marcus followed her, watching her walk with a great deal of pleasure. A well-made woman, that wonderful flesh wasted if she kept to her determination she wouldn't wed! He followed her into the tower and experienced the odd, from-the-inside-out chill he'd felt often, in varying degrees, since that first occasion when she'd fainted dead away at his feet. It was disconcerting, those fingers trailing up his back, teasing the nape of his neck, rousing his interest in a woman . . .

In one particular woman.

Marcus eyed the gentle sway of Winifred's hips as she climbed steadily a few steps ahead of him. The straight back, the long black hair tightly controlled in braids which circled her head like a crown. What would it look like if he undid it, let it fall about her shoulders, down her back? How far down her back . . . ?

"There, my lord, on a day such as this, one can very nearly see as far north as Chester. And in that direction—" Lady Winifred moved away from him as he'd been about to reach for her waist and stood at the parapet on the west side of the round tower. "—we have a wide panorama along the Welsh border. Do you see the River Dee? A lovely scene. I've often wished I were a decent artist and that I might paint it."

Marcus approached warily. Once again he raised his hands, ready to clasp her waist and once again, just as he was about to touch her, Lady Winifred moved away. "I think I like the view in this direction even better," she said and turned a questioning look on him, a look which changed as she read what his expression revealed about his intentions. Her eyes widened . . .

"A telescope!" exclaimed Lord Ramsbarrow, crossing the roof of the castle's tallest turret to where it stood on a tripod. "Do you study the stars, my lord?" he asked his host.

"The moon, mostly," said Lord Wickingham in a deprecating manner. "Been mapping it. For the fun of it, you know?"

Ramsbarrow bent to the eyepiece. He swiveled the tube slowly along the horizon. "Fascinating. Amazing what one can see. Would you care to try, Lady Pelling?" he asked, but spoke without lifting his head.

"When you've finished," said her ladyship, chuckling slightly.

Ramsbarrow moved the telescope a bit and then swung it back. "My lord?"

"Hmm?" Wickingham asked absently. He'd been talking softly to Lady Westerwood. "What?" he added when Lady Westerwood poked him.

"What is this? A cloudy crown to a hill? I've never seen the like."

Ramsbarrow moved aside to allow Wickingham to get at the machine and was astounded by Wickingham's reaction, which was one of outrage: "How dare he?" Wickingham straightened from the telescope to look out over the wall and then bent back to it. "What does he mean by it?"

"What does who mean by what? I mean—" Ramsbarrow rubbed his nose. "—all I wanted to know was what that fog might be at the top of the tallest hill there. You expect fog in a low-lying area, perhaps, but right up on top of a hill? Er, Wickingham?"

Lord Wickingham was busy capping the lens and covering the telescope with a heavily waxed cover. "Seen enough. Try another day," he said shortly and herded his guests toward the stairs. "Enough, enough," he added and grabbed Ramsbarrow's arm when his lordship hung back. "Boring. Bring you up on a good night to see the moon. Fascinating, the moon. Won't be any nonsense about the moon."

Muttering about fiends and devils and boiling in oil, his lordship fumed and sputtered and, firmly, shut the door.

When they reached the room below the roof, he stared at his guests. "Now, let's see. What to do . . ." Finally Lord Wickingham turned to Lady Westerwood, casting her, if he'd only known it, a look of desperation.

"I don't know about your other guests, my lord," she said quietly, "but I've a yen to—" She thought quickly. "—to go fishing. I remember once when I visited here, you took us all to the banks of the Dee and we had a glorious day's fishing."

Lady Westerwood smiled when Lord Wickingham relaxed. Not only had she helped him but she'd have the opportunity to spend a day at one of her favorite occupations. Luckily it was the only thing she'd been able to think of. Ah, if only everything one must do for the man in one's life were equally pleasant . . . or, that is, for the man one *hoped* might be in one's life?

". . . in this direction even better," Winifred said and turned a questioning look on him, a look which changed as she read what his expression revealed about his intentions. Her eyes widened and instantly her ladyship's features blanked into the expression of idiocy he'd come to think of as her armor. The moment he saw it, he realized what he'd had in mind to do. He turned from her, moving back toward the view she'd just left.

Had he really meant to attempt her seduction? Surely not. Why would such a thing even cross his mind? Particularly when she was far from help if she wished it? It was against every rule he'd ever made for himself, to corner an unwilling woman, and *worse,* an unwilling *unwed* woman, in a place where she'd be unable to free herself from his presence if she desired to do so.

What in heaven's name had he meant by it?

"We had better go," he heard her say, her voice as cold as dripping icicles.

"What made me behave that way?" he asked, bewildered. He ran his fingers through his hair. "It is out of character. I don't understand it. I won't apologize because I'm sure it wasn't *me!*" He swung around. "Wini—Lady Winifred, believe me, I do not wish to hurt you, to upset you, to . . . do anything you wouldn't like. I swear it. *I do not understand what just happened!*"

For a long moment Lady Winifred simply stared into the distance. Then she shuddered. "I see."

"I don't!"

She glanced at him and then away, turning back to meet his worried gaze and smiled weakly. "I don't suppose you do. It is equally out of character that I brought you up here when Jed wasn't here. That was an outrageous act on my part. So we have both acted against our natures, have we not? Don't concern yourself, my lord. Nevertheless, I think we should go. Now."

"Winifred . . . Lady Winifred, is it too much to ask that you explain?"

She eyed him thoughtfully. "Yes," she said, slowly. "Yes, I think it is." She turned toward the trap door opening from the stone stairs spiraling down through the tower.

"You think it is? Too much to ask?" Marcus scowled. "Lady Winifred, is that fair?"

She hesitated, then, stepping onto the first step, she responded. "I haven't a notion what is fair and what is not. We are caught in a circumstance I never anticipated, one I've never experienced. But I will *not* be caught in it, my lord, and that is that." Her last words were slightly muffled as she disappeared around the first curve, and the next barely understandable. "Remember to close the door, please."

"Lady Winifred, come back. Explain to me!"

But she was gone and wouldn't return and he knew it. Sighing, Marcus started down the steps, lifting the trap as he went and dropping it with a clatter when he was far enough down it wouldn't land on his head. Disgruntled both with himself and with Lady Winifred, he stomped down to the bottom and out the door.

The door had the key in it and Lady Winifred and her gelding were gone.

How, he wondered, had she mounted without help, but that was easily explained. There were several large slabs of stone and she'd used one as a mounting block. For a moment he thought of riding off after her. Then he changed his mind. He really truly didn't understand what had gotten into him and he didn't like it one bit that he'd acted so thoroughly out of character.

If anything were needed to convince Lady Winifred the male of the species was interested in only one thing and didn't care a jot how he managed to satisfy that interest, then his behavior today was just the thing to convince her. Of course, he'd begun to guess she was *already* convinced, so he'd only confirmed her beliefs!

Deciding he really didn't want to see anyone anytime soon, he put the key in his pocket and went back inside the tower, climbing still again to the top. He looked toward the village and saw Lady Winifred riding as if all the devils in hell followed her. He watched as she gradually slowed, then, as he continued watching, she reached the edge of the village green where, riding in from the direction of the castle, Jed joined her.

Marcus watched her confront Jed, who had his hat off, wringing it between his hands and, even from this distance, looking dejected.

What *had* happened to the groom? The young man seemed devoted to Lady Winifred. It wasn't at all like the lad to have allowed his mistress to ride off, alone with a man. Certainly not with a man with a reputation! Come to that, why had neither Lady Winifred nor he himself noticed Jed wasn't following, that they were without a chaperon? It did not make sense. None of it made sense.

Not a bit of sense.

Marcus put his elbows on the crenelated wall and his face in his hands and stared at nothing at all. He felt a bit dejected himself and couldn't make any sense of that either.

Nigel escaped the other guests by the simple means of slowing his steps until they disappeared around a corner ahead of him. Instantly he returned to the turret, climbing the worn stone steps at a reckless pace. He uncovered the telescope and turned it in the direction of the highest hill.

A tower, hidden by the cloud the last time he'd looked, sprang into clear view. He tipped the long tube a trifle, working his way up to the top. Then he froze. He stood up and stared at the distant tower.

"Marcus? *Marcus* is there?"

Had Lord Wickingham seen Marcus there? But what if he had? It occurred to Nigel he hadn't seen his friend that morning. In fact, when he thought about it, he hadn't seen his friend early in the morning for the past several days, which was unusual. Usually the two men enjoyed a morning ride together when both attended the same house party.

"Now what's my oldest friend up to, then?" he asked out loud and rubbed his nose hard, which, as he scented a mystery, began to itch.

A sparrow, hopping along one of the crenelations topping the turret, stopped and cocked his head when Nigel, an outlandish thought crossing his mind, bent again to the eyepiece. But Marcus looked distraught. So, if Marcus *had* been stealing a march in the widow stakes, he wasn't winning any battles! Not if that expression meant anything! Nigel watched Marcus lean both elbows on the wall, his chin in his hands, and grinned at his friend's expression of resignation.

But Nigel's curiosity was roused and he still wondered what Lord Wickingham had seen to upset him so. "He's up to something—I'll have to find out what!" Nigel straightened, noticed the sparrow, and, with much the sparrow's cheeky manner, told it, *"I will, too."*

Then, since he'd no intention of joining the fishing party, he played with the telescope. Tiring of the general view, Nigel moved the telescope to focus on the village and discovered Lady Winifred approaching it—from the direction of the tower!

Nigel straightened, staring at the distant and indistinct view before bending again to the eyepiece.

"Where's that over-sized groom of hers?" he asked sharply and the startled sparrow hopped away, half flying, to the other side of the turret. Nigel moved the telescope back toward the hill and the tower, then so that he could see more of the village, and finally, when he didn't find the man, he left the telescope and bent over the wall, searching.

"There!"

The old gray mare—Sal, they called her—pounded toward the village, Jed on her back. Nigel instantly returned to the telescope which was still trained on the village and watched Jed meet up with his mistress, watched her scolding him, watched the lad hang his head and wring his hat between his hands . . .

"Hmm."

Nigel took one more look at the tower where Marcus stared down toward the village with something of a hang-dog air about him. Then, thoughtfully, Nigel capped the lens and covered the telescope. Still more thoughtfully, he went, with far more caution then he'd come up them, back down the spiral staircase. And *then,* his mind still coursing around and among the oddest of notions, he made his way to the stables where he ordered his mare saddled.

As Nigel waited, it occurred to him it was getting on to lunchtime so he asked a stable boy to run to the kitchen and ask Cook for a bite of something. The lad returned with a small feast which he put into a saddlebag and hung from a strap on the saddle.

"There you be, my lord," he said cheekily and deftly caught the coin Nigel tossed his way.

Ramsbarrow met Lady Winifred and her groom as they returned from the village, but they did no more than exchange the commonplace greetings one said at such a meeting. Lady Winifred would not be drawn into deeper conversation.

But that was all right. He'd no intention of quizzing Lady Winifred. She wasn't one who took well to questioning! No, he'd save his questions for Marcus, who was still at the top of the tower, still staring at nothing in particular, when Nigel climbed still another set of circular steps, this time carrying a saddlebag.

Six

Marcus turned his head, recognized Nigel, and turned back to stare over the countryside.

"Nice view," suggested Nigel.

"Hmm."

"Picturesque."

"Hmm."

"Not your usual perky self, are you, Marcus? But perhaps *this* will catch your interest. Lord Wickingham showed us his telescope. Amazing what one can see through a telescope . . ."

"Hmm."

"Whatever *he* saw made him angry."

"Hmm." There was a brief pause. *"Hmm?* It did? He was?" Warily, Marcus asked, "What did he see?

"Haven't a notion." Nigel looked at his nails. Then he peered more closely at a broken corner, swearing softly.

Still more warily, Marcus asked, "Umm, Nigel . . . What direction was he pointing his plaguey device?"

Nigel glanced up. "Toward this tower, but I don't see how he could have *seen* anything." His face expressing utter candor, he added, *"I'd* been looking this way just before he did and the top of the hill was covered in a funny sort of cloud. A ball of fuzz, you might say. Couldn't see a thing."

"But *his lordship* looked this way and *did?"*

"Hmm," Nigel mimicked his friend.

"And he was angered by what he saw?"

"*Hmm!*"

Marcus turned away to lean on the parapet. Once again hands and elbows propped up his chin. "Fiddle."

Nigel chuckled. After a moment he asked, "You weren't attempting the impossible, were you?"

"The impossible?"

"Oh, something like maybe you were trying to warm up the icicle?"

"I don't think she's so much frozen as frightened. And—" Marcus sighed. "—my behavior this morning won't have helped that."

Nigel ignored the latter part of Marcus's comment, which only confirmed his suspicions, in order to probe the first part. "Afraid? You're talking about Lady Winifred?"

"Hmm."

He rubbed his nose. "Marcus, make sense."

"Why?"

"Because, you *aren't,*" said Nigel patiently. "I am of a curious nature, as you know, and I want to know what's going on."

"If *I* ever figure it out you'll be the first to know." Marcus thought about that. "Or maybe the second," he amended.

"You don't *know* what you're up to?"

Marcus sighed. "A number of things have happened I don't understand. I was thinking about that when you arrived. Trying to remember them all, you see, and get them straight in my head. But my head is one of the things that's not right. I keep doing things I'd have sworn I'd *never* do, except . . . except I do do them." Again he paused. "Or say them."

"You make no sense."

Crossly, Marcus retorted, "I agree. It doesn't make sense!"

"Had breakfast?" asked Nigel after studying his friend with a considering eye.

"Breakfast?" Marcus had to think about it, decided he

hadn't, and, finding himself surprisingly interested in the subject, turned toward Nigel. "Don't believe I have."

"Cook put up a luncheon for me." Nigel hefted the bag. "From the weight of this there's plenty. Want some?

Finally. Something Marcus didn't have to think about. *"Yes."*

Nigel unbuckled a strap and pulled out a napkin which he spread across the top of a crenelation. Then he set out boiled eggs, tapping the bottoms slightly so they'd not roll off, apples, delicate slices of ham wrapped in well-waxed paper, and a small loaf of bread which had been sliced and wrapped in another napkin. Cheese, a small tin with a brandy-soaked fruit cake in it, and another tin with twists of condiments. And, finally, a bottle of wine.

"A feast for a king," said Nigel appreciatively.

But Nigel only nibbled. He was still bemused, a state he much disliked. Nevertheless, he held his tongue while Marcus took a bite, stared off into nothing at all, and chewed and chewed, swallowed, took a second bite, merely chewed, and finally began eating with gusto.

"You were hungry," suggested Nigel when Marcus finished the miniature fruitcake all by himself.

"I think I must have been. Thank you."

"Now you can tell me all those things that don't make sense and maybe together we can figure them out."

Nigel's sly suggestion reminded Marcus of his earlier attempts to explain things like nonexistent curtains and breezes. Or words coming from his mouth he'd *never* say to a lady— except he had, of course. And his stalking that same lady with base intent when he *knew* she'd hate him for it. Particularly that last action was something he'd never done before and a thing for which he despised others.

Now he despised himself.

And then there were the other, somewhat less bothersome things, such as cards which *always* fell as badly as they could when Nigel dealt them and laughter when no one was there . . .

"No, I don't think I *will* tell you," decided Marcus.

"Why not?"

"Because you'd have me clapped up in the nearest Bedlam," said Marcus with exasperation, "and then, too," he added, a trifle belligerently, "because I'll be damned if I'll satisfy that irrepressible curiosity which will one day, my fine friend, get you into a great deal of trouble!"

"Why not?"

Marcus eyed his friend. "I remember when we were boys and you'd get started on that 'why not' game of yours. You'd ask and ask until it drove me crazy and then I'd give in and tell you what you wanted to know." He glared. *"Not this time."*

"Why no—?" Nigel stopped when Marcus held up his hand. "But, Marcus, why . . . ?" Again he stopped. This time the hand had turned into a fist. "Oh well."

"When all's *well,*" said Marcus, his mood a trifle lighter at besting Nigel's determination, *"then* maybe I'll tell you."

"So you won't tell me." Nigel gave Marcus a considering look. "So be it. Then, I won't help you figure out what you mean to tell Lord Wickingham since it's my guess he saw you doing something with or to his daughter which upset him . . . rather a lot."

Marcus's lighter mood faded. Instantly. "Drat." He turned to the wall and again leaned chin on fists and elbows on stone. "And drat again."

Nigel chuckled as he packed up the bits and pieces left from their feast. "I'll leave you to figure out your excuses. While you're at it, you might also think up what you'll say to Lady Winifred. When I saw her, she was riding into the village like a vixen chased by foxhounds. In my opinion *she* was in more of a temper than her father was. *She,*" said Nigel smugly, "looked angry enough to chew a hole in the farrier's anvil."

Nigel's mirth, in the form of chuckles, floated up the stairway as he disappeared as fast as he dared. Old stone stairs were notoriously dangerous and he wasn't about to break his neck—but he'd no desire to remain where Marcus might break it for him. Or merely bend it a trifle.

Or, which was far more likely, give him a black eye.

Once Lord Wickingham settled his guests to their fishing and saw that the footmen knew what to do about the al fresco luncheon, he returned to the castle. He stormed straight up to the room his daughter used as an office and banged open the door.

Lady Winifred, frowning, turned from her desk, a pen dripping ink across the page on which she'd been writing. "My budget doesn't include replacing broken doors, so must you bounce them off the wall that way?"

"Yes, missy, I must. I want to know what you mean by having assignations and, even worse, keeping them right out where anyone could see you at it!"

"Having . . ." Winifred blinked. "Are you out of your mind?"

"*I* saw you. On top of Old Tower. You and that rake. Anyone could have seen you."

"Fine. You saw me and that rake. In that case, you saw that I left him the instant I realized what he had in mind and *before* he'd so much as touched me."

Deflating, her father frowned a frown which matched hers exactly. "You did?" he asked cautiously.

"Of course I did."

"Why?"

Winifred blinked. *"Why?* What else could a lady do but leave?"

Her father's ears turned bright red. "Well . . ." He flicked a guilty glance in her direction.

"Father," she scolded, her voice quite as icy as it ever got, "if you wish to suggest I should have stayed there to be seduced, then you are well on your way to living in Great Aunt Murr's room." To make certain he understood her, she added, "The one with the barred windows and the extra lock?"

"Don't see that," objected Wickingham. "A rake, after all. Used to seducing reluctant maidens."

"He claims he's never bedded a woman who didn't wish it," contradicted his daughter without thinking how it would sound.

"He what!"

Realizing what she'd revealed, Winifred blushed ever so slightly. "It was an apology, you see."

"An apology for *what?"*

"Why . . ." she elaborated rather hesitantly, "I believe it was for saying something he should not have said to me."

"And just what," growled her father suspiciously, "did he say to you that was *worse* than explaining to you, an unmarried woman, his philosophy of proper raking?"

"Er . . ." Winifred's expression blanked and she stared at nothing at all. "You know, I cannot recall?"

"Daughter, you'll wed that rake if it's the last thing I do!" his lordship growled and added, virtuously, "The impudence of him! He'll not be allowed to corrupt your innocence and then pay no pipers!"

"You and Lady Gwenfrewi must put your heads together," said his less than dutiful daughter in her most frigid tones. "She appears to have the same stupid notion. I will not be forced into marriage. *I won't have it.* Do you hear me? Not you and not that . . . that . . ." Winifred ceased ranting. She stared at her father's broad grin. "What have you got into your head now?" she asked, highly suspicious. Seeing her father become his usual jovial self set a touch of fear prowling the edges of her anger. "What are you thinking now?"

"Why, that I don't have to do one diddly-dabbly thing, do I?"

"What sort of, er, diddly-dabbly thing don't you have to do?"

"Some trick to get you wed," he said, scowling fiercely, but it was a false frown. The grin reappeared instantly. "Lady Gwenfrewi has decreed you'll wed the rake, then, daughter, by all that's holy, *you'll wed the rake.* Will ye, nill ye, you will wed him."

Lord Wickingham turned on his heel and left the office, leaving his half frightened and half disgusted daughter shaking her head.

"You didn't listen," she called after him. "Not even that impertinent excuse for a castle matchmaker will make me this match. Or any other. I'll not have it. Besides," she added, almost shouting, *"ghosts don't exist.* So there." If she'd been standing, Winifred would have stamped a foot to punctuate the childish phrase with which she ended her tirade. It was wasted. Her insistence on spinsterhood and the impossibility of ghosts existing didn't reach her father's ears.

Lord Wickingham had already turned the corner and was well beyond the sound of her voice. He was satisfied that, at long last, his daughter would not escape Parson's mousetrap and, what was still better, she'd fulfill the latter part of his promise to his wife. Whether she would or no, his daughter would wed *and* she'd be happy.

Lady Gwenfrewi had so decreed.

Marcus didn't return to the castle until very nearly time to go up to change for dinner. Although he'd thought of little else, he hadn't a notion what to say to his host who would, undoubtedly, accost him with demands for his head the moment it was available for a good washing.

Wishing he knew how to make himself invisible, Marcus crossed the old hall to the main staircase. Halfway up he heard footsteps above and, glancing up, saw what he least wished to see: Lord Wickingham.

Marcus groaned softly, straightened his shoulders, and prepared himself to face what was coming.

Whatever it might be.

"Well, well," said his lordship jovially. "Had a good day? Hmm? *Son?*" he finished on a sly note.

Marcus blinked. "Er, a good day? Why, mmm, not too bad."

Wickingham, reaching Marcus's side, clapped him on the shoulder. "Fine. That's just fine. Good it wasn't *too* bad. Tomorrow will be better. No doubt about it." He reached for Marcus's hand and shook it vigorously. "Yes, sir. Better and better. Well, my boy, you just run along now. Don't want to keep you standing around in this draft."

Marcus shivered as, for the first time, he realized there *was* a draft. He nodded. Actually, it wasn't so much a draft but that bone-chilling cold he'd felt when Lady Winifred collapsed at his feet. And then again, to a lesser degree, whenever he did something he knew was out of character—almost always when Lady Winifred was about.

As he wondered where the chill came from he noticed Lord Grenville Somerwell wandering down the hall ahead of him. Forgetting the draft, he picked up his pace. "Somerwell! Hold up."

Grenville turned. He saw who accosted him and shook his head. "Can't," he said, his face set in stubborn lines. "Gotta change."

"So do I, but I've a question for you."

"Don't *want* to answer questions," said Grenville pettishly. "Want to change for dinner."

"That ghost you said you saw—"

"Don't want to talk about ghosts."

"Well," said Marcus, exasperated, *"I do."* He caught and held Grenville's gaze. "I want to know more about that ghost."

"You don't believe in ghosts."

"That doesn't matter. Tell me about him. Her? It?"

"Her."

"We progress. What did you see?"

"When?"

"When Lady Winifred fainted."

"Oh. Then."

"Well?"

"Well what?"

"What did you see?"

"When?" At Galveston's growing exasperation, Grenville pulled his cane up under his chin and backed away. "Oh. Then, you mean. Well, er, the ghost, of course."

"But—"

"Got to go get dressed," said Grenville and, turning, rushed down the hall at something just short of a run.

Sighing, Marcus glared at the receding form. Ever since Waterloo, trying to get sense from Somerwell only led to frustration. He'd have to try again when he himself wasn't about to be late.

Lord Galveston was returning somewhat later to the main staircase when he met up with Lady Winifred and Miss Tillingford. "Good evening, ladies," he said cautiously, nodding to Miss Tillingford, his eyes on Winifred.

"A very good evening, I think," said Miss Tillingford when her cousin refused to respond. "We mean to organize charades after dinner, my lord. I've always enjoyed charades."

"I do, too," said Marcus. "And you, Lady Winifred?"

Once again Miss Tillingford responded for her determinedly silent cousin. "Charades are Winifred's favorite party game, are they not, cousin?"

"Hmm."

Miss Tillingford giggled. "I think you must be getting in practice!" she told her cousin.

Winifred passed a scornful look in Clare's general direction, which bounced off Lord Galveston in passing. "Fiddle," she muttered.

"May I be on your team, Lady Winifred?" asked Galveston, politely.

"No."

Even as Winifred snarled the denial, Miss Tillingford overrode her cousin's voice, by quite loudly saying, "What a very good idea. You and Winifred will, I think, come up with excellent titles and portray them beautifully . . ." Her voice trailed off at the new look Lady Winifred turned on her. She glanced around, up, down. "Winifred."

"Don't Winifred me! You *know*—"

"But *Winifred*," insisted Miss Tillingford with another glance around, "if you'd just listen—"

"I want nothing to do with—"

"*Freddy,* listen to me."

The use of her nickname stopped Winifred's growing tirade. She stopped walking, too. "Clare Tillingford, you *promised* me you'd never use—"

"I *know*," interrupted Clare, "but you must listen. I didn't mean to say that. About it being a good idea. *Truly.*" Again her gaze darted up and down and all around.

Lady Winifred's skin paled. Then she too looked around and about, up, down, to both sides. "You mean . . . ?" she asked softly.

"I think so." Clare put her hand on Winifred's arm. "I . . . felt her."

"Drat."

"Her?" asked Marcus softly.

"Lady Gwenfrewi," responded Miss Tillingford absently, her mind still on her cousin. "Winifred, you *know* I wouldn't—"

"I know," said Winifred, interrupting.

"I'm sorry."

"If it was something induced by that . . . that . . . !" Lady Winifred shook her head. "No, I will *not* believe." Her glance lit on Lord Galveston, who made no pretense he wasn't interested in their conversation. "Oh, never mind." Lady

Westerwood turned a corner into the hall and Lady Winifred relaxed. "My lady," Winifred said, her tone revealing her relief. "Good evening."

"Is everyone else as hungry as I?" asked her ladyship, brightly. "An afternoon's fishing in the refreshing air has given me a great appetite." She glanced from one to another of the younger people. "Have I interrupted something?"

"No," said Lady Winifred in the same instant as Lord Galveston said, "Yes."

He continued immediately. "But it isn't a subject we can continue just now anyway. Did you have a good catch?"

"Merely acceptable. Only three keepers, but those were good-sized."

As the four strolled down to the drawing room in which the party would meet before dinner, Lady Westerwood described not only the fish she'd caught but every one which got away as well. "I'm greatly addicted to fishing," she admitted a trifle ruefully, as, much to the relief of her auditors, they entered the drawing room.

Lady Winifred, a hand on his sleeve, detained Galveston for a moment. "It is not a subject we will discuss *ever,*" she said firmly and, turning on her heel, walked away to join several young ladies clustered around the pianoforte.

Lord Ramsbarrow observed the little scene between Marcus and Lady Winifred. His curiosity was roused still further by the look of frustration on Marcus's face. Could his old friend truly be interested in the icicle? Unlikely. Galveston had never had dealings with unmarried wenches, preferring a willing widow, as Nigel did himself—except, of course, for the occasional adventure with the sort of chit who made her living that way, which wasn't the same thing at all. So *why* did Marcus pursue Lady Winifred?

Ramsbarrow's nose itched. It always itched when there was a mystery and he could find no satisfactory solution to it. Rubbing his nose, Ramsbarrow moved in careful stages until, seemingly by accident, he was near where Lady Winifred talked to Miss Moorhead-White.

Or rather, where Lady Winifred *tried* to talk to Miss Moorhead-White. She was getting no better response from the girl than Lord Galveston had the previous evening. The girl had no knowledge of how to converse, the comments one drew from her stopping the conversation rather than carrying it forward. For half a moment Ramsbarrow, who shamelessly eavesdropped, considered helping Lady Winifred out of her difficulty, but he quickly reconsidered. His plan relied on accosting Lady Winifred at just the right instant so she'd have no time to evade his offer to escort her into dinner!

Persevering with her guest, Lady Winifred asked, "And do you go from this party up to London for the little season or will you have your come out next spring?"

"Neither."

"Neither?" Winifred noticed the girl's eyes glistened and wished she'd thought of some other topic. "Perhaps you will go to Bath, then," she said in a calm voice.

This comment merely brought the tears to fruition and they rolled down the chit's cheeks one after another, great glistening pearls which made no change in her complexion or her nose or any other part of her face. Winifred, watching, wished she could cry so prettily.

"No," said Miss Moorhead-White. There was no particular emotion in her voice when she actually volunteered, "I'm not to have a season."

"But whyever not?" Lady Winifred instantly added, "No, forgive me. I'm sure such private matters should not be discussed between people who are barely acquainted."

"Oh, it isn't *money*," said Miss Moorhead-White earnestly, that one word proving she was not stupid. "It's me. I'm . . . I'm a nothing, you see. Quite unworthy of a season. My father has said so over and over and over again."

"Fathers can be the bane of one's existence, as I know! Does he wish you to remain unwed and at home, perhaps?"

"Oh no. Not at all. It's just that he doesn't think anyone would want me, you see, so why bother showing me off in the marriage mart?"

"What does your mother say?" asked Lady Winifred. Having experienced her own father's machinations, it had never before occurred to her a father might do other than his very best to get a daughter married and off his hands.

"The same of course." Miss Moorhead-White's eyes widened. "What else could she say?"

For a moment Lady Winifred thought of telling the chit exactly what her mother might say, but, not only did the butler appear in the doorway just then and clear his throat, she recalled that Mrs. Moorhead-White always seemed a frightened little mouse. *Not* the sort who would contradict her husband!

As the butler announced dinner Lord Ramsbarrow moved to the exact spot which put him into position to offer his arm to Lady Winifred who, as he'd hoped, lightly placed her fingers on it and *then* looked up to see who it was she'd accepted as escort.

"You!" she exclaimed.

"It was the last time I looked," he said, an eyebrow quirked.

Lady Winifred sighed. "I suppose I deserved that."

"Deserved what?" asked Nigel, curious.

"Your smart-tongued jest. Obviously Lord Galveston has joked about how I always greet him that way and told you how he responded."

"You are fair and far out with that. Marcus refuses to discuss you."

Lady Winifred was silent for a long moment. "You have asked, then. Why?"

"Because my dearest friend is acting very strangely, quite unlike himself, and I want to understand why."

Lady Winifred opened her mouth to make a sharp retort

but closed it without speaking. She tried again. Again she didn't say anything. Finally, "I don't understand. Why do you say he acts out of his usual way? He is a rake, is he not?"

"Certainly he is a rake. To one degree or another, we are all of us rakes. Marcus and I limit our raking to certain restricted circles. It is constrained by the rules by which we live. At least, we always *have* lived by them. It is only here and now that Marcus behaves in ways he'd never ever have done in the past and, as I said, I want to know why."

"I don't know why," said Lady Winifred quickly. Too quickly.

Ramsbarrow glanced down at her. "Not so much as a guess, is that it?"

"That's it."

"Hmm. I had not thought you a liar, Lady Winifred."

"I'm . . . not."

He chuckled. "Well, I cannot press you just now. We have arrived and, if I mistake not, I am placed by your ewe lamb, Miss Moorhead-White. I fear I am in for a long boring . . . ah, but I see that Lady Pelling is seated at my other hand. That will liven things up a trifle."

"How so?"

"I will flirt with her and she will snub me and I will tease her and . . . and we will see, will we not?"

Lady Winifred laughed. His expression was so wryly self-deriding she could not help herself. "You are a rogue, Lord Ramsbarrow."

"Oh, I *try.* I do try," he said softly as he pushed in her chair.

Then, leaning a trifle nearer than necessary, he blew lightly into her ear.

Lady Winifred blinked. What in heaven's name had the man done to her? Why did such a silly thing send such very odd shivers up her spine?

Rather . . . enjoyable shivers?

"How very odd," she muttered.

"What is odd?" asked Galveston who had just seated himself beside her and was engaged in unfolding his napkin.

"Lord Ramsbarrow just—" Lady Winifred shut her mouth with a snap. "Why are you sitting there? I told Beagle he was to check, the very last thing, that you were seated down the table by Lady Pelling—whom you seem to admire," she finished a trifle acidly.

"Should one not admire that which is so attractive to the eyes?" he asked blandly. "I deem *you* easy to look upon, too. Should I not admire you? For that, and—" he added before she could berate him for impertinence, "—also for the intelligence you've revealed and the gentleness I've seen in you and your truly excellent seat on a horse and for . . . No." He paused only a moment. "Perhaps *not,*" he mused, giving her a slanting glance, "for the chilly demeanor you present to your father's guests. His unwed male guests, that is."

"They are not *my* guests. *You* are not my guest."

"If you had your own establishment, you could invite whom you please."

"Oh yes," she said and, instead of the anger Marcus had rather expected, he heard a wistful note. "It is what I dream of. Not a large place. Perhaps Morningside Hall."

"Morningside Hall?"

"Yes. At the moment it is merely part of my dowry but it will be *mine,* free and clear of any strings, when I reach my thirtieth year. I dream of living there with my cousin. We would have a garden and a fine library and she'd see to the house and I would oversee the home farm . . ."

"Hmm. And does Miss Tillingford also dream of such an establishment?" He noticed that her dreamy look faded and, a trifle slyly, added, "Or does she long for a home where she is truly mistress? A husband and, perhaps, children?"

Lady Winifred seemed to wake up. She turned toward him.

"I have no notion what Clare *longs* for, but if she had even one sensible bone in her body, it would *not* be a husband."

"You say that as if you suspect she *isn't* sensible?"

"You say *that* as if you were laughing at me," she retorted.

"No. Not at you. But—" He eyed her. "—perhaps I would enjoy laughing *with* you?"

For a long moment Lady Winifred sat silent, toying with her soup, her spoon sliding back and then around and then back and then around . . . and not drinking a drop of it. "I don't know. I don't believe I've ever trusted a man enough I might laugh *with* him."

"I wonder what has happened that you believe men are all, every one of them, to be distrusted. Do you think every woman trustworthy? That all females are people with whom you might laugh? Or do you find some you like and some you do not?"

The man dared chide her! Worse, she'd no ready answer, because obviously she *didn't* like or trust *all* women and the corollary that men, too, weren't all alike was inescapable. Since she didn't dare respond to his last comment—at least not honestly—she waited until first her own and then his lordship's soup dish had been removed and said, "We speak of serious things when we should be conversing lightly. Tell me, my lord, are you like Lady Westerwood who enjoys fishing so very much?"

"I think," he said, matching his tone to hers, "that I only like to fish when I am fishing with interesting companions."

"But isn't that rather nonsensical? When one fishes, one is alone. Silent. Waiting and waiting for some particularly stupid—or do I mean particularly *hungry*—fish to bite. One must have patience to be a fisherman," she said in a tone which revealed she had it *not.* "Ah! I have just concluded you do not like fishing."

"How did you reach that notion?"

"Because you are *not* patient."

"When have I given you reason to believe I've an impatient nature?"

Lady Winifred thought over the various occasions she'd dealt with the man, her brows arching. "I haven't the least notion," she concluded revealing some confusion. "Still, I think it true."

"Might you be wrong? I often fish with Nigel. Lord Ramsbarrow, that is."

"I cannot imagine either of you at all interested in an occupation where a woman was not involved."

Winifred was a trifle surprised by how difficult it was to put an acid bite into that and, on the other hand, the difficulty she had restraining a teasing note. She bit her lip as she studied the fish offered her by the footman. Salmon. It was one of her favorites, but her stomach was in knots and she felt she couldn't eat a bite. She shook her head.

Marcus took a large portion. He saw her glance at it. "Have I been greedy? Salmon is a favorite of mine. Every year I visit a friend in Scotland who owns fishing rights to an excellent salmon stream. We allow ourselves to gorge on our favorite fish day after day until we are sated for another year—" Seeing a faintly wistful expression, he stopped and, when he continued, spoke more softly. "What is it? What have I said?"

"We used to go up to Scotland for the salmon fishing," she responded, a dreamy, faraway expression in her eyes. "Not recently, however. Father hasn't liked to take such long journeys for some years now. I miss the Scottish *braes* and the wild free wind blowing over rugged land."

"Ah, yes. Those magnificent hillsides. Did you take long walks?"

"*Very* long walks. There is something particularly bracing about the Scottish air, I think. And then to come home to salmon caught fresh that day. Food for the gods, I think."

"But you didn't take any tonight?"

"I'm not hungry. I don't know where my appetite has gone."

"Try a morsel," he urged and placed a nice flaky, orangey-pink piece of fish on her plate. "Just a bite?"

Reluctantly, not certain why her stomach was so unsettled, she took a bite. The juices instantly flowed and she took another. "It is good, is it not?"

"Something we have in common, a love of salmon and of Scotland during salmon season," he teased.

Lady Winifred laid down her fork. Her stomach had reacted to his words but in such a way she hadn't a notion what it meant. It wasn't at all a sick feeling such as she was used to feeling when a gentleman attempted to flirt with her. It was something quite different. Butterflies, yes, but not sickmaking butterflies.

What could it mean?

The meal seemed endless. Very nearly everything Lady Winifred ate came from Marcus's plate because she'd have refused whatever was offered and he'd insist she try a bite of something he thought particularly good. It was the oddest situation. Why she didn't simply get up and leave she didn't know. Why she put up with his solicitous attempts to get her to eat was beyond her.

She concluded that it was the fact she was her father's hostess which kept her in her seat. Besides, good manners required that she turn to converse with the man on her left whenever the courses changed. And that was just often enough she could bring her emotions back under control before she was required to turn back to Lord Galveston and his questions about Scotland: where she'd been, whom she'd visited, had she been to Stirling and did she know the woolen mills in another place, and had she attended a *ceilidh* when the local people gathered to sing their Gaelic songs, drink their Gaelic whisky, and dance?

Which she had not, but he had and he willingly described

such an evening of fun among the true Scots, both young and old.

By the end she felt quite relaxed. Galveston made it easy to respond naturally and showed just the right amount of interest in her answers. In fact, Lady Winifred realized as they reached the end of the meal, he'd made it *too* easy.

Dangerously easy. With a hidden sigh of relief, she gathered feminine eyes and, rising, led the women out. She directed them to one of the larger drawing rooms where she set Clare and Miss Smythe to planning the charades and excused herself. She really could not be around others until she'd figured out what had happened at the dinner table. Until she understood why she hadn't wanted to run from Lord Galveston and hide far from where he'd ever find her.

Assuming he bothered to look, of course.

The thought, sliding into her head from nowhere, brought Lady Winifred up short. Why was it . . . *distasteful,* the notion he might *not* try to find her? She shivered in a sudden chill and suddenly wondered why she was allowing a guest in her father's home to chase her away from an enjoyable evening. An evening devoted to one of her favorite pastimes.

Well, he *wouldn't.* She wouldn't allow it. Lady Winifred marched back to the drawing room, determined to have a good time if it killed her.

Lady Gwenfrewi, having successfully tricked Lady Winifred into joining the others in the drawing room, spun into a triumphant spiral, exuberantly bounded down the hall, turned the corner, another, another, and then the last, completing the square and arriving back at the drawing room door just as the men strolled up the hall. She perched on the ornately carved lintel, watched the men enter, moved inside and perched on that lintel. What next, she wondered, could she do to forward her plans for Lady Winifred?

Aha! *This* would never do.

The sprightly little ghost did a quick trick and Miss Tillingford, who had been about to choose Lord Ramsbarrow as her next teammate, choose Lord Galveston instead, which put him on Lady Winifred's team, whether her ladyship, would or no.

"Now," mused Lady Gwenfrewi, *"we'll see what we can do."*

Charades was such a fruitful game for pushing forward her plan, a fact that excited the little ghost greatly. It took great effort to restrain herself from becoming visible and joining in! Since that would frighten more than half the guests into leaving the room—and very likely the castle— she kept herself unseen, and kept careful watch for occasions when she might next influence the outcome of her private game.

Whenever possible that evening she'd maneuver dear Freddy into pairing with dear Marcus and see that the two of them were forced to act out a clue requiring properly amorous behavior . . . which would put Lady Winifred into the mood, surely, for some quite *improper* but equally delicious amorous behavior!

Seven

"Really, Clare!" said Winifred testily. "This has become far too complicated."

Clare was organizing a pile of props for her team's first charade. "Will you stop fretting? It is an excellent charade. I've always believed that the more difficult to guess the better," insisted Clare, peering out the door. "Why are they taking so long to find us a spade?"

"Everyone will assume Lord Galveston is Heracles," fumed Lady Winifred.

"Wonderful! You know the idea is to keep them from guessing correctly while not giving false clues." Clare took another look out the door and smiled. "Here we go. All right, you two," she said, looking from Lady Winifred to Lord Galveston, "do you know what to do?"

"Lady Winifred is to make demanding motions and I, obediently, go off and do the task set me," said Lord Galveston.

"Excellent. But which task should come first?" Clare's forehead wrinkled and she put a finger to her lips, thinking.

"Killing the Nemean Lion was first," mumbled Grenville.

"What was that, Lord Somerwell?" asked Clare.

Red around the ears, Grenville repeated himself. "And killing the Hydra of Lerna was next," he finished.

"Hmm. Killing something doesn't seem an appropriate labor," mused Clare.

"Then Heracles fetched the Apples of the Hesperides and cleaned the Stables of Augeas," said Grenville.

"Excellent. Thank you, Lord Somerwell. That will confuse them nicely. It is good to have a scholar among us. You'll be a great help when guessing the answer to the other team's charades."

The blood flowing up into Somerwell's ears now wasn't so much from shyness as it was embarrassed pleasure at Clare's approval. "Not a scholar," he objected. "Just like to read."

"Well, thank goodness you do," said Clare and turned to Winifred. "You do know what to do?"

"I act imperious and give orders."

"While I act the lovelorn lover," put in Marcus.

"And at the end?"

Winifred only compressed her lips, obviously not about to answer.

Marcus said, "I get down on one knee, enumerate the tasks I've done at her orders, lay hand on heart, and make it obvious I'm asking her to wed me."

"And?" asked Clare, turning to her cousin.

"And I spurn him." Winifred said that with immense satisfaction.

"Excellent," said Clare, although she eyed her cousin somewhat askance. *Love's Labour's Lost.* We'll see if it's as obvious as we fear or if we fool them into thinking of Heracles!"

"Thought you said it was Heracles," said a confused Grenville to Clare as the others moved toward the door.

"That's a red herring, Lord Somerwell," she explained. "To mislead the other team."

Lady Gwenfrewi, about to follow Lady Winifred along the hall to the salon, stopped. She looked back. Lord Somerwell, she recalled, had been there when she'd used the Effect on Lady Winifred and Lord Galveston. So had Clare. Oh dear. She'd have to think about that, check the future, decide . . .

But not now. Right now she had to keep an eye on dear Freddy and Lord Galveston. Lady Gwenfrewi flitted on her way.

"Red herring? Ah. Well then." His features relaxed only to tense back up. "Hmmm. We *want* to mislead them?"

"Oh yes. The harder it is for them to guess, the better for us."

"Is it fair?" he asked a trifle anxiously.

"Have you never played charades, Lord Somerwell?"

"Hmm . . . well . . ." He fiddled with his cane. "No," he finally admitted.

"Ah! The point is for the team not acting to do the guessing. When it comes our turn to guess, we watch them act out their offering. If you think you've discovered their title you are to tell me because I'm our team's leader, you see. At the end of their charade, they leave the room while we agree on our solution. When they return we see if we are right. We get three guesses the way we play it here at the castle."

Somerwell exhibited alarm. "They do it differently elsewhere?"

"There are several versions of the game, but the rules are stated at the beginning," soothed Clare. "Miss Smythe and I agreed our subjects must be titles from literature and that we'd have three guesses. We must go now, Lord Grenville, because I must announce the charade before it can be played out."

"Three words," she said and nodded to where her team waited. "First word." A newly married couple took the center of the room. They sat on chairs placed close together, holding hands and looking deep into each other's eyes before getting up and exiting.

"Second word."

Three men entered, including Lord Grenville, who still appeared rather confused. Each carried one of the tools Lord Galveston would use while performing the mimed playlet with Lady Winifred. Each acted as his tool implied he should and then laid his burden down some way from the others.

"Third word," said Clare.

The last three members of their team, excepting Lord Galveston and Lady Winifred, entered. They peered one way, started off, stopped, conferred and one of them pointed. They were off again. A different woman stopped them. The three took a few steps the way she pointed and the third woman stopped and pretended to cry. The other two comforted her while peering this way and that. Giggling, the three women left the room, but peeked back around the door to watch their hostess and Lord Galveston.

"The whole," announced Clare and stood aside.

Winifred and Marcus did very well. Perhaps, thought the ghostly Lady Gwenfrewi, because Lord Galveston, although he wasn't yet aware of it, was already beginning to fall in love with dear Freddy and poor dear Freddy, fighting her feelings every inch of the way, was determined to spurn him.

And spurn him she did, which would *not* move the pair in the required direction!

Fuming, an invisible Lady Gwenfrewi sat cross-legged on nothing at all, her elbows on her knees and her hands supporting her chin. She searched her memory for a title requiring that Lord Galveston take Lady Winifred into his embrace and hold her lovingly. It was surprisingly difficult.

She needed help, she decided, and flitted off to the castle library. But when she *did* find what she wanted, she faced the far more difficult problem of getting the team to use it *and* making her unloverish pair behave in a properly loverlike way! Lady Gwenfrewi sighed loudly, but since she was perched high in a chandelier, no one heard her.

Miss Smythe's team chose the difficult title, *As You Like It*. They managed "you" and "it" and, finally, "like," but it was only their opponents quick thinking which added the "as" to the beginning. Clare's team accepted congratulations from those watching and left the room.

"Antony and Cleopatra," suggested Clare once they were out of the room. The play's title had been running around her head for at least five minutes. Not *inside,* but *whispering all around her* . . . but surely that was nonsense, a bit of whimsy.

"That's too easy," objected Winifred. She'd no desire to play Cleopatra, the beloved of Antony—not if Galveston were chosen play the handsome Roman—and she feared she'd be tricked into the role.

"Besides, everything so far has been from Shakespeare. Shouldn't we try another author?" asked Marcus, who wanted no one else playing Antony and feared he *wouldn't* be chosen for the part. He thought quickly and suggested, "What about *Pamela?*"

"We could use Joseph Highmore's paintings and design tableaus to match rather than making up skits," added Winifred, instantly agreeing.

"Does everyone know those paintings? I only saw them once," said one of the older gentlemen. He grinned as he pretended to hold reins and have a team in hand. "I'd like to play the tricksy coachman! I've a greatcoat and we can find a whip. I'll sit on the edge of a table and we'll set Pamela under it!"

"For that scene, Mr. B. would have to be up high, looking out his window," objected Lady Westerwood, who had also seen the paintings. "How would we manage that?"

"A ladder perhaps?" suggested Galveston after a moment. "Whoever plays the part might hold a small window frame and peer through it?"

Grenville tugged at Clare's sleeve. "What paintings?"

"Do you know the novel *Pamela?*" she asked quietly.

"Hmm," he said, nodding several times, the head of his cane tucked near the point of his chin.

"Highmore painted a series of pictures telling the story in visual form. It was his contention that pictures told a story better than words do because a picture could say many things all at once whereas words had to tell *consecutively* things which actually happened *at the same time.* They are quite dramatic."

"Never saw them."

"That's not surprising, Lord Somerwell. I haven't a notion when they were last exhibited. *I* viewed them in Canterbury when a friend suggested I ask their owner if I might. People do that, I understand. The paintings are quite famous."

"Never heard of them." Grenville looked up, casting her a worried look. "Don't mean they aren't famous. Just never heard of them."

"No reason why you should."

"That's all right then." Having Clare's permission for his ignorance, so to speak, Grenville relaxed.

While they spoke suggestions were made for other scenes: the scene in Pamela's bedroom when Mr. B. invades it and she faints, the one with the cook where Pamela tells that lady she must leave and, of course, her wedding.

"That should be enough," said Clare. "Surely they can guess from four scenes. Does anyone disagree?" No one did. "So. Now to choose our actors."

Winifred was, although she demurred, chosen to portray Pamela. She didn't argue too hard. She *liked* acting parts in charades and plays. Marcus, needless to say, was asked to play Mr. B.

"So suitable," whispered Winifred. "A rake playing a rake!"

"Ah, but if you recall, this particular rake reformed and lived with his true love happily ever after."

"I'm sure *he* was happy," she retorted, her smile fading.

Before he could comment on this, *another* hint Lady Winifred thought a married woman's lot unhappy, Clare had them organized and ready to begin.

Fortunately for the other team, one of their members had also seen the paintings. He chortled when the second tableau was presented and could barely contain himself until the last.

Then he called out that the other team needn't leave the room. Whispering, he conferred urgently with Miss Smythe, others in their team bending near. Miss Smythe nodded and generously gestured for the gentleman to announce the title. He correctly identified *Pamela* and his team, in high spirits, left to prepare their presentation.

The preparation took forever. Clare's team, meanwhile, discussed possibilities for their next charade. Several offerings were suggested. None seemed to please everyone. Once again Clare offered *Antony and Cleopatra,* which she couldn't seem to forget and again it was spurned.

Then someone suggested Byron's *Childe Harold's Pilgrimage.*

"Surely it would be too easy," said one.

"Everything else has been by dead authors. Maybe they wouldn't think of something current," said another.

"I want to play a child," said the eldest lady, giggling. "I haven't been that young for so long it should be a challenge!"

"And we could present a herald wearing a tabard and blowing a horn. That might make them think this was another tale from olden times, maybe."

"I'll play the herald," said a young, would-be Corinthian. "Perhaps we can borrow a yard-of-tin from the coachman!" he suggested, a wistful look in his eyes. "I can blow one. I've done it before."

"I'm sure you have," said Clare, "but *not* in a drawing room, please!"

"Oh well then," said the disappointed player.

"You can still be the herald—" Clare glanced around. "—that is, you may if we've all agreed on the title?"

Nods all around indicated they'd made their choice. It then became something of a problem how they'd mime a pilgrimage, but that problem was eventually solved.

Lady Gwenfrewi, sitting on the back of the couch between Winifred and Marcus, almost forgot herself and just barely restrained herself from heaving a loud sigh of frustration.

Why would the group not agree to do *Antony and Cleopatra* when they had such a perfect pair to play the primary roles! At least, thought Lady Gwenfrewi ruefully, *she herself* believed Lady Winifred and Lord Galveston would be perfect.

Lady Winifred had another notion entirely. Although she'd enjoy playing Cleo, she *wouldn't* enjoy it with Lord Galveston as Antony. Lord Galveston, on the other hand, couldn't understand why he found the notion he might *not* be Antony so hard to bear.

The game continued, each side guessing the other team's offerings with relative ease. Clare continued suggesting they do *Antony and Cleopatra* and her team continued to demur until their very last charade. Then Lord Somerwell came in on her side. "Miss Tillingford has suggested several times that we do this title," he said with unusual firmness. "She must really wish it. *I* think we should do as she asks."

The rest looked at each other, a trifle shame-faced at the thought they'd been denying Clare something she particularly wanted. Clare stepped forward to explain she didn't really know why she'd mentioned the play so often, but Lady Gwenfrewi firmed up her substance just in time and appeared behind the group.

Clare saw the little ghost wave her hands and shake her head before she faded away. She'd been about to suggest they'd do something else, but the ghost's actions told Clare that the whispers she'd heard were Lady Gwenfrewi's, and, instead of demurring, said it was only that she thought Lady Winifred would make a delightful Cleo and that Lord Galveston would do very well indeed as Antony.

"Can I play the asp?" asked the Corinthian slyly, his eyes twinkling.

Lady Westerwood stared him down and the young man became quite red around the ears. Satisfied, she asked if she might play Cleo's maid.

The scenes went as planned until the very last. And, from

the point of view of those watching, *even that* appeared steeped in propriety.

In actual fact, however, Lady Winifred felt Lord Galveston's arms go around her in something far more amorous than planned. He actually tugged her close to him, looked down at her, stared into her bemused eyes and then, so slowly she nearly died from simple anticipation, he bent his lips to hers.

It's all wrong, some small part of her mind screamed.

Winifred told the voice to shut up and soaked up the wonderful sensations Marcus's touch induced.

He's only supposed to place a tiny peck on your cheek, yelled that bit of her mind not preoccupied with the actual kiss.

So what? asked this new Lady Winifred.

And then, long before she'd begun to understand what was happening to her, Galveston loosened his hold and lifted his face, looking almost as awed as she felt. Unfortunately, when he was no longer bemusing her with the kiss, that other part of her mind wrested control. Instantly she struggled. A stunned-looking Lord Galveston hesitated only a moment before releasing her.

The sound of a giggle registered and Lady Winifred blinked. She looked around at the grinning girls, the smirking men, and the very slightly horrified faces of the older women. She had kissed Lord Galveston. *In front of every guest at the castle, she had kissed him.*

Winifred reached up and slapped Marcus's face. Hard. And then felt further embarrassed by that action, because *it had not been Lord Galveston's fault.*

Winifred had felt Lady Gwenfrewi hovering even as his lordship approached her for their last scene. She'd felt the family matchmaker surrounding her and Lord Galveston. And then, except for that tiny voice which she'd ignored, she'd not thought of anything but Marcus's nearness. She'd reveled in his strength, which contrasted so well with his unbelievable tenderness. And that kiss! She'd felt . . .

What had she felt?

Winifred realized everyone was staring at her and raised her fists into the air. "I'll have you exorcised, you interfering busybody!"

As Lady Winifred ran from the room, she quite distinctly heard a heavily accented voice say, "Do your worst, my dear child. *I won't go.*"

Eight

"Clare, what is wrong with me?" groaned Winifred. She raised the damp cloth decorating her forehead and opened one eye to stare at her cousin, who had opened her curtains to a brand new morning's sunlight.

"I don't see anything wrong," objected Clare. She hoped to avoid a discussion of the preceding evening's events. After all, what *could* one say? Freddy had become nearly hysterical for no reason at all.

"Moonbeam, don't lie to me." Winifred sat up, throwing the rag to one side. "Tell me I didn't kiss that man."

Clare gave her a surprised look. "Well, you *didn't* kiss him, did you?" Lord Galveston had, of course, as everyone saw, placed an innocent-looking peck on Freddy's cheek.

Winifred's mouth dropped opened. Slowly, she closed it. "I didn't?" she asked cautiously.

"Freddy . . ."

"Moonbeam, how can you say I didn't kiss him?"

"But Freddy—" Clare's eyes narrowed "—I saw nothing more than exactly what we planned. If something else happened, you must tell me. What you think really happened, I mean."

"He . . . I . . . We . . ."

"Freddy."

"I don't understand how you cannot know. You were there."

"Maybe I do understand," muttered Clare, remembering that she'd seen Lady Gwenfrewi hovering near the pair just before Lord Galveston approached to place the planned kiss on Winifred's cheek. Lady Gwenfrewi must have played one of her tricks. "Freddy, so far as anyone knows, it wasn't a real kiss."

Winifred lived again those moments in Marcus's arms, the gentle warmth, the undeniable but tender strength, his accelerated heartbeat matching her own. "If it wasn't," she muttered, "then I've no desire to experience the real thing."

Even as she said the words, Winifred knew she lied, knew she wished to explore again the melting sensation she'd experienced all too briefly. Wanted him to carefully, gently, tug her near, bend down to her, touch her mouth with his . . .

He'd been supposed to do no more than touch her cheek briefly . . . but Lady Gwenfrewi had interfered. Winifred had felt the ghost surround them. And, unplanned, he'd truly kissed her. How *could* Clare say no one would call it a real kiss? Or perhaps Lady Gwenfrewi had somehow masked it?

But what, exactly, had Galveston done to her? What magic had made her feel such truly odd sensations? How had his hands on her waist, then his arms surrounding her, his lips brushing lightly across her own once again, then holding hers until she'd leaned into him, willing him to . . . Oh! Winifred's hand crept up to her cheek.

Wide-eyed, she stared at the faded embroidery decorating the bed's tester. *She had actually begged that he deepen that kiss* and was it that which led to that oddly warm and enticing feeling deep within her?

"How *could* I . . ." she muttered.

"Freddy, you aren't listening."

"Listening?"

"You are off in your head somewhere," accused Clare.

"If I was," said Winifred, not exactly denying it, "I'm not now. What did you say to me?"

"You asked how you could have kissed Lord Galveston

and I said you'd agreed to that little peck. And I don't know why she did it, but you must have felt Lady Gwenfrewi because I saw her surround you. But then everything was just as we'd planned." Clare frowned. "Except you say it wasn't, so she must have done something. At least, after you slapped Lord Galveston, you told Lady Gwenfrewi you'd have her exorcised!"

"I'd forgotten that bit." Winifred moaned softly, then caught Clare's gaze. "And she said she wouldn't go!"

"She did?" Clare almost succeeded in hiding a smile.

Winifred lifted the wet rag, peering at Clare. "You didn't hear her?"

"I don't suppose anyone but you heard her." Clare's smile grew.

"You think it funny. *Traitor.*"

"But, Freddy, it is funny." Before Winifred could respond with the heated words on the tip of her tongue, Clare added, "Shouldn't I call Maud in? If you are to ride this morning, it's high time you left for the stables. If *not,* we should send down a message so Jed needn't delay his other chores."

Winifred threw aside her covers and leapt to her feet. She was late for her ride with Galveston and he would be *waiting.* She plopped back onto the mattress. Lifting her feet to the bed, she lay against her piled pillows.

He would be waiting. Where had that thought come from. Deeply suspicious, Winifred looked around the room, but caught no hint of Lady Gwenfrewi's presence. But if *not* the ghost's doing, then why had she felt concern at that thought?

"No ride?" asked Clare.

"No ride. Moonbeam—" Winifred turned her head and looked at her cousin, a sad-eyed look. "—send down the message for me, will you?"

"Are you not getting up?"

"Not just yet."

Winifred's thoughts edged back to that kiss. For something she'd feared and therefore avoided, her first real kiss had been an oddly agreeable experience. She'd looked into Lord Galveston's eyes and seen a warmth she didn't understand, a tenderness, a . . . something. And she hadn't a single clue as to what it was which had happened between them.

"If only I understood," she said just a touch pettishly. "If only it made sense."

Clare had gone into the sitting room to ask that Maud send a message to the stables, returning to hear only the last bit. "If *what* made sense?"

"How can I possibly actually *want* that . . . that *rake* . . . to take liberties? How can I actually hope he tries—" She glanced at Clare. "Oh. Well. Hmm. Forget I said anything."

Clare ignored the order to forget. "You *do?*"

Winifred scrabbled for the damp cloth she'd laid aside and placed it back over her eyes. "Moonbeam, I don't understand what is going on."

"Maybe you are falling in love."

Winifred sat straight up, her spine as rigid as one of the posts holding up the tester above her head. *"Moonbeam! Wash out your mouth!"*

Clare chuckled. "I haven't said anything bad."

"You *did.* It is terrible for a woman to fall in love. You know my beliefs—"

"I know," said Clare, interrupting, "that you've a bee in your bonnet and you must shoo it away before it ruins your life. You've avoided men and with reason, but *not* the reason you *say* is your reason." Clare's voice softened, losing the scolding tone. "Freddy, you've had fortune hunters wooing you and, since your father became desperate, tricks played on you. I'll admit his lordship has gone about the business with no tact, but you, Freddy, have wallowed in your fear until you are in danger of actually losing the one man who could provide you with the love and tenderness you crave."

"Love, tenderness, and that other business," snapped Winifred, turning her head away.

"You mean the way men and women make babies," said

Clare placidly. "Have you no desire to hold your own child in your arms, Freddy?"

The wistfulness in Clare's question was so very obvious that Winifred, preoccupied as she was, couldn't avoid hearing it. She removed the cloth and stared at her cousin. "Are you suggesting you are willing to allow a man to do *that* just so you can suffer all the pain, horror, and dangers of child bed?"

"Unlike you, I don't believe what a man and a woman do together need be all that bad. You know we disagree on that. And to have children I will suffer every pain and torment." Her rounded chin settled into a stubborn shape. "I want a husband. And I want children. Very much."

Again Winifred heard something in her cousin's voice which she'd never heard before. "You surely aren't thinking of bringing the idiot up to scratch merely so you may marry and have children, are you?"

"Do not speak disparagingly of Lord Somerwell, Freddy," said Clare with dignity and a trifle coolly. "You do not know him as I have come to know him. You've no notion what he suffered during the battle at Waterloo and what nightmares he still endures."

Winifred sighed, turning her eyes to the medieval scene which decorated the tapestry above her head. "Lord Galveston told me Lord Somerwell was never the brightest soul, but that before Waterloo he was a competent officer and well liked for his good nature."

"You see?"

"What do I see?"

"Lord Somerwell merely needs love and care and he will return to being the excellent man he once was."

"And you think you might provide that love and care?"

"I think it very possible," said Clare. "I am sorry if you think me foolish, Freddy, but you have never understood my needs, just as I don't yours."

"I have been selfish that I haven't really tried, have I not?" Winifred reached her hand to her cousin, grasping the quickly extended palm. Realizing she'd hurt Clare, Winifred spoke gently. "Do tell me now. Please, Moonbeam."

Still holding Winifred's hand, Clare sat down on the side of the bed and stared out the narrow window toward a ride cut through the castle's oak forest. After a moment she began speaking slowly, a trifle hesitantly. "I have been treated very well here at the castle, Winifred. I don't want you to think I have ever felt as if I were the poor relation put up with because of pity or duty or whatever. But it is not truly my home. It can never be my home. And——" She turned toward Winifred, reaching with her other hand to clasp it too around her cousin's. "Winifred, I want a home to call my own."

"But couldn't you find someone better than——"

"Freddy!"

Winifred sighed. "You mean to have him."

A mischievous smile flickered across Clare's face. "Yes. I think so. He hasn't a notion of it, but I'll bring him up to scratch. See if I don't."

"And it is what you want?" asked Winifred, curious.

"He and I have a great deal in common, you know. We both see ghosts, but that was only the first thing we knew about each other. I have introduced him to most of the castle ghosts now and told them to stop teasing him, that I do not like it."

Winifred grimaced.

"Yes, I know you do not want to believe in ghosts, but they do exist as I've told you for years."

"I've never seen one."

"Not true. And you've heard one, according to what you said a bit ago."

Winifred blushed. *"I did not see or hear a ghost."*

"You keep telling yourself that and maybe you'll make yourself believe it," said Clare, her voice dry as dust. She continued before Winifred could respond. "What you *should* do, of course, is get down on your knees and thank the good Lord that Lady Gwenfrewi has found you your own true love. And after you've done that, you should do whatever you must to assure that he remains truly your love!"

"Even if I wanted to," said Winifred, not meeting her cousin's eyes, "I wouldn't know where to begin."

"You might begin by relaxing when he's near instead of bristling like a hedgehog who has had its sleep disturbed."

"I . . . can't."

"Can't? Or won't?"

"Don't scold. I said can't and I mean can't. Sometimes, oh for minutes at a time, we are talking and I forget he is a man and a rake and I enjoy speaking with him. He has six sisters, you know. And I forget how many nieces and nephews, but a lot of them . . ."

Even Winifred heard the enthusiasm in her own voice and let it trail off to nothing. She turned her eyes sideways, saw her cousin smiling. A groan rising from deep inside her, she stared straight up, unseeingly, at the tester.

"It sounds," teased Clare, "as if the trick may be to keep him talking."

"Keep him talking." Winifred drew in a deep breath. "If I kept him talking, then he wouldn't try . . . wouldn't expect . . ." Again she glanced at her cousin and quickly looked away.

"Expect *that,* as you so succinctly put it. I don't think it would work on your wedding night."

"No one has said word one about a wedding."

"Except Lady Gwenfrewi." Clare chuckled at the grimace marring her cousin's face. Her laugh grew louder when Winifred scowled.

The teasing was not appreciated. "Lady Gwenfrewi does not exist."

"That's the way, Freddy. You keep telling yourself that." Clare stood, "Well, I've the flowers to see to. If you are not getting up, then I'll send up a tray, shall I?"

"Don't bother. I'm not hungry." Winifred toyed with the cloth, which was nearly dry. "Besides, I *must* get up soon.

We've the ball to prepare for." Winifred sighed. "Go along, Clare. I just want to be alone for a bit."

Clare nodded and quietly closed the door to Winifred's sitting room where their shared maid waited, working at some mending in the light from a window. "She'll call when she's ready for you," she told the middle-aged woman who had been the cousins' maid since both left the nursery. Clare went into the hall and turned toward the intersecting hall which led to the main staircase. At the corner she found Lord Somerwell hovering in indecision.

"Good morning, my lord. Have you breakfasted?"

Grenville's eyes lightened and a smile crossed his face. "Hmm," he said, nodding. Then he looked confused. "I think." But the confusion faded. "Yes, I did. *You* weren't there," he finished, the faintest of accusatory notes in his tone.

"I ate early and have been talking to my cousin. Lord Grenville, last night in Lord Galveston and Lady Winifred's last charade, did you see Lady Gwenfrewi nearby? Just before my cousin said she'd have her exorcised?"

"Oh, yes." Grenville nodded his head rapidly. "She clouded what happened and made almost everyone see what they were expected to see."

"Most everyone?" A touch of horror chilled Clare. "Not *everyone?"*

Lord Somerwell, hearing that she was displeased, raised the ivory head of his cane to his mouth and shook his head. "Oh dear . . ."

"I think," said Lord Somerwell, trying to mend matters, "that only Lord Ramsbarrow saw the true situation."

"No one else?" asked Clare, worried.

"Besides me? I always do." He sighed.

"Is that bad?"

"Isn't it a bad thing to know secrets you should not know? And have to remember not to tell anyone about them?"

"That is a pretty heavy responsibility, is it not?" she asked sympathetically. She patted his hand and offered, "I'm going to do the flowers now. Would you like to come help?"

Lord Galveston, just around the corner and unashamedly listening, closed his eyes. He felt relieved most people hadn't a clue what had happened. It had been clear, almost at once, that those watching believed he'd merely kissed Winifred's cheek.

Why people believed that when he'd actually done what he'd done was, at the time, lost in the relief flooding through him: no one expected an immediate announcement of marriage!

Which was just as well. Winifred wasn't ready for such an announcement.

Winifred wasn't ready. He wondered where the thought had come from, but put it aside. Later he'd wonder what he meant by it. At the moment he must worry about that kiss. Miss Tillingford obviously knew, but she wouldn't talk. Somerwell did, but he'd just said he wouldn't tell. He'd also said *Nigel* knew what really happened. If *Nigel* knew . . . !

Marcus moved silently but at speed down the hall. He had to find Nigel. Not that Nigel would *tell,* but he did love to tease and he mustn't tease Lady Winifred. She wouldn't appreciate Nigel's jesting. Not at all!

Nigel wasn't in his room. His valet would only admit to the fact that his master had been dressed for riding. Marcus, who had returned from his own ride but hadn't yet changed, retraced his path to the stables. Jed gave him the added information that Lady Winifred had not gone riding that morning and another interesting detail: Nigel was riding with Lady Pelling.

If Nigel was riding tête-á-tête with Lady Pelling, he'd be exceedingly upset if interrupted. Worse. If interrupted, he'd feel vengeful. He might hint to Lady Winifred what he knew.

Almost as bad, he'd roast Marcus and Marcus had no desire to be teased unmercifully about that kiss.

A kiss which had taken place before a roomful of house-guests who, for the most part, hadn't seen a thing out of the way. How could that be?

"Jed," said Marcus, "something I don't understand is going on. Things . . . happen. I do things I've no intention of doing. I feel things which . . . I won't say they frighten me, but I'll admit they've an eerie feel to them. Explain, if you can, what is happening."

Jed eyed Lord Galveston. He looked all around, up, down, even stood and picked up the bucket on which he sat. Then, in a whisper, he said, "It's the ghost. Lady Gwenfrewi. You've heard of Lady Gwenfrewi?"

"Should I have heard?"

"There are stories," mumbled Jed, not looking at Galveston.

"I like a good story."

Jed glanced up, then back down at his work and mumbled, "I'd rather not if you don't mind?"

Galveston frowned. "You'd prefer that I hear it from Lady Winifred?"

"It's just that, if you don't already know, I don't want to be the one to tell you." Jed seemed to realize what he'd said and glanced up at Lord Galveston, who merely grimaced.

After a moment Galveston prompted, "Lady Gwenfrewi . . ."

"That's right."

"A castle ghost?"

"Yes."

"Gwenfrewi. That's Welsh, is it not?"

"Hmm-hum."

"And it is a form of Winifred, is it not?"

"It is?" Jed looked up. "Do you suppose our Lady Winifred is named for that one?"

"It's possible, is it not?"

"No wonder Lady Gwenfrewi is so determined . . ." Jed glanced around, up, around. Once again he stood and looked under his pail. "Not that I'd see her if she don't want to be seen," he muttered.

"Jed, what are you doing?"

Jed's ears reddened. "Don't want *her* knowing I'm talking about her."

"The ghost?"

"Hmm-hum."

"Do you truly believe ghosts exist?"

Jed looked up, his eyes wide and his mouth hanging open. He closed it. A scornful expression crossed his features, but it too was quickly erased. "If you *don't,* you *will,*" he said. Cautiously he looked all around again. "If that's all, my lord," he said politely, "I've work to do."

"It isn't half enough, but I've tried your patience too long and you've work to do and—" Marcus turned at the sound of hoofbeats to see who approached. "—here comes the friend for whom I'm waiting."

Almost Marcus moved to help Lady Pelling from her horse. Just in time he remembered he didn't wish to rile Nigel. There truly was no telling what Nigel might do if irritated. Falling back into their old competitive habits was the *last* thing he should do just now.

On the other hand, old habits wouldn't instantly die and a compliment tripped off Galveston's tongue before he could catch it back. "Such beauty so early in the day!" He smiled and asked, "Your ride was agreeable, then? Your cheeks have lovely color so I think it must have been. Hello, Nigel," he finished quickly, before Lady Pelling could respond. "I don't suppose you've a moment this morning when you might allow me a few moments of your time?"

Nigel gave Marcus a searching look. "Lady Pelling has promised to show Miss Smythe how to tie a love knot and is a trifle late for their appointment. I'll just see her into the house and join you in . . . the rose garden?"

"Back here," said Galveston shortly. "We'll ride."

One of Nigel's brows arched. His lips twitched, but he merely nodded, offered Lady Pelling his arm, and the two walked off. While Marcus waited, he paced an area where long usage had smoothed the ancient cobbles into reasonably even footing. Back and forth. Back and forth . . .

And trailing behind, holding on with one hand to the tail of his coat, was Lady Gwenfrewi. Earlier the ghost had overheard Lord Ramsbarrow and Lady Pelling talking. Lord Ramsbarrow's surprise that Lady Pelling didn't know why Lady Winifred had slapped Lord Galveston. had decided Lady Gwenfrewi she'd better take this ride with Lord Galveston, even though she hated like anything sitting pillion behind a rider!

That had been true even when she lived. Now, when it was so difficult to keep her lack of substance anywhere near a horse without the horse seriously objecting to her presence, it was to be doubly disliked.

But perhaps she could slide in under his lordship's hat? Lady Gwenfrewi awaited an opportunity and, when Lord Galveston lifted his beaver to stroke back his hair, she quickly melted inside it. *Now* she needn't worry she'd lose contact.

Not that she couldn't catch up, of course, but she might miss something!

Nine

Lord Ramsbarrow returned to the stable where his friend paced. Nigel grinned and, hands on hips, said, "Really, old man, just what *have* you been up to, anyway?"

Startled, Marcus turned on his heel. "Nigel!"

"The very same," said Nigel on a dry note. "But answer my question," he coaxed. His fingers went to his nose, which he rubbed furiously.

Marcus eyed that clue to the fact his friend was dying of curiosity. "I haven't—"

"Tut, tut, tut. Ladies do not slap a gentleman for no reason. At least, most don't. They say Lady Winifred is an exception to that rule."

There was a laugh in Nigel's voice that put Marcus on edge. To avoid an immediate response, he mounted Princeling, waited for his friend, and trotted off. Marcus thought about the way Nigel had phrased his dry comment. When they were well down the drive toward the front gate, he cautiously asked, "You think she's . . . an exception?"

"Lady Pelling believes you whispered something outrageous in Lady Winifred's ear and that is why she reacted outrageously in return."

"Something outrageous. And what do you think?"

"Lady Westerwood," continued Nigel, half teasing but also informing his friend of the gossip, "is convinced that, perverse as her ladyship can be, Lady Winifred merely objected to even a pretend kiss to the cheek and that is why she slapped you."

"I didn't ask what the Ladies Pelling and Westerwood say—" Marcus was relieved, nevertheless, at this proof that, somehow, no one seemed to know the truth. "—but what *you* think?"

"What do I think?" Nigel heaved a hugely dramatic sigh. "If I were you, my boy, I'd ride, *ventra à terre,* to the nearest port and take ship for a distant destination. If you don't—" He glanced sharply at Marcus. "—well, then, I'll offer to stand witness to your marriage, of course. I haven't a clue why no one but myself seems to think a wedding is in the wind. I mean, that sort of kiss leads to a lady strolling down the aisle, does it not?"

Discovering Nigel had indeed witnessed the truth, Marcus ignored both his friend's conclusion and his question, asking one of his own. "Just what is this business about Lady Gwenfrewi?"

"Lady Gwenfrewi? What about her?" asked Nigel. "A castle ghost, is she not?" When Marcus merely grimaced, he added, "You mean more than that?"

"Something . . ." Marcus heaved a true sigh, not a pretense as Nigel's had been earlier. "I'll discover the whole somehow. No one seems to want me to know the truth, but I *will* find out."

"Maybe Amanda Longfellow at the Wickingham Arms would know."

"Is that where we're headed?" asked Marcus, realizing. finally that they weren't idly riding, going nowhere in particular.

"Hmm. Molly—" Nigel gave Marcus a bland look, "—informed me she'd be cleaning the end bedrooms this morning."

"And you think I might keep Mrs. Longfellow busy while you are otherwise occupied? Nigel, I am not your whipping boy!"

"But you do have questions she might answer and there is still a bit of that really excellent ham available . . . ?"

"I wish she'd be making bread."

"She does that in the evenings for some reason."

"If she does it in the evening then she doesn't have to get up at four in the morning to bake it before breakfast," explained Marcus.

"It takes so very long to make a loaf of bread?" asked Nigel, truly astounded.

"Hmm. A long, involved process."

"How would you know?"

"Cook let me help when I was little."

"Oh." Nigel lost his interest in bread-making just as quickly as he'd found it. "Well? Are you coming? To the Inn?"

"I suppose." Marcus pretended disinterest, but the instant they arrived he headed for the kitchen. He went to the sideboard where he sliced several lovely thick slices off the end of the ham and lay them on a plate. Picking up a bowl, he went next to the hob, where he filled it with a thick barley soup, sniffing appreciatively at the mouth-watering aroma. Taking soup and ham to the table, he slid onto the end of the bench before he glanced up.

Manda, hands on hips, stood grinning at him. "Make yourself right at home, why don't you?"

"Thank you." Marcus grinned back. "I will." She handed him a spoon and he dug into the soup. "Hmmm! Are you *certain* you'd not like a new position? I'm sure I could find work for your husband as well . . . ?"

"Get along with you. That would never do, now would it?"

"I don't suppose he'd like leaving his inn, would he?"

"I'm quite sure he would not."

"Ah well, if you ever change your mind?"

"I'll keep you in mind, my lord," she promised and chuckled. She went toward the sideboard for another bowl. Turning, she asked, "Now then, is it my good cooking that brought you to our inn?"

"Always that, but I'll admit I also have a need for information. Do you know anything about Lady Gwenfrewi?"

"That old ghost up at the castle, you mean?"

Marcus, his mouth full of ham, nodded.

"Seems I've heard some tale." Manda dipped up a bowl of soup for herself and brought it to the table. "Let me think, now." She dunked a crust of bread into her broth and chewed it slowly. "It's coming back . . ."

"A Welsh lady, I'd think?" hinted Marcus.

"Oh yes. With that name? What else? One of the first Alistaires—I think he was called Sir Rafe—kidnapped her. There's something about her being taken from her home on the very eve of her wedding to another, but that's not the whole—" Amanda was distracted from her tale by a shuddery sort of shiver. She looked around. "—I'm sure there's something more." After a moment she shook her head. "It's gone right out of my head!"

Heaving a sigh of pure relief, Lady Gwenfrewi settled herself on the edge of the buffet. At the very last instant she'd realized what was happening and managed to stop Mrs. Longfellow from telling all. Lord Galveston was *not* the sort to appreciate the notion his wife was chosen for him. Even *less* would he like it that the lady was chosen by a ghost!

Lady Gwenfrewi concluded she was going to have to stay alert. It appeared dear Freddy's threat the evening before had roused his lordship's curiosity to a dangerous degree.

Have her exorcised? Ha!

Lady Gwenfrewi's thoughts moved on and she scowled at Marcus, who was not behaving as he should. Even with her prodding he was taking ever so long seducing dear Freddy and convincing her she wasn't really averse to marriage. It was too bad of him to be so dilatory. Perhaps she should have chosen Lord Ramsbarrow? But no. That would not lead to a happy marriage. Lord Ramsbarrow was not yet ready to settle down and dear Freddy would not like a man with a wandering eye. Lord Galveston *was* ready and this pairing *would* be happy. It was just too bad neither of them had any understanding of that simple fact!

If they did, thought Lady Gwenfrewi, *my task would be ever so much less difficult . . . But what,* her thoughts continued, *would Lord Galveston do next? Who else might he question?*

Oh dear, she'd have to be on guard every moment to be certain he didn't discover even a hint about her matchmaking. He was obviously not one who would find it a delightful tale, but would think her manipulative and deceitful and would do his best to thwart her wishes. He was strong enough he might succeed, too.

"Which," muttered Lady Gwenfrewi, "would be a sorry shame."

Lord Galveston and Mrs. Longfellow swung in her direction making Lady Gwenfrewi realize she'd spoken aloud. Drawing herself into a tight ball, she rolled off the buffet, out the door, and found a corner in which she could thoroughly berate herself.

I really must watch myself, she thought. *I myself will give away my aims to Lord Galveston if I'm not more careful!*

Back in the kitchen the turned heads turned back so they stared at each other. When they realized what they were doing, they bent their heads and stared at their soup. After a long silent moment, Marcus cleared his throat.

"Er, Amanda?"

"No," she said in a firm tone. "I didn't."

Marcus blinked. "Didn't what?"

"Didn't hear anything." After a moment she asked, "Did you?"

"Hear something? What was there to hear?"

Again they stared at each other and then, simultaneously, turned to look at the ham.

Nigel strolled in just then, moved to the sideboard, and

cut himself a slice. He turned, found the others staring at him, and blinked lazily. "Should I slice some for you, too?" he asked, smiling sweetly.

Amanda Longfellow lost all interest in voices that weren't there. She was far more worried about what the dratted Lord Ramsbarrow might have been up to while his friend asked questions she couldn't answer. She quizzed him, attempting to discover if he'd been doing what she feared he'd been doing.

Lord Ramsbarrow, however, was an old hand at misleading the curious and easily misled Amanda.

Long before Lord Galveston had settled himself in Amanda's kitchen, Lady Winifred forced herself from bed and called in her maid, giving orders for a morning gown instead of the habit she'd normally have donned first thing.

Picking up the habit she'd laid out while Lady Winifred still slept, Maud hurried into a tiny room, once a rather large powder closet, but now used for her ladyship's wardrobe. As usual, the plump woman grumbled about the outrageously inadequate suite of rooms; moving her ladyship from a proper suite had been no punishment for dear Lady Winifred, who didn't much care about her surroundings—so why didn't Lord Wickingham allow her young lady to return to rooms where a body could do a proper job of work?

Maud picked up the newly selected pile of clothes and returned to the bedroom where she found her ladyship drying herself. "Here now, you don't want a bath then?"

"Not this morning. There is the ball this evening to which we've invited half the county. I'll bathe before changing into that new gown."

"The new gown, is it? The one that comes down to here—" Maud laid her hand just over the tips of her breasts and eyed her charge. "—the one you said you wouldn't wear if wild animals tried to force you into it?"

Winifred blushed. "That's enough of your sauce, Maud. I've decided I'll wear it and no more need be said. *Not even by you.*"

Lady Winifred rarely gave even so mild a scold as this one. "Well, then . . ." Maud bit her lip. "I'll see it's pressed then." Maud shut her mouth, but didn't stop her thinking. And what she thought was that, for once, maybe the castle gossips had the right of a situation. Maybe Lady Gwenfrewi really had taken a hand in getting their young lady married off!

And not before time.

Maud's gaze flitted nervously around the room whenever she needn't pay strict attention to dressing Lady Winifred. The cousins' maid might have lived over half her life in the castle, but that hadn't been half long enough to get her used to the notion of ghosts. Especially not ones with the habit of interfering with those still enjoying life!

The notion Lady Gwenfrewi might, right that moment, be hovering around her mistress didn't sit too well with Maud. But, since she wanted very much to see both her young ladies happily married, she sincerely wished the ghostly matchmaker well.

Maud just hoped she, herself, was elsewhere whenever the phantom went about the business.

Lord Grenville Somerwell watched Miss Tillingford step back from the last bouquet. She stared at it, just the tip of her tongue showing between her lips and a faint line drawn between her brows.

"What's the matter?" asked Grenville, worried.

"This needs something. Something dramatic."

Miss Tillingford was upset. Grenville was bothered by that and wanted desperately to see her smile again. He glanced around at the few remaining blooms. Nothing among them looked the least bit dramatic.

"Is it important?" he asked, his cane clutched in a stranglehold.

"There's to be a ball this evening, remember?"

Grenville nodded several times.

"And we want the castle to look its best."

"Always looks its best," said Grenville.

"Thank you. But this evening it must be special." Clare picked through a stack of discarded blooms in the hopes she'd missed something. She sighed. "There is nothing for it. I must find old man Black." She sighed again.

"Gardener." Grenville had met the curmudgeon on a previous occasion.

"Lord Wickingham's head gardener. He's very possessive about his blossoms. He hates to have them cut, but I must have at least a single spray of . . ." She stared at the bouquet. "I just don't know. Something."

"Go look for it. Then find Black."

Clare smiled. "Yes. Just the thing. Then I won't have him grumbling and muttering and uttering curses all the time I'm searching!"

"Help?"

Grenville opened his eyes wide and stuffed the head of his cane in his mouth, removing it when Clare nodded and beckoned him to follow her. They left the castle through a door which led to a steep set of stairs rising to the level of the gardens. He looked around and found they were in the castle's vegetable garden.

"We've a glass house where Black grows flowers all year round. This way."

Clare approached the conservatory with caution. Her nervousness communicated to Grenville and he too looked around, although he hadn't a notion what he looked *for*. But Clare relaxed once she was inside the warm and humid structure so he was able set aside this new concern and enjoyed watching Miss Tillingford go about her business.

"Something white? Or perhaps a blue?" she muttered as

she moved around a table holding pots of some plant just sprouting mature leaves. "The blue flowers are over there if I remember correctly."

Grenville goggled. "I didn't know flowers came in so many colors."

"Amazing, isn't it? Black is a genius when it comes to flowers . . . Ah! What about these?"

Clare stood before a display of delphinium which shaded from white to a deep blue, the tall flowers marching in rows as if at one of Prinny's military parades.

Grenville pictured the bouquet. "Those," he said with authority. He pointed his cane at a group of blossoms verging away from white and into the required blue.

"Just the thing. If Mr. Black will only allow me to cut three stems . . ."

Grenville frowned. "Don't need him."

"What?"

"Don't need permission. I'll do it for you."

Before Clare could demur Grenville had taken out a pen knife and, selecting three perfect stems, cut them. He turned and presented them to her.

"Oh dear."

His Miss Tillingford wasn't happy? Why? "What's wrong?" he asked.

"Mr. Black will skin us alive."

Grenville relaxed. "No, he won't."

"But he will."

"You *need* them. It's his job to provide what you need—" Grenville's expression firmed into a stern visage. "—is it not?" he asked.

A growled response indicated it was, but also revealed its owner wasn't too happy with the conclusion.

"So that's all right, then." Grenville offered his arm. "Shall we go finish your bouquet, Miss Tillingford?"

Clare, her eyes wide, felt her spine stiffen. Mr. Black had crept up behind them. She was convinced he'd lay a switch to her legs as he'd done when she and Freddy were children and picked his flowers. She waited. Nothing happened and, very slowly, she turned.

"That all you be needin', Miss?" growled the scowling gardener.

"I . . . think so."

"Good." He turned on his heel and stalked off, not bothering to be silent about it.

"Well!"

"What is the matter, Miss Tillingford?"

"He didn't scold." Come to think of it, the last time he'd laid a switch across her legs was when she'd still been in short skirts! Why, wondered Clare, had she continued to fear him so? She beamed at Grenville. "You are wonderful."

"I am?" he asked cautiously, not having heard such sincere praise for a very long time. Maybe never?

"*I* think so. You were so firm. So . . . properly authoritative!" She smiled. "I think that's the way you behaved around your soldiers and that's why they liked and respected you."

"They did?" Grenville remembered back before Waterloo, back to when he had been in the Peninsula. "Maybe they did."

For the first time since that last battle he could think of his life in the army without cringing. Miss Tillingford had given him back his memories of the good times. He looked at her with new eyes. She was so soft and warm and . . . and cuddly. Except he wouldn't dare cuddle her, of course. Not a proper lady. Proper ladies didn't like to be cuddled.

Did they?

Once the thought of cuddling Miss Tillingford entered his head, Grenville discovered he'd a great deal of trouble getting it out. In fact, it wouldn't budge. He followed her back to the steep stairs leading down to the room in which she did the flowers. Hurrying ahead, he insisted on going first, helping her, assuring she didn't take a tumble on the badly worn steps.

Not only did it give him an excuse to hold her hand, but he received one of those gloriously beaming smiles when they reached the bottom. Grenville felt as if he were in a dream. And, he decided, freckles *were* pretty. At least, Miss Tillingford's freckles were pretty. He liked them.

"I like your freckles," he blurted.

Clare felt herself blushing. "You do?" For the most part she managed to ignore her skin, which she detested. But here was a man who actually liked her spots? She tipped her eyes sideways and studied him. He seemed sincere.

"I never thought about it before," he said, "but they are nice. They make you . . . comfortable and warm and . . . nice?" It was, for Grenville, a sincerely complimentary speech. But he'd never been very good at giving compliments and perhaps Miss Tillingford wouldn't like it? He stuffed his cane in his mouth, apprehensive about how his words would be received.

"I'm glad you like them," said Clare gently and, laying a hand over his, tugged the cane down.

"Did I say it right?"

Clare ignored that his compliment was, perhaps, just a trifle awkward. She smiled. "Just right. I've never before liked my freckles, but if you do, then I won't mind them anymore."

"Like them," he said firmly. He felt his spine stiffen, something of his old, more self-assured posture returning.

"Good." Rather flustered by the change in him, Clare stuffed the last flower stem in just anyhow. By accident, it was the exactly right spot. "I'll tell a footman where to put these and to fill the vases with water once they are in place. Perhaps you'd care to come with me to the church? It is my turn to put fresh flowers near the altar."

Lord Somerwell nodded, moving his cane up toward his chin. Clare tugged it down gently and grinned at him. Grenville grinned back and, swinging the cane the way a man on the strut would swing it, he strolled beside her through the gardens, down the lane, and into the church.

It was a relatively new building. Even Lord Somerwell, who had no particular interest in architecture, could tell that. He asked about it.

"Yes. The old was torn down because of a fire a little over fifty years ago. I've seen an etching of the old and, believe me, this is *not* an improvement!"

As she spoke, Clare's hands poked blossoms and greenery into a pair of lovely urns. She placed them beside the steps going up to the altar and then filled them with water. Then, for a moment, she stood there, head bowed. Grenville realized she was praying and hastily bowed his own head. He looked up when she turned aside, picked up the bucket and ewer, and headed for a side door.

"There's a place in the vestry where I keep these. Next we'll visit the Inn. Mrs. Longfellow makes very good soup. After doing the flowers I usually have a bowl while I chat with her." Clare grinned. "Mrs. Longfellow knows all the local gossip and I discover what's going on in the neighborhood!"

Ten

"Well, now, I don't know if you'd consider it news if *you* could tell me more than I already know!" said Amanda Longfellow after settling her two new guests at one end of her kitchen table. She went back to rolling out dough for her justly famous goose pies.

"What could we know you do not?" asked Clare.

"Why, about that nice Lord Galveston and his—" Amanda glowered. "—not so nice friend, Lord Ramsbarrow. That man! You daren't turn your back on him, but what he's, hmm . . . pestering the maids. And Molly! I wonder about that girl." Amanda whomped another lump of dough on the table and put a little more energy than needed into pressing it out. She reached for her rolling pin. "She'll find herself with a bun in the oven for sure the way she's carrying on." Amanda glanced up and discovered Clare was a trifle red in the face. "Not that I should be saying such things to *you,* of course."

"But," asked Clare, changing the subject from what might or might not be Ramsbarrow's peccadilloes, "you mentioned Lord Galveston. And you think we might know more than you do?"

"Ah! Yes! Now, is that Lady Gwenfrewi up to her tricks or is she not?" asked the inn-keeper's wife, setting both hands on the table and leaning forward. "That's what I want to know."

"Tricks?" muttered Lord Somerwell, with a quick glance at Miss Tillingford.

Clare ignored him. "Lady Gwenfrewi made her choice—I know *that*—but in the past when she's chosen, there's been no question about everything coming to a proper conclusion. This time . . . well, neither of them is acting like April and May, which they should be doing."

"Choice?" asked Somerwell softly, his eyes narrowing.

"Should be! Oh my yes indeed! But you say they are dragging their feet, like?"

"More like outright rebellion on my cousin's part. I'm not quite certain about his lordship."

Amanda's eyes widened. "Well now! What a situation."

"It is, is it not?"

"Situation?" asked Lord Grenville and this time wasn't ignored.

"That old matchmaking ghost isn't having it all her own way." Amanda Longfellow chortled and turned back to Clare. "But what an odd pairing it is, or would you disagree?"

"I certainly thought so. To begin with, that is. But then it occurred to me—" Clare's face turned rosy again. "—that there might be *advantages,* if you know what I mean?" She got a frown from Amanda. Her lips a tightly compressed line, she glanced at Lord Somerwell. She couldn't say more. Not before a man.

Mrs. Longfellow took the hint and didn't press her. "Well, now, isn't that a right kettle of fish? We'll just have to hope it all works out. But it will. After all, Lady—"

Amanda and Clare finished together.

"—Gwenfrewi is *never* wrong!"

The women grinned at each other. They both ignored Grenville's softly spoken question: "Never wrong about what?"

This time Somerwell hunted up Galveston, finally locating him in the library. "About what," he said, barely getting Marcus's attention first, "is Lady Gwenfrewi never wrong?"

Galveston closed his book over a finger. He rolled his eyes. *"Now* the man wants to talk about ghosts. Why now?" he asked no one in particular. "Why not when *I* wanted to talk about ghosts?"

"Now I've heard something," said Somerwell, answering what was really a rhetorical question, "and I want to understand. She chose you. She is never wrong. What did she choose you for and why is she never wrong?"

Galveston laid aside the book, his brows drawn tightly into a line. "Chose me? When and how did she choose me?"

"I don't know. If I knew I wouldn't have to ask you."

"Somerwell, why don't you back up and begin at the beginning and tell me the whole thing?"

"Miss Tillingford and I went to the church and did the flowers there, and then Miss Tillingford said we'd go on to the Inn and we did, and that cook there, she wanted to know what that matchmaking ghost was up to and Miss Tillingford said she'd made her choice but the pair wasn't smelling of April and May and they should be and then . . . hmm, er . . ." Looking up at Galveston, who was glowering at him, Grenville's words trailed off.

Galveston had, as Somerwell's words ran on, slowly risen to his feet until he towered over the smaller man. "And then?"

Grenville gulped, his cane coming up under his chin. "And then they said she was never wrong."

"Never wrong."

"I didn't understand it either," said Grenville. "Want to know." He got a slightly desperate look about him. A hunted look. *"Need* to know."

"Why do *you* need to know?"

"Maybe she chose me too?" A blissful expression took up residence on Grenville's face as he moved off aimlessly, his thoughts having taken a quick turn toward Miss Tillingford.

Lady Gwenfrewi, sitting on top of a bust of a Roman noble, smiled down on him. She'd taken time from her worry about Lady Winifred and Lord Galveston to do some research into the future and had discovered Grenville and Clare would do very well together.

Galveston took a step and caught Grenville by the shoulder. "Somerwell, put your mind in order, will you? I need to know a bit here and there, too." When he once again had Grenville's attention he asked, "Do you really see ghosts?"

Warily, Somerwell eyed Galveston. Then, resigned, he nodded.

"And that day Lady Winifred fainted, you saw one?"

"Lady Gwenfrewi."

"She was there? When Lady Winifred fainted?"

"Before. Then you came. Then she pushed Lady Winifred back against you and then she—" He spoke the last words in a rush. "—went right through the two of you."

Galveston's brows snapped together. "That cold . . . ?"

"Hmm."

"And you and Miss Tillingford both saw it happen?"

"Hmm."

"And, somehow, that means I've been chosen?"

Grenville started another 'hmm' but paused . . . Instead: "I think so."

"Chosen for what?"

"A match? Perhaps? They called her a matchmaker." After a moment he added, "And maybe I have been, as well?"

Grenville said the last with such a hopeful look Marcus simply couldn't bring himself to loose the string of expletives hovering on the end of his tongue. "Why you too?"

"Think it must have something to do with being with an Alistaire? And experiencing the ghost? Lady Winifred kept saying things like 'I don't believe in ghosts' and 'You don't exist' and 'I've avoided you for years' and that sort of thing? She didn't want to see Lady Gwenfrewi. It was when she realized *you* were there, too, and *before* the ghost surrounded you, that she fainted. Before that she was merely angry. Must mean something?"

For Somerwell it was a very long statement. Having said the whole he put the end of his cane in his mouth and eyed Galveston with the wary look which, since Waterloo, was so much a part of his character. Then Grenville realized Galveston was paying him no attention. He lowered the cane; Miss Tillingford didn't like him to put it in his mouth so he was trying to remember not to do it. He straightened his spine.

"Galveston?" he asked when the silence had gone on too long. "You think maybe I'm right?"

"A matchmaking ghost?" Galveston glowered quite dreadfully.

"Hmm." It was the best Somerwell could do when glowered at, but he did keep the cane at his side and himself upright. He was rather pleased with himself for doing so.

"A—" The profanity which followed would have done a coachman proud. "—ghost is supposed to have chosen me my wife?"

"Don't think so."

Marcus, about to spew out a curse of the ripest sort, closed his mouth. He opened it and, a trifle confused, said, "That's what you said."

"Huh-uh." Grenville shook his head.

"Then what *did* you say?"

"Think the ghost is supposed to choose Lady Winifred a husband."

"That's the same thing."

"No, it isn't," insisted Grenville.

"It is."

"Isn't."

"It most certainly is."

Grenville merely shook his head.

Galveston glowered.

The door opened and Lord Wickingham strolled in. He

ignored Somerwell but beamed at Galveston. "My boy, what
are you doing here? Didn't know any of my guests were
interested in my library."

"My boy?" asked Galveston. In turn, he felt wary.

"Hmm? Said that, did I?" Wickingham grinned. "Meant
to say Galveston, of course."

Somerwell edged slowly toward the door. He didn't want
to be in the middle of the dust-up he feared was coming.

Marcus, seeing him slipping away, once again caught him
and drew him back. "Somerwell has a rather strange tale to
tell about a matchmaking ghost and your daughter and myself and I want to know the truth of it." Then he barked a
command as if he were still an officer. "Now!"

Lord Wickingham pouted for a moment, glowering at
Galveston. Then he brightened. "Might as well. After all,
nothing you can do about it now. You, my boy, have been
chosen. Welcome to the family!"

Lord Galveston drew in a sharp breath on a quickly
made decision. "Lord Wickingham," he said, his voice as
icy cold as Winifred's ever was, "I've word of a family
emergency. I fear I must leave on the instant. If you'd be
kind enough to order around my carriage while I help my
man pack?"

"Leave?" Wickingham's face fell into lines that indicated
he wanted to cry. Then the expression cleared. "Oh well, if
you must. Won't make any difference. You'll still wed her.
Maybe not so soon as I'd expected." He sighed. "I wanted
her wed before the little season this fall so I could do my
own wooing!" Wickingham's eyes widened. *"Wooing?"* He
blinked. "Did I say I wanted to woo . . . ?"

"You did."

Wickingham's overly expressive face achieved one of deep
thought. "Do you suppose . . . ?" he mumbled. And then he
muttered, "But twice in one life? Has that ever before happened?" He wandered off. "But she's a very nice armful and

quite comfortable to have around and—" The door shut, cutting off more words.

"You are actually leaving the castle?" asked Grenville cautiously when Marcus merely stared after his host.

"What?" Marcus drew his puzzled gaze from the door and asked, "Leaving?"

"You said," said Grenville patiently, his cane once again in a stranglehold, "you'd a family emergency?"

"Emergency? Oh yes! The emergency." Marcus grinned. "Wouldn't you say it's an emergency if you discovered you'd about been tricked into parson's mousetrap?"

"But it isn't a trick, is it?"

Marcus scowled. "Ghost or no ghost, I choose my own wife! If everyone and his mother's uncle thinks a proposal is due, then I'd better run. Fast. Maybe to the nearest port!"

"Port?" asked Grenville, confused.

"Nigel recommended a ship to a far destination. He may have the right of it! Do you suppose the Antipodes might be far enough!"

"Don't see how *you* can get far enough away even if you go to the moon." Grenville sighed. "Thing is, wonder do I dare believe I've been chosen for Miss Tillingford."

"Lady Winifred's companion?"

"Her cousin. Thing is, if I marry her, will my aunt approve, and if my aunt don't approve will Miss Tillingford be willing to live without the elegancies she should enjoy as her right, and even if she will should I ask it of her?"

"I think," suggested Galveston with a deal more kindness then he'd ever expected he'd feel toward Lord Somerwell, "that that is something you will need to discuss with Miss Tillingford. Your aunt holds the purse strings?"

"Hmm."

This time when Somerwell wandered off Galveston let him go. He'd a good deal of thinking to do. Because although part of him wanted to shake the dust of the castle from his boots on the instant, there was another part of him that wasn't

quite ready to go. He'd still to discover what it was Lady
Winifred hid behind that mask she wore, what fears, what
pain. . . .

Marcus sighed. If he stayed he feared he'd find himself
riveted to the icicle when what he wanted more than anything
was a warm and loving wife and children and . . . and what
in heaven's name was he thinking? A wife? *Children?*

He was, decided Galveston, going mad.

The door opened and this time Lady Winifred entered. "I
am told you wish to leave instantly?"

Galveston eyed her. "Will you tell me something?"

"If I can," was the polite if rather cold response.

"Do you wish to wed me?"

Red flooded up Winifred's neck. "I don't wish to wed
anyone. Ever." Her voice rose. "It is a trap women endure
and I'll not allow myself to fall into it." She shook her fist.
"I won't, I tell you. I don't care what Lady Gwe—" Winifred
gasped and fell silent.

"All you need do now is stamp your foot," said Galveston,
his eyes narrowed.

"I am not having a tantrum," said Lady Winifred and
sighed. "I discovered long ago I want nothing to do with
men. They are brutes."

"All men?"

Lady Winifred frowned. "You know, I've never asked myself that question."

Galveston felt a chill up his spine as he closed in on Lady
Winifred. Well, why not? He was leaving. Why not show her
what she'd be missing simply because he refused to allow
himself to be manipulated. "All right, Lady Gwenfrewi. On
your head be it," he muttered, and gently pulled an exceedingly bemused Lady Winifred into his arms. He stared down
at her, his eyes hooded. "I'm going to kiss you again," he
said.

Lady Winifred nodded. She still couldn't quite believe in

the strange sensations which filled her the last time he kissed her. She waited.

Very gently Lord Galveston lifted her chin. Very slowly he lowered his head. And very, very gently he touched her lips with his own. Touched them again. Soft as a feather, he brushed his mouth across hers, back. Finally he felt her rise slightly on her toes, felt a trifle of her weight against his arm. This time he allowed the kiss more range and her weight increased, her mouth actually reaching for his when he lifted his head. He stared down at her until she raised heavy lids and, a glazed look in her eyes, lifted them up to stare at him.

"Not what you expected?" he asked softly.

"Not at all."

"Would you like to try that again?"

Shyly, she nodded.

So they did it again. This time Lord Galveston gave Lady Winifred opportunity to order the extent of the kiss and was rather surprised at the strength of the passion she roused in him.

A dangerous degree of feeling, he decided when, her arms sliding around his neck, she drew herself closer to him. But one more kiss . . . ?

Marcus couldn't see where another kiss could hurt and he was enjoying her kisses a great deal indeed . . . and the feel of her, her long, firm body pressed against him, her hands playing with his hair, her back under his hand, then her waist, and then her—oops!

"If you slap me," he said to the outraged Lady Winifred, "I swear I'll slap you back!"

"Brute."

"Because you led me on to believe you wished more of me?" he asked blandly, finding his balance far more quickly than the inexperienced Lady Winifred could do. "And don't cry. It doesn't become a woman who has just done her best to seduce a man. She shouldn't cry when she's changed her mind and wants to blame him."

"Seduce! I *didn't*."

"Did you not? Did you not press against me? Did you not put your hands in my hair? Did you not return my kiss with a great deal of ardor?"

An arrested expression widened Lady Winifred's eyes. "Ardor? Is that what I felt?"

"I don't know about you, but I certainly did. Usually," he explained, "such feelings are mutual or they don't exist at all."

"Men . . . lust . . ." Her voice faded and she eyed him through her lashes from under lowered lids.

"Lust?" He shook his head. "No, Lady Winifred. Lust is not the same thing. Not at all. Lust needn't be mutual."

"I . . . see."

"Do you?" he asked, curious.

"I think perhaps I do," she answered slowly. Then, suddenly, she was all business. "Lord Galveston, we are forgetting your emergency. Must you leave immediately or can you wait for morning? It's well into the afternoon now and you'll not travel far before you lose the light and, although there will be a moon, it is never easy traveling at night."

"I believe," he said slowly, eying the woman he'd just kissed with such unexpected and mutual passion, "that I might wait for morning—" Morning . . . and a wedding? No! Never! "—but truly, I must leave."

"Very good. I'll give orders that breakfast be brought to your room at an early hour and that your carriage be harnessed and ready for you. Now I must prepare for the ball." She grimaced. "I hate balls."

Startled from thoughts he'd reluctantly, if silently, admitted were lustful rather than ardent, he asked, "You do?"

"Balls are merely an excuse for flirting and for matches to be made. They are insidiously dangerous to young women. They let down barriers which a woman should never—"

"Never?" he interrupted. "I thought you'd come to understand there was a difference between lust and ardor, but your words indicate you've again misplaced the distinction."

A faint rosy tinge brightened her cheeks. "Perhaps you are correct. I must think seriously about the beliefs I've held for years. It will not be easy to instantly change opinions after a fifteen year duration."

"Just so long as you do change, Lady Winifred. You will grow into an ancient hag, unhappy, bitter, and lonely if you cannot find it in your heart to accept there is a very great difference."

The rosy hue deepened. "Thank you for your . . . er, kindly meant words of . . . hmm . . . advice, Lord Galveston. I will keep them in mind." She turned on her heel and stalked from the room.

Galveston returned to his chair and picked up his book, but didn't open it. Instead he lay it in his lap, rested his head against the back of his chair, and closed his eyes. "Lady Gwenfrewi? Are you there?"

A faint chill crept over him, disappeared.

"Is that you?"

The chill returned, lasted a trifle longer, and then again vanished.

"So, you wish me wed to your protegé, is that it?"

This time a warmth crept up from his toes to the top of his head, fading away in the same sequence.

"I presume that means yes. Well, Lady Gwenfrewi—" His eyes closed, he frowned. "—you can take your wishes and put them where they'll do you no good, do you hear me? I'll not be told by a specter whom I'm to marry!"

Galveston rose to his feet and he too stalked toward the door. It was not a triumphant exit, however. Suddenly he found himself sprawling over a footstool which, only moments earlier, he'd have sworn was nowhere near. Stretched out full length on the floor he waited for the cold to flood into him and was surprised when it didn't come. Carefully he rose to his feet.

"You, Lady Gwenfrewi, don't play fair."

Faintly, Lord Galveston heard the sound of a chuckle. He sighed. "You don't play fair and I only amuse you, do I not?"

The warmth swept up him once again.

"I do not wish to amuse you. Nor do I wish to be toyed with. You, Lady Gwenfrewi, may go to the devil!"

"Won't."

The disembodied voice sent a shiver up Galveston's spine. Not the usual shiver. What on earth did he think he was doing, talking to a ghost? Hearing one answer was worse!

Did ghosts actually exist?

Galveston, who had always thought such beliefs the delusion of a weak mind, found himself forced to admit, if only to himself, that ghosts existed. Not only did they exist but they could, he feared, play a role in the lives of the living.

Or should one say play havoc with the lives of the living! But no ghost would chose him his wife. Only he knew what he wanted in a wife.

And Lady Winifred wasn't it . . . was she?

Eleven

"Well, my boy, *I've* no objection."

Lord Wickingham stared at the man sitting across the desk from him. He wished he could get his hands on that cane! He'd break it over his knee and toss it on the fire! What did Clare see in the fellow?

"Have to tell you, though, I mean to tie up Clare's dowry right and tight. Only let you have the income. Principal will go to Clare's younger children."

A stricken look crossed Lord Somerwell's features. "Forgot."

"Forgot what?"

"Only a competence. May not be able to keep Miss Tillingford in the elegancies of life?"

"You have an estate, do you not? Seemed to remember it's up in Nottinghamshire?"

"Neat little manor," said Somerwell, nodding multiple nods. Then that worried look returned. "Not too big though? Not like this?"

Lord Wickingham sighed. "Just so long as the roof is tight and there is room for a garden, my little Moonbeam won't object!"

"Roof don't leak," said Somerwell with something approaching outraged dignity. "Nice gardens. M'father had them kept up after m'mother died." he said. Then, more anxiously, he added, "Not a lot of land, though. Couple of farms.

Some grazing. Goodly amount is in forest, but I don't like to cut it if I don't have to? *Like* trees."

Lord Wickingham nodded. "Add Clare's income to yours and I'm sure you'll do very well," he said with more of a dry note than was normal to him.

"You certain?"

"Boy, don't you have a notion . . . ?" Wickingham goggled at the innocent look of inquiry he got. "None at all, do you?"

"Should I?" asked Somerwell cautiously, not at all certain what it was to which Lord Wickingham referred.

"Talk about it if she says you yes," decided Wickingham. He stood. "Well, lad, if that is all?"

Somerwell hurriedly rose to his feet, nodding, but didn't move.

"Should I send for Clare?"

Somerwell, who had thought himself steeled to the necessity of putting the question to his wonderful Miss Tillingford, suddenly felt as if his feet were freezing. He discovered he didn't want to find out that she didn't feel the same about things as he did. "Better wait," he decided.

"You'll find Clare in your own time, then, and settle it. One way or the other?"

"One way or the other." Somerwell nodded half a dozen times, lifted his cane and then, before it could reach his mouth, remembered Miss Tillingford's gentle discouragement of that action. He dropped it to the floor and leaned on it. "Soon," he added when Lord Wickingham seemed to require more of him.

"That's all right then?"

Somerwell nodded.

Wickingham decided the boy hadn't a notion how to get himself out of the room. He walked around the desk and, an arm around Somerwell's shoulders, led him to the door. The door closed with the suitor on the other side, and Wickingham heaved a sigh. He moved toward another door, one which led to an inner cabinet and which had stood ajar throughout the meeting. He opened it wider, and stared at his ward.

Clare sat behind a smaller desk, correspondence strewn across it, her elbows on it and her chin resting on her clasped hands.

"Well, Clare? *Is* that strange creature what you want for your life?"

"He needs me, my lord," she said with simplicity. "And, when he isn't frightened or nervous, he's perfectly sensible. We have much in common, too." Clare suppressed the fact they could both see ghosts. It wasn't a talent of which Lord Wickingham approved. "He has a lovely sense of humor and he knows a great deal about herbal remedies which Freddy and I have studied. He has a great interest in forestry which I've learned about through helping you with your reforestation." She shrugged, as if that should make it all obvious.

"I'll miss your help, Clare."

Clare smiled. "You'll finally have to get around to hiring that secretary you've mentioned from time to time. I think Mr. Addlestone's middle son might do."

"The vicar's boy?" Wickingham thought about it and then, wary, looked at Clare. "The middle one ain't the overly tall one, is he? The beanpole?"

"No, that's the youngest. The middle one has curly red hair."

"Oh. That one. Can't keep 'em straight."

"There are only three of them."

"Seems like more."

Clare giggled. "They were rather loud and boisterous when younger, were they not?"

"*Very.*"

"But that was years ago. They are all quite sensible now." Clare looked at the watch pinned to her gown. "Oh dear, I hadn't realized how late it had gotten. I must run, my lord, or I'll not be ready for dinner. It takes forever to dress for a ball, you know."

"Frippery nonsense. You always look the lady, Clare."

In a mocking tone, she pertly informed him that at a ball one didn't wish to look merely a lady! "One wishes to look a very special lady and with my freckled skin and fly-away hair, that is a somewhat difficult goal to achieve!" She smiled impishly, her eyes twinkling, and stood on tiptoe to put a kiss on Lord Wickingham's cheek. "You have been the best of all possible guardians, you know."

Lord Wickingham's ears turned bright red. "Run along now, Moonbeam. You needn't turn *me* up sweet, you know. Save that nonsense for your young man."

His suggestion led to thoughts which turned Clare's ears quite as rosy as Lord Wickingham's.

Lady Winifred stalked from one end of her father's bedroom to the other and turned. She glared at her father. "I'll open the ball with you or not at all."

"But I told you. I wish to ask Lady Westerwood to stand up with me."

"You can ask her for the second dance. I'll not give the gossips more to talk about!"

"Won't." Her father's jaw jutted.

"If I dance the first dance with one of our male guests, it won't give rise to gossip?"

"Only confirm it," muttered her father, eying her warily.

Winifred's eyes widened in response and she sighed. "Tell me what is being said."

"Mostly that Lord Galveston seems to have laid siege to you."

She waved that away. "He leaves in the morning. Early."

"Family emergency," nodded her father, with a melancholy aspect. "Really thought he might be the one—"

"I have *told* you—"

"Know that," interrupted her father. "Nonsense. All young women want to marry. You're a young woman. Follows."

"What follows?"

"You want to marry, of course. Forget what it's called. Logic thing."

"You need a valid premise or it comes out wrong. All women do *not* wish to marry, so the notion that I must want to as well doesn't follow."

"Want to what?"

"That I must wish to wed, of course! Father, I don't know how we got onto that logic nonsense. You still haven't said you'll lead me out for the first dance or if it will be *you* who gives the gossips food for grinding in the mill!"

A faintly stricken look in his eyes, he asked, "I would?"

"Lady Westerwood would definitely be the subject of gossip."

"Hmmm."

"Father, you do *not* wish it."

He sighed. "No," he said sadly. "Don't suppose I do, do I?"

A feeling of panic tied a knot in Winifred's tummy. Ignoring the sensation, she said, "If you wish to ask her to wed you, then that is what you should do, not play games with her reputation!"

But what, she wondered, would *she* do if her father rewed? It rarely worked, two women trying to run a household. She and Moonbeam had managed it pretty well, but add another, and one with the authority of his lordship's wedding ring on her finger, and there would be no bearing it. She herself would be relegated to being a mere daughter of the house! When, nearly a decade earlier, she'd taken the reins into her own hands, it would be next to impossible to return to such a nothing position!

"So?" she asked her father, wondering if perhaps she and Moonbeam might set up house together elsewhere, *"Do* we open the dance?"

"Guess it's for the best." He glanced at his daughter. "Winifred . . ."

"Very good," said Winifred and quickly exited from her father's suite before he could tell her he truly did want to marry Lady Westerwood. She went to Clare's rooms.

"Are you ready?" she asked when she'd been admitted.

"I suppose so. I do wish I could find a remedy for all these freckles," said Clare more crossly than Winifred had ever heard her speak of them. For just a moment she covered her cheeks with her palms.

"Staying out of the sun seems the only way," said Winifred.

"With me that means that, on a sunny day, I dare not even approach a window!" Clare turned from her mirror where she'd been tucking a loose strand of hair beneath the neat bands holding it in place and looked at Winifred. "Well! I thought you said wild animals wouldn't get you into that dress."

"My godmother was kind enough to send it to me," said Winifred rather defensively. "I suppose I must not insult her by not wearing it?"

"That's as good an excuse as any," said Clare, hiding a smile.

"Between you and Maud, I may change it yet!"

"You look lovely, as you well know."

"I don't feel lovely. I feel . . . nervous." In an abrupt manner, she then asked, "Clare, do you know the difference between ardor and, well, hmm, *lust?*"

"I presume ardor has more of a mutuality to it? Lust, I think, must be a very selfish emotion?"

"Selfish . . ." Winifred wandered to where a chintz-covered chair sat before the fireplace in which a small fire burned. At no time of the year was the castle really warm and even at the height of the summer fires were lit whenever anyone wished for one. Freddy stared into the flames, not feeling the heat of the fire but, in memory, the heat generated by Lord Galveston's body, his arms around her, his mouth on hers . . .

Could she have been wrong all these years?

Winifred glanced up when Clare approached her. Clare had always said she'd overreacted to that ridiculous and disgusting scene between their maid and footman. Had she? It was certainly true she was deeply intrigued by Lord Galveston's kisses. Whatever she'd felt, it certainly didn't include disgust!

She sighed.

"What is it, Freddy?"

"I wish I knew."

"I think you do know."

"He's leaving. In the morning. A family emergency."

"Will he be back?"

"I . . . didn't ask."

Clare cast her cousin a worried look. "Freddy . . ."

Winifred didn't want to talk about Lord Galveston. "Were you aware Father is thinking of remarrying?"

"He is? Who?"

"Lady Westerwood, or I miss my guess."

"Oh dear."

"You don't dislike her, do you?" asked Winifred.

"What's to dislike?" asked Clare, her response rather random. Clare wasn't the least worried about Lady Westerwood. She was worried about *Freddy.* If she herself married and then Lord Wickingham married, where would that leave her cousin?

"Moonbeam, what is it?"

"Hmm . . . well . . . Oh, nothing, Freddy."

"Something is bothering you."

"Hmm." Clare glanced at her mantel clock. "I don't think we've time now," she demurred. Just then the gong clanged its call throughout the castle. "See? We must go down. In fact, we should already be down."

Winifred sighed, wondering what it was which had upset

her unflappable cousin. Something, but as Clare said, now was not the time to go into it.

"Later, then," said Winifred.

Clare nodded. She was quite frankly relieved she didn't have to tell dear Freddy she'd soon desert the castle and her cousin and set up her own establishment elsewhere. With a husband. And, in time, *children*. Clare very much wanted to hold her child in her arms and lavish love on it.

But dear Winifred understood none of that and would only see she'd been abandoned . . . which had been bad enough when one assumed dear Freddy could carry on as she had done for years now. But if her role as castle chatelaine was about to be taken from her . . .

Oh dear.

"Well," said Lord Somerwell, "I'm glad that's settled." He beamed at Clare.

"I too am glad, my lord." She was pleased she'd managed, tactfully, to lead him up to the point and through it. She beamed right back.

"Moonbeam," said Somerwell, reverently. And then, stricken by the thought he'd presumed, he asked, "I may call you that? Now we're engaged?"

"In private, it could be allowed," she agreed. "It is not a name I would like bantered around by just everyone. It is a private name, you know?"

He nodded, that quick, multiple nod of the head. "Wouldn't like just anyone calling you that."

"It wouldn't be seemly." When, for a change, he simply nodded once, Clare looked around the anteroom which a set of waltz music had cleared. "Shall we return to the other room now?"

Again he nodded. This time he put out his hand and helped her rise to her feet. She put her fingers on his arm and they strolled toward the ballroom doorway in which a tall thin girl appeared. She stood there like a statue except for the tears rolling down her cheeks, the only indication she wasn't one.

Clare stopped, stopped Somerwell, and sighed. "Miss Lemiston," she said softly.

"Why's she crying like that?" asked Somerwell, perturbed.

"She does that. It could be a ripped hem, a torn fingernail, or a death in the family. She is waiting for someone to fix it. Whatever it is. I think I'm chosen to find a solution."

"Why don't she do it herself?" asked Somerwell, now a trifle angry. "Not your business."

"Well, I suppose in a way it is. My cousin is hostess, but I've always been a sort of assistant hostess at castle parties?"

Somerwell sighed. "Oh well, then."

"You'll await me here? I promise I won't be long."

"Wait for you here." Somerwell nodded another series of nods.

Clare had been gone for no more than a minute when another figure loomed in the entrance. Somerwell ducked farther back into the anteroom.

"Numbskull!" boomed a voice from the doorway.

Grenville winced.

"Booberkin! Come here."

Grenville remembered his conversation with Clare when he'd asked her to marry him. He'd warned her he couldn't give her the elegancies of life and she'd said he could. He'd demurred, mentioning his aunt. Clare had said he needn't worry about the woman. His aunt wasn't important. He didn't need her. And that his aunt couldn't do a thing to hurt them.

"Can't hurt us." Grenville straightened his shoulders and turned to face Lady Baggins-Keyton.

"You great lump. So. What are you up to?"

Grenville blinked. "Up to?"

"Up to. How dare you get yourself entangled with some chit and not ask my advice? A fortune hunter. A feather-head."

"Ain't a featherhead. Doesn't want a fortune."

"Nonsense. Either a schemer out to feather her nest or an empty-headed chit whose mother is telling her what to do."

"Clare don't have a mother," argued Grenville. "Not important," he added in a mutter.

"A fortune hunter isn't important?" asked Lady Baggins-Keyton with well-honed sarcasm.

"Didn't say that. Besides, don't have a fortune."

"Well, I do, Blockhead. It's my fortune your bit of fluff is wanting. Well, we'll just . . ." Lady Baggins-Keyton pointed her cane at Clare, who had just come though the door. "You. Take yourself off. Want to talk to my neffy."

"Oh, I don't think I should. You see, I'm the bit of fluff about whom you're talking. My lord?" said Clare placidly. "Will you introduce us?"

Grenville nodded. "Introduce you. Lady Baggins-Keyton, be pleased to meet my fiancée, Miss Clare Tillingford. Or," he said adopting a more belligerent tone, "don't be pleased, but meet her anyway."

"Fiancée," groaned Lady Baggins-Keyton. "It's worse than I thou—" She broke off. Her eyes bulged. *"Tillingford?"*

"Clare Tillingford," repeated Clare, softly.

"Remington Tillingford's only daughter?"

"Yes and, far more important to *you,* Barr Grafton's granddaughter."

"Grafton! Stinks of the shop! You will forget that connection from this day forward."

"I don't think so. I love my grandfather very much. A wonderful man."

"But not a . . . a *person* to be admitted into *my* family," insisted Lady Baggins-Keyton, looking down her nose.

"My lady, he's a hard-working man who doesn't think highly of people like you who have never had to lift a finger. I haven't a doubt he'd *scorn* to be part of your family! So," Clare added with well-feigned innocence, "it is a very good thing, is it not, that he'll only be part of *Lord Somerwell's* family."

"Hoity-toity!" Her ladyship glared but her favorite expression for cowing the opposition didn't work on Clare, who merely studied her ladyship with an interested look on her round freckled face. "Somerwell, go get me a glass of wine. And none of that slop they're feeding the masses. You get me some good wine, hear me?"

A footman just then passed the doorway and Clare beckoned. He entered, giving her a querying look. Clare, holding Grenville's arm in a firm grip, gave the servant his orders and, nodding, he departed. "You'll have your wine in a moment," she told Lady Baggins-Keyton, once again all innocence.

Her ladyship realized she'd met her match and, surprisingly, found the thought didn't displease her. "Boy," she said, prodding Grenville with her cane, "take yourself off. Want a few words with your Miss Tillingford. And you needn't worry I'll eat her if that's what that frown means!" She surprised the young couple and herself as well, by adding, "I like her."

Grenville turned his worried look on Clare, who smiled at him with the beaming smile that always made him feel good. "You'll be all right?" he asked in what he thought was a whisper.

"I'll be fine. Remember we have the next dance but one. Return for me here, if you will?"

He nodded, dared to cast a warning glare toward his aunt and then, gulping at his temerity, took himself off.

"Blockhead," said Lady Baggins-Keyton, but without heat. "At least he had the good sense to get himself an heiress, although how the devil he managed it, I'll never guess."

Clare smiled at the lack of subtlety in the questioning tone. "I wish to wed your nephew because he is a very nice young man. Gentle and loving. Then, too, he isn't yet aware I am an heiress."

Lady Baggins-Keyton goggled. "Doesn't know!" She sighed. "I suppose I might have guessed as much. Boy had good luck wished on him by the fairies when he was in his cradle. At least, that's what I've always believed. Last of seven, all the others stillborn. An eight-month babe at that and never thought *he'd* survive. But he did. And then he lived through three years, an officer you know, in the Peninsula, and then the Battle of Waterloo." Her ladyship grimaced. "I'll never understand how such a dullard managed it."

"I don't think he is dull. Nor is he stupid. But he has a nervous nature and, particularly since the horrors of Waterloo, he cannot stand loud noises or controversy. So, when you yell at him it reminds him of battle noise. I'd appreciate it if you'd moderate your voice when you talk to him?"

"You would, would you?" asked Lady Baggins-Keyton crossly. "And what if I won't?"

"Then I doubt if we'll visit you very often. Something will interfere with our accepting your invitations. And somehow," said Clare, a look of pretend wonder in her eyes, "although I don't know how such a thing could happen, I fear your name won't manage to make it onto our guest list."

"Quick-tongued lass, ain't you? Sharp as a tack."

"Perhaps, but what *I* think is that I'm determined you'll no longer bully my Grenville."

"Won't allow anyone but yourself to do that, hmm?"

"If I bully him, it will only be in the nicest possible way and to help him, and never in a way which upsets him."

"Enough," said Lady Baggins-Keyton, sighing. "I know when to give over. What's more, I like the fact you've a backbone. Suppose one reason I bully Grenville is that he's got a spine made of tomato aspic. I can't resist making him tremble like a blancmange!"

"But—"

"I said, *enough*. He was a cute little boy, you know. That sandy hair was a mass of curls and he had such an innocent look to him . . ."

Clare heard the wistful note and asked, "Did you have no children of your own, Lady Baggins-Keyton?"

"None." Then she glared again. "You'd better have a houseful, Miss Tillingford. The Somerwell line's dying out, you know."

"It is my fondest hope that we'll fill our nursery to overflowing," Clare responded, smiling. "I'd like that very much. Perhaps, Lady Baggins-Keyton," she added a trifle slyly, "bringing some Grafton blood into the family won't be such a bad idea. Perhaps the Somerwell blood has gotten a trifle more blue than is good for it?"

Lady Baggins-Keyton chortled. "Not only a sharp tongue, a pert one. Ah, there you are, Somerwell. Well, don't hover. Come in or go away. As you see," she went on, "your Miss Tillingford has survived my bellowing very well."

"Clare is brave enough to be up to anything, Aunt," said Grenville with simple pride and, with no thought to insult, added, "Even you."

"Thank you, Grenville, but it is merely that I know your aunt doesn't mean the half of it," said Clare.

"She doesn't?" He thought about that as he led her toward the door. "Well, there's still the other half," he decided and, admiringly, added, "Brave woman to face that much, Miss Tillingford!"

"Nincompoop," muttered Lady Baggins-Keyton. But she did so very softly.

Twelve

"She's going to marry him, that's why," Lord Wickingham said in answer to Winifred's shocked question as to how Clare dared take the floor for a third dance with Somerwell and, worse, two of them waltzes.

"Marry him? Nonsense."

Winifred watched her cousin smile up into Somerwell's bemused but glowing face. It wasn't nonsense. And it was the decision to wed him which had had Clare so worried when they'd spoken of the possibility of Lord Wickingham wedding Lady Westerwood. Clare had realized how difficult Freddy's position would be once both weddings took place.

"And you, Father? Have you made your decision?"

Wickingham eyed his daughter from under ragged brows. "Hurumph. Have to wait and see, won't I?"

"See what?"

"Whether Lady Gwenfrewi is right or if, for the first time in her whole tenure as castle matchmaker, the Effect don't take!" Chortling rather sourly at his daughter's expression of outrage, he strolled off. "After all," he grumbled, "if it *don't* take where does that leave me?"

A touch of guilt crept into Winifred's mind as she realized her father understood her situation, that he would not put another woman over her when she had held the authority of Mistress of the Castle for so long!

But why *should* she feel guilty? Winifred sent a scowl

after her father and then turned to look at the dancers. Her cousin and Lord Somerwell were passing by again and the scowl faded. The knowledge Moonbeam would soon take the light of her smile away from the castle sent a pang through Winifred, which was followed by another, still sharper stab, when she noticed Lord Galveston dancing with Lady Pelling, the two laughing about something.

Dejected, Winifred turned aside. Everything was changing. Nothing would ever be the same again. She used the excuse that she must check the tables in the dining room in order to escape the ballroom. The music stopped just as she left. She turned a corner and, no sooner was she well around it, when an arm encircled her shoulders, guiding her into a convenient room.

"You!"

Galveston sighed. "I'll ignore that. We only have an argument when I respond to it. Instead, Lady Winifred, tell me what is wrong?"

"Wrong? I planned this ball to the last crab roll. What could possibly go wrong?" she blustered. Realizing her tone wasn't exactly conducive to belief, she went on more evenly. "Everything is running smoothly. To insure that it stays that way, I must check that all is ready for the supper which everyone will be wanting quite soon now."

"You weren't thinking about the party."

"I wasn't?" She eyed him warily. How did he know what she was or was not thinking?

"Lady Winifred, I know we have our differences, but I rather thought that, nevertheless, you and I had reached something approaching friendship. I, as a friend, am asking what is bothering you. As a friend, you are supposed to tell me. Then, friends together, we are supposed to come to some solution."

"Friends?"

"We have talked of many things, as friends do," he said softly. "We have spent agreeable time together doing things we both liked, which friends do. We have felt that liking—" He frowned slightly. "—at least *I* have, that friends feel for each other. I truly believe we are friends." He paused, but she said nothing. "So?" She still didn't speak. "Won't you tell me?" he coaxed.

Winifred struggled with herself and lost. "Moonbeam—" She admitted the least part of it. "—is to marry Lord Somerwell."

"She is?" He blinked. "Why?"

That brought a weak chuckle from Winifred, but she sobered as she remembered her other concern, that her father wanted to wed. She might explain that, too. But she wouldn't. One bit of revealing idiocy was surely enough.

"Why will she have him?" she asked. "I don't know why. She says he's nice. She says he isn't as stupid as he seems."

"He couldn't be as stupid as he seems." This sally only drew a smile. "What else bothers you, my dear?"

"What makes you think there is more? Isn't that enough to make me sad?"

"I think there's more."

She flung a glare his way. "How do you get inside my head that way?"

"Do I? I haven't a notion." When she said nothing, he added, "It isn't the ghost's doing that worries you. I haven't felt her presence all evening."

Winifred nodded. "I know. For some reason Gwenfrewi doesn't like balls. She always disappears when we hold one."

"You mean she's nowhere near?"

"I haven't a notion where she goes, but she's gone."

"She won't suddenly appear here? Now?"

"I said she disappears when we hold a ball," said Winifred crossly. "I meant it. No one has ever experienced her until the following day. Not that it isn't nonsense in any case," she finished on a mutter—but with a wary glance around.

While Lady Winifred was preoccupied, Galveston reached for her and tucked her carefully into a warm embrace. For half an instant he hesitated. What if their kisses weren't so fiery when the blasted ghost wasn't there to encourage them? What if there was nothing between them but the ghost's mischief?

But wasn't that exactly what he needed to know? If there was no true fire, then it was best to discover it before they did something utterly stupid.

Somewhat later, he lifted his mouth from hers and raised his head. He stared blankly across the top of her braids. Lady Gwenfrewi might have manipulated them into those first kisses, but if one could assume she truly wasn't near, here was proof positive she'd nothing whatsoever to do with the resulting passion! Why, it might take the rest of his life to fully explore such incredible sensation . . .

"Freddy?" he murmured into her hair.

"Why did you have to do that?" she muttered into his chest.

Her question pushed him from a sudden impulsive decision to ask her to marry him. Instead, he responded, "I had to know . . . I needed to discover . . ."

"What?" Her question had an urgency to it. She pushed away and stared more than a trifle anxiously into his face, her expression revealing confusion and . . . something more?

"I had to know if it was merely that ridiculous ghost or if we ourselves set off the fireworks I feel whenever we kiss."

"And?"

"You know! We just set off the display of the century and you promised she'd be nowhere near!"

She stared at him.

"You *must* have felt it too."

"Fireworks. Is that what you call that . . . that bubbly feeling in your middle? That . . . shivery feeling up your spine?"

"To say nothing of a few other rather enticing sensations?" He grinned down at her.

"Lord Galveston," she asked sternly, with no hint of humor, "are you attempting to seduce me?"

He blinked. "Actually, it hadn't occurred to me to do so—" He grinned still more widely, one brow arching. "—but I'll be happy to oblige if you'd like me to try?"

For the barest instant Winifred hesitated.

"No! Of course not," she exclaimed, blushing that she'd even for a moment thought of saying yes. "You are absurd." She pushed and he released her. Crossing her arms, she walked away. With her back to him, she said, "I think this must be goodbye, my lord. You will leave early in the morning. I am required to stay up until the very last guest has decided to call it a night. I doubt very much I shall be awake to see you off."

"Leaving . . . ?"

She swung around, frowning. "Your family emergency?"

"Oh." Why didn't he feel the expected relief? "That." He *should* feel relief, that reminder of his excuse for reaching a safe harbor. "Yes."

"Then?"

He ignored her question, wondering if he should also ignore his decision to leave. "Have you a waltz remaining unclaimed?"

"I never dance waltzes."

"Dance one with me?"

"And have the gossips talking more than they already are?" Her arms, which had dropped to her sides, crossed again, one hand rising to her shoulder, a protective gesture. *"Never.* I won't do it."

"Are they talking?"

"About us?" The hand crept to her neck, an endearingly revealing self-protective stance. "Somehow it has gotten about that Lady Gwenfrewi is playing games with our lives. Everyone is watching us and, very likely, laying wagers on when an announcement will be made."

Marcus exclaimed, "I'll not have a ghost dictate to me whom I choose for a wife!"

Winifred's frown matched his. "Nor will I be forced by a spectral matchmaker into a match I don't want."

His frown deepened. "You *don't* want it?"

"Well, *you* don't. Why should I?"

"I . . . see."

"What do you see?"

"That I must leave in the morning for more reasons than I'd thought." He bowed. "And since an early start is of the first importance, I shall take myself off to my bed now. This is good night and goodbye . . . my friend."

Galveston turned on his heel and walked toward the door. Behind him he heard something that, if it had been any other woman, he'd have thought was a choked back sob. Given it was Lady Winifred it must have been something quite different. Still . . .

He turned. "My lady?"

"I shall miss our friendship," she said in a small voice.

"I believe I shall too. Which reminds me . . ." He took a few steps back toward her. "I never did discover that other thing bothering you."

"It is nothing."

When she didn't go on, he sighed.

"Truly," she insisted, consciously prevaricating.

This time he waited only a moment before, a muscle jumping in his cheek, he said, "You leave me nothing to say." He bowed again and this time disappeared out the door, closing it quietly behind him.

Instead of following, Winifred moved toward a heavy curtain covering a corner of the room. Behind it a narrow circular staircase was hidden. She took it to the top of the castle where, shivering in the cool air, she moved across the stone-floored tower room. She stared down through an unglazed arrow slit at the massive, three-story-high gate complete with long unused portcullis, and then across moonlit land beyond. All lay revealed in glowing golden light shed by the moon, which hung like a lantern above the world.

For a long moment Winifred blinked back tears brought on by too many shocks, each following too quickly on the heels of the last. Then, here where no one would find her, no one see her, she decided it didn't really make one bit of difference whether she was strong or weak. She let the first tear fall, another, that one followed by a flood.

When the last tear traced its path down her cheek she went to her bedroom where she washed her face thoroughly, checked that her crown of braids was unruffled, either by Lord Galveston's embrace or when indulging her bout of self-pity, and finally, straightening both her skirts and her spine, she returned to the ball.

It was too late to check that the dining room was well prepared because supper had begun in her absence. Lady Winifred discovered a place had been saved her at her father's table where he sat with Lady Westerwood, Clare, and Lord Somerwell. And Lord Ramsbarrow.

"Not to worry," whispered his lordship when she rather hesitantly took the seat beside him. "I am merely here to fill out the numbers, the odd man, the agreeable soul who . . . Ah! At last. A smile!"

They bantered back and forth for some minutes, Lady Winifred making herself participate, but then she could stand it no longer. "Do you know," she asked, "what family emergency forces Lord Galveston to leave our party?"

"Family emergency? I'd not heard of one." Nigel quickly passed over their mutual family tree. "Unless someone has had an accident . . . ?"

"That must be it."

Since she'd been delayed, everyone but Winifred had finished eating. Faintly, drifting from the ballroom, came the sound of instruments tuning up. The dining room emptied quickly. Finally only Lady Winifred and Lord Ramsbarrow remained.

"You needn't wait for me," she said.

"No. But it's an odd thing," he said, musingly. "I had this

really nasty nurse, you see. She swore that if I ever forgot the manners she taught me, she'd return from the grave and haunt me."

"Then please remember them while you remain here," said Winifred with a touch of acid. "We've quite enough ghosts of our own."

"Well, there's a problem."

"Yes?"

"She isn't dead yet. I don't think you can haunt a person until you have died?"

Winifred's lips tightened. Then relaxed into a smile. "You, my lord, are a complete hand—as I've heard the stable boys say, of course!"

"Oh," he said earnestly, "I try. I really do try." He rose to his feet. "If you've finished stirring up your food, come dance with me?"

"If it is not a waltz," she said, wary. "I never dance the waltz."

"Someday," he said gently, "you should try one. You'd find you enjoy it a great deal. I've seen you dance, you see, and you are very graceful and have a good sense of time. You'd do it well, I think."

"I don't think—"

"Try it with Marcus," urged Ramsbarrow. "He's the best man with a waltz you'll find. And he has the patience to teach it, which I do not."

"Oh, I've been taught." Winifred sobered. "However, since I am unlikely to meet Lord Galveston again, I doubt I'll have the opportunity. Ah," she added, relieved to be done with talking about Galveston, "they are making up sets for a reel. Shall we join one?"

Winifred went through the motions of enjoying the rest of the ball. She managed to convince everyone, even Clare, that she was having a good time. And she danced—except for the waltzes—every dance right into the dawn. When the last guest had either left or taken themselves off to bed, she found a shawl and took herself back to the tower room which had served her so well once that night. She stood straight and tall, hands clasping the stone window sill, and waited.

And waited . . . and was finally rewarded.

She stared down into the courtyard and watched Galveston's coach pull under the sallyport, heard it rumble over the drawbridge, and watched as it trundled down the drive, disappearing among the trees. For a long time she stared at the spot in which it vanished, her mind a blank.

She was still staring when the coach reappeared. Her heart surged, her eyes widened, hope burgeoned . . . and then the vision, for it was merely a vision, faded. Winifred swung on one foot, her eyes darting up, down, and all around. "You!"

"Yes, it's me," said a disembodied voice. "Have I shown you what you feel for him?"

"Does it make any difference what *I* feel? He called me his *friend*. That is not, surely, the sort of word a man would use if I were more to him."

"You, my dear child, are an utter idiot. I wash my hands of *yooouuuuu*."

The word faded in a long drawn-out wail and Winifred knew she was alone. Worse, she feared she'd always be alone.

What was she to do?

That she had to do something became still more obvious over the next few days as the castle gradually emptied of most of its guests. Finally only a handful of her father's cronies remained. These were not men who required or wanted a hostess cluttering up their days, requiring they do the polite, so Winifred searched until she found Clare.

"Dreaming again?" she asked dryly, when she discovered Moonbeam in her favorite garden but simply holding her trowel, staring at nothing at all, and accomplishing nothing as well.

"Hmm?" Moonbeam smiled. "Hello, Freddy. I suppose I

am." She seemed to realize more was wanted. "Grenville says there are gardens at his home and I may do anything I wish with them."

"Good," said Winifred. "But you aren't wed yet and you need to order bride clothes. I think we should visit my god-mother in London."

"London?"

"Bride clothes."

Clare set her trowel in her basket and stood up. "A London modiste? I hadn't thought of it."

"Well, do so now. I've had a letter from Lady Belemy. She says she is bored to tears and why don't we join her and we'll all go on to Paris. Perhaps you might buy some of your gowns in Paris?"

"Paris gowns? For Grenville? I wonder if he'd like that," breathed Clare. Suddenly she laughed. "Yes. Why not?"

"Shall I write my godmother that we'll arrive on the heels of my note?"

"An excellent plan."

"Jed must be told to organize a carriage. And to send horses on ahead so we needn't suffer the slugs so often offered travelers."

"I'll set Maud to work on our trunks."

"That task won't take so long if you detail a couple of maids to help her," suggested Winifred, far more anxious to be gone than she'd willingly admit.

The young women separated and went each to her own task. After a brief stop in the stables, Winifred went to the game room where she found her father and the other men playing billiards.

"Father, a word, please?"

Lord Wickingham motioned her to be still. The man making the break sank several balls before he missed an easy shot. Winifred's father stood up to the table. He sunk his first ball, but left himself in an impossible position and missed the next. Shrugging, he turned to Winifred.

"What is it?" he asked a trifle testily. He'd been cross ever since Lord Galveston left.

"Clare and I have decided to join my godmother in London. We may go on to Paris."

"Nonsense," he blustered. "Why go to a place like that? Nothing but foreigners there!"

"Clare must purchase her bride clothes. A Paris wardrobe would be a wonderful thing to have."

"Well," scolded her father, "no need for *you* to spend a fortune on *your* back. Seems like *you'll* never have need of a Paris wardrobe!"

"Perhaps not," said Winifred evenly, "but I'll enjoy helping Clare chose hers. We'll leave day after tomorrow."

"You can be ready that quickly?"

"The notion is to buy new clothes. We needn't take so many old ones if we are to have new, do you see?"

"I see you'll need a huge bank draft to cover expenses," he said rather gruffly. "See you don't forget to get it from me."

Winifred smiled. "You are a truly excellent father. It is too bad you were ill-wished such a daughter as I."

He hurumphed and then, looking first to see there was no one who would observe him, he leaned forward and kissed her forehead. "You're a good gal except for the one silly notion in your cockloft."

Winifred didn't tell him that the 'silly notion' had a dent or two in it. Thanks to Lord Galveston and Lady Gwenfrewi. "I'm sorry I'm such a burden to you."

"And so you should be!" Lord Wickingham glared, wishing to cancel any notion his impulsive kiss implied he was weak. He turned on his heel and returned to his friends. Winifred spun on her own heel and went in search of the housekeeper who would need advice and direction before taking up the housekeeping reins and ordering the castle's daily life.

Finally Winifred's carriage passed under the wall and she could breathe again. It was strange how . . . how *bound* she felt by the castle which had been her home forever. The idea she was free of it, free of the duties which made up her life, free of the heavy weight of tradition and, most of all, that she no longer need feel, when in his presence, that she'd let her father down . . . well, everything had become all too much.

"Freddy?"

"Hmm?"

"Will you be all right?"

"All right? Whyever should I not be just fine?"

"I don't know. But ever since the ball, well, you've been running here and there and back and forth and . . ."

"In circles, perhaps?"

Clare giggled. "Perhaps you have. What is it, Freddy? What is bothering you?"

"I suppose I am adjusting to the coming changes. You will wed your Somerwell before Christmas. Father will eventually understand that if he is to rewed he cannot wait for me to accept a husband first. And then . . ." Winifred searched her mind for a substitute for the fact Galveston's departure had left a huge hole in her life.

A hole she feared she might not be able to fill. A hole that, perhaps, a change of scene might at least shrink? Thus the journey to London and later to Paris. Surely new places, new people, new routines would make life more bearable?

"Freddy?"

"Hmm."

"You've gone off into your head again."

"Hmm?" Winifred turned to look at her cousin. "What do you mean I've gone off into my head?"

"Just that. You are going along fine, speaking much like a sensible person, and suddenly, well . . . you *aren't.*"

"Aren't sensible?"

"Aren't speaking."

Winifred chuckled. "Then I *am* sensible, am I not? I am not chattering on and on with nothing to say?"

"You don't wish to tell me what is bothering you?" asked Clare in a rather small voice.

"Bothering me? Good heavens, Clare! What could possibly be bothering me?"

"If you do not wish to talk about it," said Clare, very much on her dignity, "then you only need to say so. You needn't lie about it."

"I haven't a notion of what you speak!"

Clare turned an incredulous look her way and Winifred found she felt guilty. Again. It was becoming a habit, she thought crossly. But then, before she could bring herself to confide, even in Clare's excellent ear, Clare had turned a stiff shoulder and stared out the window.

Then after a long and convoluted debate within herself, when Winifred was almost ready to give in and ask that Clare forgive her and help her, Clare pulled a slim volume of poetry from her oversized travel reticule and began reading aloud. Taking turns reading was one of their usual ways of passing the miles when traveling.

Or they'd set a particularly appealing poem to memory.

Or they played chess on a travelers' board.

Or any of the things a traveler does to pass the time.

And none of the time-filling nonsense offered Winifred another opportunity in which she might have opened her heart and soul to her—usually—understanding cousin.

Thirteen

Winifred climbed, in the most dispirited fashion possible, up the stairs to the Belemy guest bedrooms. In deep dismay, and long after her goddaughter had disappeared, Lady Belemy stared after her. "But . . . but such a little ride into London!" she exclaimed.

"*Little* ride, Lady Belemy," said Clare gently. "We left at cock-crow two days ago. It is now nearly four in the afternoon and today we had only one goodly sort of break in late morning. You can call that a little ride?"

Lady Belemy turned a smiling face toward her other guest. "I suppose what I meant is that it is not enough to tire our Freddy. You and I? Yes! Like any sensible person, we find ourselves exhausted by such a journey, but not Freddy! Except . . ." Although they were now in her small salon and facing each other across a well supplied tea tray, Lady Belemy turned a frown in the general direction of the stairs.

"I think this year's party at the castle was a bit more than she'd expected," said Clare, gently.

"How so?" asked Lady Belemy, holding the hot water over the teapot, but not pouring. She looked up and what she saw made her set aside the just barely boiling water. When Clare still didn't respond, her ladyship coaxed, "Moonbeam, I've heard such wildly impossible rumors. The Gwenfrewi *Effect?* Her ghostly ladyship actually—"

"I was there, as it happens. I saw it," admitted Clare.

"You watched." Lady Belemy had long known of Clare's ability, so that it wasn't Clare's seeing a ghost which startled her. It was that she verified the unbelievable. "You actually watched a Gwenfrewi Effect in the making? How brave of you."

"Not at all. Lady Gwenfrewi would never hurt anyone."

"But who . . . ?"

Clare smiled. "You don't mean rumor has not supplied the man's name?"

"I denied there was any possibility of a match in *that* direction!"

"Who?"

"Lord Galveston. A totally impossible situation. Now, if *you* were not engaged to Lord Somerwell, *that* might be a possibility. Winifred could rule that particular roost and not have felt—" She frowned. "—what is the word I want? Threatened, perhaps? Oh, but Lord Galveston? Oh dear."

"Dear Grenville would never do for our Winifred. I'll admit I don't understand Lady Gwenfrewi's thinking, but it is true Freddy seems . . . different. Around Lord Galveston, I mean. There isn't yet a match, but as to *no possibility*—" Clare, knowing Lady Belemy's penchant for the card tables, smiled. "—I'd not put my blunt on it. Lady Gwenfrewi is never wrong."

"You mean to say it *was* Lord Galveston?"

"Yes."

Once again Lady Belemy turned her gaze in the direction in which her goddaughter had disappeared and stared as if, somehow, she'd see through two floors and several walls and into Winifred's heart. "She turned him down?"

"I don't think an offer was actually made."

"But you do think there will be a match? That somehow or other, the two of them will agree to wed? Each other?"

"Lord Galveston sought her out on every possible occasion. I believe he kissed her, although I can't be certain." Clare smiled. "It's not anything she's *said,* but you'll admit she is *acting* totally unlike the Freddy we know and love. Whatever happened, she still stubbornly insists she'll never wed. I think—" Clare dropped her teasing tone. "—there was also something *Galveston* didn't like about the situation. The problem, of course, is getting them back together long enough they can agree to anything!"

"You think Freddy will avoid Lord Galveston if she can?"

"Don't you?"

"Oh dear me, yes. She *will*, will she not?"

Lady Belemy rose briskly to her feet and strode to the bell pull. She yanked it so firmly Clare feared it would come down. It didn't. On the other hand, she must have set the bell clattering in such a way as to alarm her servants because several burst into the salon.

One quick glance around, a search for a disaster which didn't exist, and Lady Belemy's butler quietly told her ladyship's personal maid and two footmen they might return to their dinner. "Yes, my lady?" asked Philbert once he'd closed the door behind the others. "You wish me to do something?"

"I most certainly do. Today's papers," said Lady Belemy somewhat abruptly. "Find them all. *Every last one.* Burn them, Philbert. I am very sorry to ask it of you, but you must accomplish this task before you yourself return to your dinner."

"Yes, my lady."

Philbert was a distinguished looking man, one who, due to his self-assurance rather than his height, oozed authority. Now he moved in stately fashion to retrieve a newspaper half hidden under a cushion on the settee on which Lady Belemy had been seated. He bowed and retreated through the door. They heard his footsteps crossing the hall to the large salon on the other side.

"He'll see not one is left where Freddy might find it," said her ladyship in a conspiratorial fashion.

"Why is it—" Clare was utterly intrigued. "—so important that she not see a news sheet?"

"You yourself said she'd avoid Lord Galveston."

"I'd not swear to it, but it's my best guess."

"Then she mustn't see the papers. It is reported in each and every paper's passenger list that Lord Galveston left Dover on today's packet and after a month or two in Paris, he'll travel on to Switzerland, Austria, and eventually Italy—" Her ladyship suddenly looked as mischievous as an imp. "—I believe that is news with which we needn't burden Freddy?"

"Certainly not," said Clare, her eyes twinkling.

"And I believe," added Lady Belemy thoughtfully, "that I'll put forward our leave-taking. You, my dear, must choose a length of good Bath cloth for your habit—" Her ladyship's eyes narrowed as she studied her young guest. "—in a pale violet, I think, or perhaps a mauve." She frowned and then shook her head. "But that isn't important. What is, is that we'll have you measured for it tomorrow, and we must order your gloves here in London." Once again the all important question of fashion interrupted Lady Belemy's planning. "Clare, I have discovered the most amazing glover. You will be exceedingly well served by him, I assure you. You can be measured for your boots although shoes must wait, I suppose, until we know the fabrics chosen for your gowns, but anything else?"

"I'm certain everything else may be found in Paris," agreed Clare, her face and voice solemn. Only the twinkle in her eye hinted she found her hostess's plans amusing.

Lady Belemy turned to making tea. "Now that that is settled," she said, sitting back, "do tell me all about your Grenville Somerwell. I'd heard he's been acting like a regular knock-in-the-cradle baby, but that can't be so if *you've* agreed to wed him."

"I suppose some might describe him so. He is still a very easily unsettled man—" Clare glanced at lady Belemy. "—from that horrid battle?"

Lady Belemy nodded, her expression one of sympathetic

understanding. Everyone knew the men who survived Waterloo had experienced hell.

"When quietly occupied with things he enjoys he is completely sensible. He's also an exceedingly kind man. And—" Clare flashed a quick grin. "—we also have it in common that we both suffer from the dread talent of seeing ghosts." Her mischievous look returned. "He too watched the Lord Galveston-Freddy-Gwenfrewi encounter, you know."

Lady Belemy blinked. *"Another* who sees the dreary things? Well! But," she asked, after half an instant's thought, "if you were there together when it happened, doesn't that mean the two of you also experienced her spectral ladyship?"

Clare bit her lip, frowning slightly. "I have wondered, my lady," mused Clare, "whether ours was a true Effect or if it were merely an accident that we happened to be there together." Then she smiled. "Whether it is or is not, it has," she said, "worked out very well and surely our lady ghost would have interfered if she disapproved?" For half an instant Clare had a rather withdrawn and worried look. She glanced up when her hostess spoke.

"Are you *certain,* Clare?" asked Lady Belemy, still thinking of the rumors about Lord Somerwell's behavior.

"Very. It won't be the most exciting of marriages, but I've never craved excitement. All I want is husband and children and enough space for a garden. I expect we'll spend most of each year at his country home."

"If that will make you comfortable," said Lady Belemy doubtfully.

Clare grinned. "I know it wouldn't do for you and very likely it wouldn't do for Freddy, but it is exactly what I want." Clare stifled a yawn as she set down her cup and saucer. "And now, if you do not mind . . . ?"

"Oh, dear, how rude of me! Of course you must go to your room for a rest before dinner. You've plenty of time, my dear. As you know I keep town hours when in London and dinner isn't served until seven."

"Excellent. I'll have a little nap."

"Well, tell Freddy that we mean to leave for Paris on—" Lady Belemy swiftly calculated the minimum time needed. "—shall we say Friday?"

"Friday will be perfect."

Gradually Clare escaped Lady Belemy's plans, explanations, and questions and reached the stairs. She'd climbed to the first landing when there was one final question. "Clare," asked Lady Belemy, hesitantly, "do you think they are . . . in love?"

Clare stared down at her hostess for a long moment. "My lady, I haven't the least notion. I couldn't even put forward a guess." Bemused by the notion, Clare turned and hurried on up the stairs.

Was that the problem? Was Freddy's malaise because she was acting the lovelorn lady? Surely not. It didn't suit Freddy's character at all, moping around after a man.

But, oh dear, wasn't that, perhaps, *exactly* what she was doing?

Paris in the late summer was lovely. Too lovely to spend all one's time at the modistes or in search of dress lengths or finding just the most delicious hat out of all the many wonderful hats available. Lady Winifred escaped the shops and shopping whenever she could discover a chaperone under whose lackadaisical eye she might enjoy the parks and woodlands.

On this occasion the rest of her party were settled some way downstream. All were resting and some were actually asleep after a huge, over-poweringly delicious pick-nick. Winifred, as usual, hadn't been particularly hungry and was among the very few who didn't sate herself on the truly excellent viands. So, instead of lying back against a pile of cushions on one of the rugs and flirting with whichever man happened to be nearest, she'd picked up her painting supplies and requested the footman carry her easel and stool.

They'd wandered up the path until she'd found this lovely spot. Once he'd set up her equipment, she told him to inform her chaperone where she could be found when the party was ready to return to Paris but until needed she was to be left alone.

The painting, however, was not developing as she'd hoped. Freddy sighed. Her paintings *never* came out in just the way she wished and yet she continued to persevere, never giving up hope that one day she'd achieve a truly excellent picture. She studied the view, stared at her painting, and, reaching out, daubed hesitantly at one of her trees. She sighed. Almost, she was glad when she heard footsteps coming down the path beyond where she sat. Someone to interrupt her work . . .

"You!" exclaimed an unexpected, long-missed, baritone voice.

Freddy glanced up and experienced a sudden lightness of heart. "Well, I *think* so," she said, impish lights shining in her eyes. "The last time I looked."

"Don't!" interrupted Lord Galveston. "Don't bring back memories of those early days of our acquaintance. They are too painful."

"Painful?"

"I was acting the ass, was I not?"

"Were you? I manage to remember them with a certain fondness."

"You do?" He approached and stood beside her. "What is this?"

"It was supposed to be a delightful watercolor painting of this lovely glade, but somehow . . ." She shrugged.

Marcus took her brush, daubed it in a couple of the watercolor pads and then here and there on the paper. He added another color and then, when Winifred stood up, sat in her place. She handed him her paint box. Absently he took it.

His lordship really didn't do all that much, Winifred decided. It was merely a question of changing the light or something, but just how did he manage that? And what was he doing now?

"Oh, I'd never have thought of adding something that isn't there!" she exclaimed.

"Hmm?" He glanced up, then at the painting. "What have I done!"

"You have fixed what was rapidly becoming a disaster under my brush. Do continue. I've learned more watching you then I ever did from my painting mistress at school!"

"You're certain?"

"Quite!"

He turned back to the picture and continued with the branch he was adding to the front of the scene as if one were looking through the lower part of a small tree toward the water and trees beyond.

"La! What have we here?" asked a light, rather brittle voice. "I see I've been all too careless in my chaperonage, Lady Winifred, when I find you solitary with a noted rake! But," added Madame de Montholon, "I have yet to see a rake behave in this particular fashion. Is it, Lord Galveston, a new way of seducing a lady?" teased the petite Frenchwoman as she approached.

"Madame?" asked Winifred more than a trifle embarrassed, "you have met Lord Galveston?"

"Oh, one meets his lordship everywhere, does one not?"

Galveston, a muscle jumping in one cheek, nodded and pretended to concentrate on adding the final touches to his and Winifred's painting.

"This one is such a one for flirting with all the prettiest ladies," Madame continued her teasing. "But he cannot seem to make his choice from among the bevy of beauties willing to lay down their, er, all before his, hmm, feet. So strange, we feel. Why, when we discovered he was coming, we all awaited, breathlessly, to see whom he'd take for his mistress and who it was he would deny." She chuckled softly. "And then, my sweet English jewel, I find him with you?"

"But not taking her for my mistress," said Lord Galveston, his voice so dry one felt an arid breeze.

Madame de Montholon's tinkling laugh filled the glade. "Instead you paint her a picture. Are you any good?" she asked coming nearer and then nearer still, and somehow moving Winifred from Lord Galveston's side.

Lord Galveston set the brush in the box and lay it down. He rose to his feet on the side of the easel away from Madame de Montholon. "As you see. Merely an amateur effort. And now I must bid you both good day. My party will believe I have deserted them." He bowed to Madame. And, turning slightly, catching her eye for half a moment, he bowed to Winifred. Then he turned and quickly disappeared up the path.

The look Madame sent after him was deeply soulful. "Ah, that one! He will drive us all quite mad before he is done. You know him well?" she asked Winifred without a break, turning a sharp look on the withdrawn young English lady she'd met only the day before.

"We met at a house party just this summer," said Winifred shortly. "He left rather abruptly—a family emergency."

And she'd forgotten to ask!

"Ah, la! Those English house parties. We all know about your English house party!" Madame gave Winifred a twinkling look. "Such delightfully sinful parties, are they not?"

"Are they?" asked Winifred and, sensing a trap, continued carefully: "I'm certain I've never attended one which could be labeled so, but then I wouldn't know, would I?"

"La, you English. So cold. So reticent. So unwilling to confide all to a friend?"

The humor underlying Madame's remarks finally got through to Winifred and she chuckled. "It seems," said Winifred, "that you are unwilling to believe what I confide. Truly, I have never witnessed anything the least bit sinful. We have these rules about unmarried females, you see. I would be unlikely to have seen or even to *hear* of a single dissipated do-ing."

"Ah." Madame's brows arched. "I will ask your Lady Belemy. *She* is not an unmarried girl who, by your English rules, must be protected. She will know. Perhaps she, too, was at this house party at which you met Lord Galveston?"

"I'm sorry to be forced to inform you that she was not."

"Ah, well . . . perhaps his lordship's friend? Lord Ramsbarrow then." Madam chuckled. "I see from your expression *he* was there. And perhaps your expression reveals you wish he were not *here?* But yes! I will ask Lord Ramsbarrow! Such a lovely flirt as the man is!"

They had rejoined the pick-nick party by then. Winifred was relieved to discover it was breaking up. She didn't know how much more of Madame's teasing she could gracefully swallow.

But Galveston was here. He was in Paris.

Winifred lost track of the conversation, which became quite general, as she wondered at her more rapidly beating pulse, at the way the sun seemed to shine more brightly, and the birds sing more sweetly . . .

When they all came together for tea later that afternoon, Winifred displayed her watercolor to Lady Belemy and Clare.

"Why, my dear, this is excellent!" said her ladyship, casting a rather surprised glance at Winifred, who was not known for her talent with a brush.

"A major improvement from the last work you did." said Clare. She sent a speculative look toward her friend. "In fact . . ."

"In fact you would be quite correct, I did only the basic brush work. It was finished by . . . another."

"Ah!" exclaimed Clare, something in Winifred's voice

giving her the clue she needed. "Someone actually took your brush from you and finished the painting?"

"Yes. He—" Winifred interrupted herself. "—I mean, this person taught me a great deal. Just watching this person add a bit of color here and there, and then add that branch to the front which makes the rest seem farther away somehow! It was . . . enlightening."

"Is that what you call it?" teased Clare.

"Don't you start!" Winifred glowered.

"Start what?" asked Lady Belemy, darting a look toward Clare and back to Winifred.

"You will never guess," said Clare, "who finished Freddy's picture for her."

"If I will never guess," said Lady Belemy, suddenly able to make a very good guess, "then you had better tell me."

"*I*," said Clare, "would guess Lord Galveston was one of the guests at Winifred's pick-nick party."

"You would be wrong," retorted Winifred.

For a moment Clare pursed her lips, frowning. "Wrong. He wasn't a guest. Then he must have appeared while you were painting." She grinned. "Your blush proves me correct in *that* guess. How long has he been in Paris?" she asked, making the question sound as innocent as she was able

"I don't know. At first I wondered if he'd followed us across the channel, but something Madame said makes me think *he* will believe *we* followed him." Winifred's face crumpled in a fashion utterly unlike the woman the others knew. "I cannot bear it if he thinks that! And—" She hid tears in her handkerchief "—what else can he think?"

"That I invited you to join me in a jaunt to the continent and the need to buy Clare's bride clothes was an added inducement for accepting. Do not concern yourself that he will not understand exactly why you have come to Paris. But do—" Lady Belemy dropped her kind voice and spoke more sternly. "—help me understand why it would be so terrible if the man thought you'd followed him? *Why* that would be so unbearable?"

"I will not have him thinking . . . thinking . . ."

"Knowing?" substituted Clare softly.

"Knowing . . ." Winifred raised her face from her handkerchief. "Nonsense. There is nothing to know."

"Then you are behaving in an exceedingly foolish fashion, are you not?" asked Lady Belemy.

Winifred drew in a deep breath. She really didn't understand why she was so unsettled by the knowledge Lord Galveston was nearby. She didn't understand why her world felt a better place, why life no longer seemed something she must simply endure. At least she'd not admit any understanding. Even in her private heart.

"Winifred, our gowns arrived for the Embassy ball. They are more lovely than promised," said Clare, drawing Winifred from her rampaging thoughts.

"The ball?"

"Tomorrow evening. We'll eat early so that we may leave a trifle early," said Lady Belemy. "I like to watch people arriving. One can see the gowns most clearly when they're introduced." She had caught Clare's hint they should change the subject although she was deeply intrigued by this new side to her goddaughter, a young lady she'd thought she knew from the inside out. But *how* she wished to probe!

Still, at this point, it would be, she decided, very like pushing a tongue into a sore tooth. There would be a pain as well as the very strange sort of pleasure one felt. Freddy might like talking about Lord Galveston—but mostly she'd feel the pain.

And it would be the pain the chit would remember, pain she'd associate with her godmother, and that would be a terrible thing. No. As curious as she was, decided Lady Belemy, she must not push for confidences until Freddy herself felt ready to give them!

There was the wee problem, of course, that Freddy might *never* feel ready.

Fourteen

The Ambassador had sent invitations to every Englishman with the least pretension to class who was currently residing in Paris. In addition, he'd invited every European who had a shred of reputation. The French were, of course, well represented, but there was a large sprinkling of Russians and Austrians, to say nothing of Dutch, Germans, Spanish, and Portuguese. Here and there in the babble of languages a finely tuned ear might hear one or another of the Scandinavian tongues and last, but by far the most exotic personage, was a high-ranking Persian who was, just then, visiting the city.

Clare clung to Winifred's side, fearing she'd become lost. Winifred, a trifle nonplussed herself, kept an eye on Lady Belemy, determined she'd not stray far from that lady's side. Neither young woman long retained the place she desired. Two lovely young Englishwomen, dressed in the best Paris had to offer, instantly drew the attention of the gallants. The two were besieged before they were well into the ballroom and the sticks of their fans filled rapidly with names, many of whom they didn't know—and some they weren't certain they wished to know.

Clare managed to escape to Lady Belemy's side and hand her her fan. Her ladyship consulted a French friend whom, fortuitously, she'd found in the crush. The two ladies crossed out two names. Clare smiled at her chaperone and, the music starting up just then, welcomed her first partner.

Winifred, rejecting several more requests for dances, managed to offer her fan to her godmother. The same two names were crossed through and Lady Belemy was returning it to Winifred when a hand plucked it from between them. Winifred had no need to see who had approached. Somehow she *knew*.

She heard a scribble, another, and reddening very slightly, accepted the fan, hanging it from her wrist as she walked off with her first partner. Lord Galveston had signed his name twice! She wondered which were his dances. With luck they'd not be far distant. She'd no interest in the puppy leading her through the stately, old-fashioned contra dance with which the ball was opened and was glad there was little time for conversation between them since she had a great deal of difficulty merely concentrating on her steps.

She managed to turn off his soulful looks with a laugh and a few well-chosen words, allowing him to laugh at himself. Winifred marveled at what she'd just done. A teasing remark or two was, she discovered, far more entertaining than her normal reaction to such flirtatious ways on the part of her partners, which was a blank look and a pretense she'd no notion what was going forward.

She practiced her new art on her next two partners. It worked on the first, but the second was an overly passionate young Russian aristocrat who took himself far too seriously. She never discovered his reasons for settling heart and soul upon herself, but she was only slightly alarmed by his threats to cut his throat if she didn't instantly retire with him into the gardens.

With something approaching exasperation, Winifred finally told him that if he insisted on cutting his throat then he was to have the goodness to do so where he'd not get blood on anyone's gown and he was to find a place where he'd not damage his hostess's carpets. It would only be polite.

She got a deep groan in response and not another word from the gentleman except a half-sighed, "Sweet cruel," as he left her at Lady Belemy's side.

"Fallen foul of Czar Alexander's cousin, have you?" asked Lord Galveston sarcastically, when finally he led her out. "I assume you realize he falls in and out of love almost as often as he changes his cravat?"

"So I guessed. His quite extraordinary passion arose too quickly to have a basis in anything except a love of being in love."

Just as Marcus led their waltzing steps out onto the terrace it occurred to her she was dancing that sinful dance! What's more, Lord Ramsbarrow had been correct. She'd been enjoying it very much! Of course, going outside and *not* dancing it might be considered still more sinful!

"Do you really think," she asked politely, "that you should have danced me through those doors?"

"I've this set and the next, the only time we can talk this evening, and I think we should. Talk, that is." He drew in a deep steadying breath. Holding her gaze, he asked, "Freddy, did you, as I hope, follow me to Paris?"

"You know I'd never do such a thing. That morning when we met over my watercolors I thought perhaps *you* had followed *me,* but—" She sighed softly. "—I soon learned you'd been here for some time."

"Yes, your, hmm, *delightful* hostess said enough you could not have failed to guess it." He was silent for some time. "I can't bear it a moment longer. I *must* know. Winifred, that blasted ghost didn't follow you, did she?"

Winifred found it necessary to suppress a giggle at the desperation revealed in his tone. "Lady Gwenfrewi," she said, soothingly, "is tied to land owned by the Alistaire who wed her, which in some directions lies beyond what the family has now and in others doesn't extend so far. It certainly," she teased, "doesn't stretch to Paris."

"Hmm. I wish I'd asked for a map when we were there."

"Why?"

"I needed to know . . ."

"Yes?"

"And although you said . . ."

"Galveston?"

"Even at the ball . . . ?"

"My lord, what is it?"

"You see I was never certain . . ."

"Lord Galveston, are you quite all right?"

Galveston groaned softly. "Never mind."

For another long moment they stared across a balustrade at a fountain, the water of which sparkled in the light of the many lanterns hung among the trees.

His hands tightened, relaxed, tightened again around the cool stone. "Blast," he said. "This will never do. Who knows who will come through those doors and disturb us. Come along," he ordered rather abruptly.

Taking her elbow, he led her down the few steps and onto a well raked path.

"Where are we going?"

"That summer house." He nodded.

Docilely, knowing she should do no such thing, Winifred followed Lord Galveston's lead. He didn't halt until he stood exactly under the middle of the pointed roof structure open on all sides. A small lantern with dark yellow glass hung above him, shedding a faint but mellow glow. Marcus stared down at her. "Winifred, I must admit I have missed you."

"You say that with more than a little exasperation, my lord," she said, holding herself a trifle more stiffly.

"Did I? Well, I'm not surprised if I did. I told you before I left your home I'd not allow a ghost to choose my wife for me. I'm still angry about that. Your blasted specter forced me into behaving in ways I would never behave toward a young and unmarried woman. I do not appreciate being manipulated. Even by so ancient a mentor as your meddling ancestor!"

"Nor do I. I have sworn, always, that such beings do not

exist." She moved and reached for the wrought iron railing surrounding the little house. "I have been forced to admit that one ghost, at least, is very real indeed."

"Hmm." He turned and they both faced the garden.

The long silence was broken by Marcus. "Winifred, are you still of the same mind about marriage?"

Winifred drew in a sharp breath. "I . . . don't know."

"I suppose that is better than I'd expected, if not what I'd hoped."

"For what had you hoped?"

"That you'd reached a more positive attitude."

"You offered friendship, my lord," she said with just a touch of her old chill. "Don't pretend it was otherwise."

"I see no contradiction."

Winifred digested that. "You believe one can be friends and . . . something else as well?"

"Given what I've been told is a long tradition of happy marriages in the Alistaire family, a tradition which should have been bred into you, I don't understand why there is any need to explain—"

She gave him a look heavy-laden with confusion.

"—but I will," he continued more gently. "My parents were the best of friends, Winifred. They were also, something I understood as I grew old enough to see the signs, the best of lovers. And, my doubting Thomasina, they've been very much a happily married couple for over forty years."

"I . . . see."

"Do you?"

She didn't answer.

"Freddy, what is it you fear?"

Winifred drew in a deep breath. "I fear being dominated by my husband," she said almost at once. After a moment she added, "I fear losing my identity, that which makes me *me*." A longer pause and she began, "I fear . . ."

"Yes?"

She sighed. "Please. Don't insist I continue."

"But there is more?"

"Yes."

He sighed in turn. "We progress, I suppose. Winifred, I've no desire to dominate anyone. Especially I've no desire to turn you into something other than you are. I like that tart tongue and your ability to stand up for yourself and the fact you've a mind and opinions of your own. I do not like people who turn themselves into mats under the feet of others. Not only, my dear Winifred, does it disgust me to my soul, observing such behavior, such people are *boring.* Think of Mrs. Moorhead-White if you need an example!" He glanced at her. "Have I reassured you?"

"Words."

"When have I ever *acted* in a way which contradicts those words?"

Winifred thought back over their relationship. She cast out those occasions when, as she either knew or guessed, Lady Gwenfrewi had manipulated his behavior and discovered there wasn't all that much left by which she *could* judge! And so she told him.

He scowled and then sighed. "You, my beloved friend, are a puzzle I'll not solve this evening—" He studied her as if he still hoped to do so. "—and, if I do not get you back to Lady Belemy, we'll find you ruined, me with my reputation as an honorable man in shreds, and both of us ostracized!"

Marcus offered his arm. Winifred took it.

As they approached the terrace, they saw Lady Belemy awaiting their return. It was obvious she'd been watching them and that they'd been as well chaperoned as if they were seated in a drawing room, their chaperon sitting quietly in a corner working at her needlework!

"Your reputation is safe, my lord," teased Winifred, looking ahead and noticing her ladyship's presence.

He grinned at her. "On the contrary. Although I'll not lose my reputation as an *honorable* man, I'll surely have lost the other."

"The other?"

"Who will now call me a rake! I didn't once attempt to kiss you."

They were chuckling when they reached Lady Belemy's side. She looked from one to the other and saw less than she'd hoped but more than she'd expected. "Come along, Winifred," she said, biting back a question about their relationship. "Your next partner will be hunting for you and rumors of the most damaging sort will fly if he cannot find you."

Later it occurred to Winifred to wonder why Lord Galveston had *not* attempted to kiss her, and to rue the lost opportunity to once again experience those strangely interesting, warm and tingly feelings which even his most innocent touch induced in her—but not in anything like the degree his kisses did!

The next few days were frustrating for Lord Galveston. Either the Belemy party were not at home or their salon was littered with young men, and a few *not* so young, courting Lady Winifred and Miss Tillingford. It was impossible to have any sort of conversation. Lord Galveston, on the third occasion when he found the salon crowded, didn't try to get close to her but, after a few words with Lady Belemy, left.

Lady Winifred watched him go and wondered . . .

The next day, when she was again surrounded, a note was delivered by a pert maid. Half an instant after scanning the message, Winifred crushed the paper and, right in the middle of one of the Czar's cousin's long-winded compliments, rose to her feet. His eyes bulging, he stopped in mid-sentence.

Winifred didn't even blush. "Gentlemen, I've done the unforgivable! I have forgotten an appointment. Everyone must forgive me, because it is imperative I depart at once." She smiled brilliantly, moved quickly to Lady Belemy's side where she bent to whisper in that lady's ear. Lady Belemy gave her a startled glance but, after half a moment, nodded. Smiling widely, Lady Winifred made what passed for good-byes as she left the room.

Fifteen minutes later, having scrambled into her habit, she hurried through the back garden to a gate where she found a gardener awaiting her. Using a magnificently wrought, oversized key he unlocked the gate and, with a wink and a smirk, bowed her through.

"How," she asked Marcus, "did you arrange that?" She eyed the mare he'd brought for her use with a critical eye. It was nowhere near so good an animal as Much More Likely, but looked a decent mount.

"Bribes." He smiled into her eyes. "I wished to spirit you away from your admirers."

"You bribed me, too. I have longed for a good ride. Where—" With not the least hesitation, she accepted his help reaching the sidesaddle. "—are we going?" Winifred looked down to where he stood by the stirrup he was shortening for her.

"Anywhere but one of the *parcs!*" He chuckled. "There I'd merely lose you to other riders wishing your attention. There is a way through the suburbs and into the country that isn't too long a ride."

She looked around and noticed no groom followed them. "But exceedingly dangerous to my reputation?"

"Ah! You have noticed the groom remained behind. I won't deny there is some danger. I think it unlikely anyone of consequence will be going this way, but it is not an impossibility."

"You do not worry that you'll be forced by convention rather than a ghost into wedding me?"

"I've come to the conclusion I no longer care how I wed you, my dear, just so long as I do." He was looking ahead and didn't see the sharp, wondering look she sent his way. "If it seems to the world that I am forced to it by the world's strict rules of convention, then so be it. I will know otherwise."

"But I will care," she said slowly, fearing that, if forced to wed her, he'd come to blame her.

He pulled up. "It is up to you, my dear."

She too drew to a halt. "I . . . will chance it?"

"And if we are caught?"

She stared a hole in the road. "I will retire to a nunnery?"

"Somehow I doubt that," he said. "Whether you are aware of it or not, my love, you've an exceedingly sensual nature. A convent is definitely not the place for you."

"And your bed is?" she responded a trifle tartly.

"Along with my home, my hearth . . . my heart."

Winifred found herself drawing in a harsh breath at that last. Did he truly mean he loved her? Unable to look at him, she stared between her horse's ears. *Truly* loved her? She bit her lip as she wondered if it made a difference if he did?

"I offer you my heart," he asked softly, "and you've no response?"

"I . . . don't know what to say."

"Perhaps that you love me too?"

"But perhaps . . . I do not?" She turned and caught a quickly hidden look of pain. "Marcus, I don't *know.* I've denied the existence of love and all that goes with it for so long I simply haven't a notion what it is I feel for you. I had thought it friendship. I liked that. It was something I could accept. But . . . more? I just don't know."

"Do you deny you find the kisses we've shared as enjoyable as I do?"

"But surely that isn't love?"

He laughed. "Oh Winifred, what will you say next? No, that in and of itself is not love. But it is part of loving. Let's endeavor to think of other clues to how you feel. For instance," he added after a moment's thought, "how did you feel when you read my note?"

"Relieved."

"Relieved?" He looked blank for a moment. "Why relieved?"

"I could escape those idiotic men boring on forever about my beautiful eyes and magnificent hair and their truly outrageous references to my lovely form!"

"And a note from just anyone would have left you feeling the same?" he asked softly.

"Of course." She heard the softest of gasps and sighed. "No, that isn't true. There *was* more. I was very glad of the opportunity to share a ride with you. With *you*. With my *friend—*" She looked at him, then straight ahead. "—*not* with just anyone."

"I am exceedingly pleased you are so honest, my love. I was very near to turning us around, returning you to Lady Belemy, and leaving Paris for the Antipodes!"

"Don't *you* start spouting nonsense. I get enough of that from the men who haunt Lady Belemy's drawing room!"

"Excepting that my destination would have been other than the Antipodes," he insisted, "it was *not* nonsense! If you'd meant it, I'd have had to leave Paris. I could not have borne to have been so near you with no hope of ever getting closer."

"I do wish you'd cease flirting with me," said Winifred crossly.

"Do you? Perhaps some day you'll understand there is a difference between flirting and my telling you my feelings, but, for now . . . as you will." He thought for a moment and then asked if she'd planned her costume for the rapidly approaching *bal masque* which was talked about by all at every opportunity.

"I can't make up my mind," she admitted—also forced to admit she was chagrined he'd taken her at her word and was no longer flirting. "Clare is determined to be safe. She'll be a traditional shepherdess."

"*Is* that safe?" asked Marcus, surprised. Winifred looked a question and his expression changed to one of mock horror.

"Safe? Here in France where it was the Queen's playing at being a shepherdess at Petit Trianon out at Versailles that was one of the last straws, breaking the French and bringing about the revolution?"

Winifred smiled. "I doubt if one English maid dressed as a shepherdess will lead to another revolution, but I will mention it to her. She is such a sensitive soul she will change her mind not because of any danger, but for fear of giving offense to some Frenchman."

"And Lady Belemy?"

"Ah! Her ladyship has decided to dress as one of Macbeth's witches. From Shakespeare?"

"That should be a sight to see."

"If she allows her imagination free rein, I'm sure it will be."

"But you have not made up your mind?"

"I've thought, perhaps, someone from our history."

"Queen Elizabeth."

"Why Elizabeth?"

"You've the same sort of presence I imagine she had. There is a problem with her red hair, of course. You'd require a wig."

Winifred considered the suggestion and nodded. "Have you decided who you'll come as?"

"Dudley, Earl of Leicester?"

"Elizabeth's supposed lover? You wouldn't dare."

"I wouldn't?"

She glared.

He chuckled. "I don't suppose I would, then. How about Sir Francis Drake? I'd like playing the free-freebooter, I think."

"That would be in character, would it not?" she teased. She fell silent, her eyes darting in every direction. They'd reached the countryside and Winifred pulled up so as to be free to look around. "This is delightful," she said. "Why do we never come this way when on a pick-nick, I wonder?"

"Oh, a variety of reasons, but the strongest, very likely, is because there is so little likelihood of seeing one's friends and acquaintances with the result that one may not be seen oneself!"

Winifred laughed, touched her mare with her quirt, and set off at an easy canter. Marcus followed, trailing just far enough behind he could feast his eyes on her straight back and the graceful movements of her body as she adjusted to the demands of the ride.

A country inn beside a canal appeared and he drew to her side. "Will you stop and drink a lemonade if they have it?"

"Or even cool well water. I am becoming overheated and that will not do!"

"Why not?"

"A lady never allows herself to become too heated, did you not know?"

"You are wrong. There are occasions when it is not only permitted that a lady become heated, but required."

"Never."

"Ah, but there is," he teased. "Think how you've felt when I've kissed you.

A becoming flush reddened Winifred's cheeks and she was almost reluctant to put her hands on Marcus's shoulders when he reached to help her down. His hands on her waist, however, were inducing just that sort of warmth which he'd mentioned, and she knew it would not go away until he released her.

Except . . . he didn't release her. She was trapped between the mare and the man she could neither deny nor give into. What, she wondered, despairing, was she to do?

Something of what she felt must have shown in her face, because Marcus instantly stepped back, holding her a moment so she'd not fall. He then suggested a stroll before they took refreshment and offered his arm.

They took a path alongside the canal, coming to an arched bridge. At the center they stopped and leaned on the balustrade. As they stared down into the waters both gasped slightly when, silent as a breath of air, the prow of a long narrow boat appeared.

The prow gradually emerged, grew to half a boat, then three quarters. A young man holding a guitar leaned against the cargo stacked in the middle and covered by canvas. He smiled up at the two on the bridge, his teeth white in sunburnt skin. Lifting a guitar he strummed a few notes, then began singing a French song Winifred had never heard. She felt Marcus stiffen beside her and glanced at him.

"What is wrong?"

"You don't understand his words?" he asked rather sharply.

"I can understand Frenchmen when they speak but have difficulty when they sing. I wasn't trying to hear words, but merely enjoying the sound."

"Good," said Marcus.

"Good?" Winifred laughed softly. "It is a naughty song?"

"Very."

"If you were a truly good friend, then you would translate if for me," she teased.

"I will." He gave her an enigmatic look. "Someday."

"You will forget," she pouted.

"When you are able to understand it, I will translate it for you."

"Is that a promise?"

"If you wish. But *only when you can fully understand* will I fulfill it," he warned.

"And when will I understand?" she asked, and wondered at herself. Was it, perhaps, something in the French air which turned her into a flirt?

"The sooner the better!"

There was something ever so slightly dangerous in the heavy-lidded look he cast her way and Winifred felt herself withdraw.

He sighed. "I fear it will not be as soon as I'd like."

Again they stared at the water for a long silent moment before Marcus straightened. He led her back to the inn and into a walled garden. When he'd seated her under an arbor, he went to find someone from whom he could order their drinks and check that their horses were being properly walked and watered.

He returned to seat himself across from her at the table. "Winifred, what can I do to resolve the situation between us?"

"I . . ." Winifred thought wistfully of the daily rides they'd taken when at the castle, where no one worried if they went off together—as would be the case if they were caught in today's prank. She put the thought aside. "Do you think it must be resolved? Can we not go along as we've been doing?"

"Tempting fate, you mean?" When she refused to admit to his meaning, he waved his hand around the inn's garden. "You do know what would be said if we were seen here, do you not?"

"Yes, of course." She looked at her hands and found she was twisting her fingers in an awkward fashion. She smoothed her gloves and put her hands in her lap.

"Or is that what you hope? That the decision will be removed from your hands and that you'll be forced to do what you really want to do?"

Winifred's eyes rose to meet his steady gaze. "Of course not!"

"Are you sure?"

"I couldn't be such a fool."

His gaze didn't waver.

"Could I?" she asked in a small voice.

"I think perhaps we can all be fools," he said, his tone thoughtful, "when our minds are in disorder and we know no way of untying the knots in which we find we've bound ourselves."

"Knots?"

"Haven't you tied yourself up in knots, my dear?"

"You mean I would feel a fool to wed you when, for a decade, I've sworn loudly, to whomever would listen, that I'd never wed?"

"I'm sure that's part of it."

"And the rest of it?"

He hesitated. "I don't know, do I? You admitted, in the ambassador's garden, that there was something . . . ?"

Winifred rose quickly to her feet and moved to look through trailing vines toward the canal.

Another barge, a twin to the one they'd seen from the bridge, passed slowly in the other direction. Two men poled it, walking along the sides of the barge and pushing it forward and then, lifting their poles, returning to their starting point and repeating the process. When it was well beyond the inn Winifred turned slightly and looked up at Marcus, who had joined her, watching in silence.

"You are very patient with me, Marcus."

"I have no choice, do I?"

"I don't think it would bother me—" She cast him a quick grin. "—at least not *too* much, to have society laughing at me for marrying after insisting I would never wed. That I could bear. I have never been too caring about the opinion of others, you see." She clutched the nearest pole holding up the arbor. "It is the other that I fear . . ."

"The other which you will not explain and because you won't, I cannot help you with a solution."

She heard and disliked the priggishness in her voice when she said, "It is not something I can discuss with you, Marcus."

"Friends can discuss anything. Winifred, it isn't fear of childbed, is it?"

She blushed. "I hadn't gotten so far as childbed in my thinking!"

"Ah."

She dared a quick look. What, she wondered, had she revealed by her thoughtless remark? Speaking quickly, to prevent his pushing where she could not bear him to go, she said, "I do not think I'd fear to bear a child if I could choose my own midwife."

"How is that?" he asked, his interest caught.

"Some seem to have less difficulty with childbed fever than others. There are some midwives where the new mother very often succumbs to it, but others where one almost never does."

"So you would choose on the basis of the woman's record. That makes a great deal of sense."

"I must remember to warn Clare to check carefully when choosing."

"Miss Tillingford!" He cast her a startled look. "She's . . . ?"

Winifred took half an instant to read his expression and then chuckled. "It is only that she wishes a large family, my lord," she said with a prim look. "I did *not* mean to imply that she will, within in a few months, be in need of such services!" She heaved a sigh that verged on the exasperated and added, "My lord, you know both Lord Somerwell and my Clare. How, for an instant, could you have thought such a thing?"

"The passion of the moment." He shrugged. "It can happen before one thinks."

Winifred sobered, visualizing that scene which had frightened her so badly. "Surely not."

"But of course. I assure you, my dear, that *not thinking* is a rather important part of the whole—" He glanced sideways. "—as you will eventually discover. But not until we are wed, of course."

Winifred's back straightened. She'd just been shockingly reminded of why she feared men and spoke stiffly. "Do not make the rash assumption that we *will* wed."

Marcus sighed. This was a step back but, perhaps, before that, they'd made as much progress as he could have reasonably hoped. "I believe the horses will have cooled," he asked, politely. "Shall we have them tacked up and return to town?"

"I suppose we must. I'd not realized, until today, how much I miss the country. I wonder how much longer Lady Belemy will remain in Paris."

"Surely for some time yet," said Lord Galveston, startled.

Winifred sighed. "So I fear." She brightened. "Ah well, Clare's wedding is scheduled for the last of September. We cannot stay here forever since we must return to make plans for it."

"You dislike Paris?"

"I liked it very well until the ball at the Embassy. Since then we've not had a moment we could call our own." She cast him a glance. "Until today. Thank you."

"I will have to arrange more time for you alone."

"Hmm. Did I hear a note of satisfaction in that?"

One brow quirked and laughter could be seen in his eyes. "I can hardly arrange it if I am not there to oversee it, can I?"

"I suspect you could, but I doubt you will."

"Very true."

She laughed at the satisfaction she heard in that. They talked nonsense the rest of way home or gossiped about mutual acquaintances. As they talked, Marcus managed to tell her tidbits about some of her suitors and why they should be discouraged and, if she hadn't been so glad of his advice in this respect, she would have accused him of behaving in a self-serving fashion!

Later that evening Winifred asked Lady Belemy what she thought of Queen Elizabeth as a possible character for her costume for the *bal masque*.

"I can think of no one more English than our Virgin Queen," she finished.

"Queen Elizabeth . . ." Lady Belemy studied her goddaughter. "The very thing. We must quickly order a proper costume—but how can we explain to the modiste what is needed?"

The three women discussed this problem for some time. They *could* describe it, of course, a costume with a high-standing ruff and a farthingale, but that was insufficiently detailed.

"Perhaps we can find a picture of Elizabeth . . ." suggested Clare finally. "Yes, that is what we should do."

"An excellent notion," said Winifred, who had tired of the chatter some time previously. What she wanted to do was go to her room and think seriously about something Lord Galveston had suggested. Surely she wasn't such a widgeon she wished to be forced into a marriage with him!

Was she?

Fifteen

During the days which followed, Lord Galveston managed to organize other, less dangerous parties into the countryside. Unfortunately, since they *were* parties, he and Winifred found only brief moments which were private enough they could speak of personal things.

Too brief. Nothing changed. Nothing was settled. Winifred felt she lived in some sort of limbo where she floated through life pulled first this way by one demand—Lady Belemy insisting she come to a fitting for her costume, for instance—and then another—by one or another of her suitors requiring her attention, for instance—but very rarely in the direction she wished to be pulled: Lord Galveston was so rarely nearby!

The night of the masked ball, the Belemy party arrived somewhat later than expected due to the difficulty of getting both Lady Belemy and Winifred into their costumes. Clare, a woodland sprite, wore a beautifully simple gown and a wreath of flowers in her hair. Ready early, she'd run from one woman's room to the other, lending a hand where she could. Finally they'd set out, only to discover that, although the wide avenues eased it somewhat, the chaos caused by carriages, all arriving at the same time to let off passengers, was as frustrating in Paris as it was at a London party. And as slow.

"I knew we should have left earlier," fretted Lady Belemy,

twiddling with her hand-held mask-on-a-stick. "Now we'll never see all the costumes!" For the fifth time she rearranged the layers of tattered strips of material, ranging from palest gray to deepest black, which formed her skirt. "I should have sat down in this silly costume," she fumed. "It is fine so long as I stand, but when I sit the panels slide around and off my lap. I don't like having my knees hidden by nothing but this petticoat, even if it is black and not at all thin."

"We can go to the retiring room and have the front panels basted to the petticoat if you like," suggested the wood sprite.

"That would take forever. No, I will simply stand."

"The whole evening?" asked a startled Queen Elizabeth.

Lady Belemy laughed. "I am being quite silly. Of course I will not remain on my feet the whole of the evening. So I will be sensible and cease to concern myself about my tatters. Ah . . . finally! I believe we are next."

His face nearly hidden in the hood of the most extraordinary of monkish costumes, a footman led them through the halls to the end of a line waiting to step through double doors onto a balcony, where they'd be announced by a lordly abbot. Even as members of the Church of England, which had split from the Catholic church in Henry VIII's reign, they found it disconcerting—if not outright shocking!

Soon they were just inside the door and looking down into the huge ballroom which appeared even larger, thanks to tall mirrors hung one after another along the inside wall. The opposite wall had sets of opened double doors along it, adding the width of terrace to the ballroom. Even with so much space, the ballroom was crowded.

"Shakespeare third Witch, from Macbeth," intoned the major domo, thumping his crozier on the floor. Again the boom of the staff. "Queen Elizabeth." And a third. "Woodland nymph."

The Belemy party swept down six steps and into the crowd at the bottom where, before she could think, Winifred found herself swept into a waltz.

"Sir!"

"Madame Queen?"

"Oh." Recognizing Galveston's voice, she relaxed into the dance which was, as Lord Ramsbarrow had once promised her, quite delightful. "You frightened me."

"You didn't recognize me," he said, making his words sound even more sad than he felt.

"You didn't give me time to recognize you." She pulled back in his arms and looked him up and down. "Hmm. Walter Raleigh, I presume?"

"After he'd been knighted, of course."

"Oh, of course." He swept her into a breathtaking swirl of steps. When she'd her breath back, she said, "A rather incredible man, Sir Walter."

"An interesting life, at least. But the Queen. A truly exceptional woman, our Virgin Queen." He eyed Winifred. "Ah," he breathed, "and you are another extraordinary woman." His tone changed from bantering to intense. "You are, you know. Those weren't empty words or a banal compliment."

"You will turn my head, my lord."

"Don't I wish!" It was Lord Galveston's turn to hold her away from him. He studied her. "Do I remember seeing that particular costume in a painting?"

"Very likely. We found a book of etchings in which it was reproduced. The modiste did an exceptional job of copying it, did she not?"

Above the wide skirts, his hand moved along her side and around her back a trifle more than was acceptable. "I think," he said, adopting a judicious tone, "that she copied more than what one could see in the picture."

Winifred felt herself blushing. "You, my lord, have no business knowing about such things."

"You do not deny it?"

"It is a very old lady who has an interest in . . . er . . . in historical costume and has studied it all her life. She knew exactly what went under the outer gown, how each layer was constructed, and was delighted by the opportunity to make it all." Winifred felt the blush returning. "She taught me to get into it, too, but I'll admit that, this evening when we were without her aid, it was more than a little difficult. I do not see how women of earlier ages managed to be ready for anything!"

"Or how men managed to get them ready for, hmm, anything else!"

"Marcus!"

"Sorry," he apologized, but his eyes glittered behind the mask covering the upper portion of his face and a rather wolfish smile, his teeth white against faintly tanned skin, suggested he lied.

Winifred decided he was in a mood where it was the better part of valor to ignore his more provocative remarks. So she said, "Then poor Lady Belemy. Her costume has tattered layer over tattered layer over tattered layer and she had them off and on six times trying to recall in exactly what order they were to be worn!"

"I must remember to take a look at her."

"But you saw us when we arrived."

"I saw *you* when you arrived," he contradicted, holding her gaze with the steady look in his own. "I saw nothing and no one else from that moment."

The feeling of warm blood returned to her cheeks. Winifred wondered at it. She'd never been one who blushed easily.

As the music came to an end, they were immediately beside one of the open doors. Before Winifred could ask Lord Galveston to return her to Lady Belemy—wherever that lady had settled herself—she was urged onto the terrace. She discovered there were any number of couples scattered along the broad flagged area and relaxed, moving toward the balustrade to stare out over the garden.

Marcus turned and half sat, half leaned against the stonework. While she stared, amazed, at the fairyland scene made visible by colored paper lanterns hung from trees and the glow of hidden lamps, the whole cooled by the tinkling waters of sparkling fountains, he watched her.

"Do you like it?" he asked.

"It is incredible, is it not?"

"Inventive, at least. The larger creatures, the fawns and unicorns, are papier-mâché. The elves and fairies, which you cannot see from this distance, but which I assure you are there, are dolls dressed in fairy costumes." He smiled when she peered, trying to discover the latter. "Perhaps we can take Lady Belemy and Miss Tillingford and explore—since there are many grottoes and nooks dangerously tempting to such as I."

For half an instant Winifred regretted that his suggestion included a chaperone, but she realized he was right. Despite what she'd almost accepted about herself since their last discussion, she didn't wish *him* to have to wed *her* at the demand of society's arbiters simply because they'd contravened some silly rule.

"Winifred, that day we rode out of Paris you . . . hesitated over the notion you be forced to wed me so you'd not have to make up your mind to it. Have you thought more about that?"

Did the man read her mind? she wondered, not for the first time. She bit her lip but then, softly, said, "You suggested it was a solution to my problem, that I'd not be seen reversing my mind which has been so very firmly made up against marriage," she said on a dry note and added, scolding, "You should say what you mean."

"I merely try to be tactful," he said and she heard both rue and laughter in his voice. He stood quietly for a moment but when it appeared she'd not respond, he insisted. "Have you? Thought about it?"

"I haven't had a moment to think of—" She sighed. "Oh, why do I lie? I have thought of little else!"

"But concluded nothing?"

"Nothing." She bit her lip. "Marcus, I fear you are never going to hear what you wish to hear. Perhaps you *should* take a cabin on that ship headed for the Antipodes."

"You wish that no more than I wish it," he said thoughtfully.

"No." Then she feared he'd read too much into that and, hurriedly, added, "I would miss our friendship."

"Is that all you'd miss?"

Winifred started to answer, but Marcus cut her off.

"Winifred, we've strayed from the topic. Do you think you would prefer to be forced to wed me rather than to change the long held creed you'd never marry?"

"It would be easier. Or it would—" She slid a quick sideways glance his way. "—I suppose, if I meant to wed you."

"But you do," he said gently.

She glanced up at him, saw something so soft and loving in his gaze she instantly felt the blood flooding up her body, her throat, and into her face. And there was, in this costume, a great deal of chest and throat to reveal the color! Winifred forced her eyes away from his and stared back out into the gardens. "I wish I could be certain of that."

"Be certain, Winifred, my love."

She frowned slightly, casting him a look questioning *his* certainty.

"You, my dear, are not an indecisive person," he answered her unvoiced question. She nodded. "When have you ever dithered for so long about anything?"

"Never."

"You see? That proves to me that, long ago, you made your decision. But now you've done so, you've the difficulty of admitting you've changed your mind about marriage."

"It is far more complicated than that."

"Yes. There is fear as well, but I have told you, we will solve that problem easily enough once we are wed."

"When you may subjugate me."

"When I may freely love you as you should be loved."

She remained silent, her knuckles white.

"I talked to Miss Tillingford, my love. Another difficult conversation, but, in the end, quite revealing." He thought of poor Miss Tillingford's blushes as she hinted around the edges of the scene which had left his Winifred convinced men were brutes and women fools to put up with them.

"I'll boil her in oil," said Winifred fervently.

"No. You will thank her. Because now I know what it is you fear and I may reassure you and help you through it."

She gave him a startled look.

"But," he added, laughing, "not until we are wed."

"I don't believe we've reached an agreement on that problem."

"True. We still have to find a means of achieving that much-to-be-desired end!"

"I cannot believe Clare would—" Her hands tightened around the stonework. "You went behind my back and discussed me with another."

"With someone who loves you and wants you to be happy, Freddy, my own true love."

"That is no excuse."

"Love is no excuse?" His voice revealed an odd combination of horror and amusement. "Winifred, you cannot mean that."

"The end never justifies the means," she said primly.

"Never?"

Winifred recalled several occasions in which she'd used devious means to achieve some end. She felt her face heating up again. "There are exceptions to every rule," she admitted.

"Believe me, my dear, this *was* such an exception."

Silently she agreed. "I just don't know . . ."

Winifred thought of his kisses, which she'd not experienced for so very long. Well, she could hardly admit to missing those! She felt a trifle angry he was pushing her for answers she could not give.

"You do not answer," he said. "Is that an answer all in itself?"

"No." That, surely, wouldn't reveal what she'd been thinking.

"Good."

Or did it? Good, he said? Just *good?* The one word sounded so full of masculine satisfaction Winifred's ire was roused.

"If," she said, exasperated, "you are once again reading my mind, I wish you would not. It is not fair that you can get into my head and I cannot get into yours."

He chuckled. "Winifred, yours is so easy to read. How can I help but take advantage of it?"

"Don't laugh at me, Marcus."

"I am not—" His voice caressed her. "—laughing at you. I merely wish it were permitted for a woman to tell a man what she is thinking when she is thinking such thoughts as you were thinking."

Winifred turned a horrified gaze his way. "What an awful world it would be if one could merely open one's mouth and say whatever one pleased!"

"Do you think so? I, on the other hand, believe it would lead to far fewer problems and complications. We tiptoe around so many subjects which, if only we dared discuss them freely, would never become problems. You, for instance, could explain to me what it is you fear and I could explain to you why it is *not* something to fear . . . ?"

"It?" The horror deepened. She stared at him. Surely he couldn't know!

He ran a finger across the back of one hand. "When I may kiss you—" His voice was soft and coaxing. "—and touch you and bring you to the very edge of passion's borders—" And then even softer. "—and then take you and myself, both, together, across that boundary and into paradise."

Something inside Winifred coiled tightly as he spoke. But words! Words could mean anything or nothing. Oh, if only she *knew!* But knew what? She didn't even know what it was she didn't know.

Winifred sighed. "Will you," she asked in something of a rush, "return me to Lady Belemy?"

Lord Galveston hesitated. Then, "Yes, I believe we've accomplished all we can." He eyed her. "Enough, perhaps."

"Enough?"

"For me to make a decision I must make . . ." He grinned. "Oh, no you don't. *You* won't confide in me and, in this, I'll return the favor." He stood away from the railing and offered his arm. "Shall we dare that crush and see if we may locate one small Macbeth witch among such a crowd?"

"We shall promenade until we do," said Winifred somewhat sternly.

"Yes, my dear," said Galveston meekly.

Winifred laughed. "You told me one day you did not care for mats in human form beneath your feet. Do not make one of yourself!"

"I will remind you of that if it becomes necessary, my love."

"I don't understand you. Surely you—" She cast him a mocking look. "—are not suggesting you'll act in an overbearing and despotic manner, tyrannizing over me and making me wish to retract my order that you not become a mat beneath my feet?"

"It is not impossible," he said.

There was a determined note in his voice which surprised Winifred, who had thought they were jesting, but by then they'd entered the ballroom and once inside there was no thinking of anything but how to remain unscathed by ill-placed elbows and feet and, on the other hand, take great care that one not harm another in a similar fashion!

Days passed after the ball with no sign of Galveston. Winifred began to wonder if, in truth, he'd taken ship for the farther reaches of civilization. But then, nearly two weeks later, another note was delivered to Winifred while among her importunate suitors. She'd thought her lack of interest would have turned them off by now. With a few, the more serious, it had worked, but there were several who, the colder the shoulder she showed them, only became more ardent.

But the note! She was relieved to discover that Lord Galveston, in a mere twenty minutes, would be awaiting her at the back gate. This time she didn't give her suitors a reason for leaving them. With a simple "excuse me" she rose to her feet and went to Lady Belemy's side. Lady Belemy read the note, nodded, and then, a hand on her arm, pulled Winifred down. She kissed her goddaughter's cheek.

Winifred was so deeply mired in the fear she'd be late that she almost failed to note Lady Belemy's odd behavior, but she did and wondered, oh, for half an instant, about that kiss.

And then her abigail was there helping her into her habit, settling her hat just so and, for some reason, wiping away a tear . . . But there was no time just now to probe into Maud's malaise. Winifred reminded herself to do so when she returned. Perhaps dear Maud was merely homesick.

The same gardener was at the gate today as before. She waited impatiently while he unlocked and swung open the wooden door set into the stone wall surrounding the gardens.

And there was Marcus. Him eyes were as alight with excitement as she felt her own to be. She went directly to her mount and put her foot into his cupped hands. He helped her to her saddle and took a moment to arrange her skirts before mounting his own horse.

"Shall we go?" he asked, restraining his prancing gelding, which obviously wished to be off.

"We shall."

Winifred touched her quirt to her horse and they set off rather more decorously than she'd have preferred, but since they were in town, it was better they not call attention to themselves. Not that she really cared. She hadn't seen Marcus since the *bal masque* when they'd danced, quite daringly, for a third time.

In the slowly dragging days and hours and minutes since, she'd realized that *not* seeing him weighed with her far more than her fear of what he could, if she gave him the right, do to her. Besides, he had assured her again and again that her fears were baseless. Shouldn't she believe a friend? And he *was* her friend, was he not?

Winifred had come to the conclusion she'd been a fool. She'd vowed to tell him when she saw him—which was today! Now!—that she'd wed him when and where he wished.

And somehow, the decision made, she had felt a light and joyful feeling filling her like the odd gas they put into those balloons men rode into the sky! She'd felt a need of something to anchor her to the ground and, once or twice since making her decision, had been surprised to discover she was not, as she'd thought, walking on air but, just as always, on solid ground.

"It is a beautiful day," she said.

She had sworn she'd not ask him what had kept him away from her. Away from everyone, if her informants were correct. He had, it was said, actually left Paris. If he'd not left word with Lady Belemy that he'd return, she'd have decided that he'd given up. But he *had* left word he'd return and Marcus had yet to make such a promise and not fulfill it. In fact, Winifred was certain that, if he ever did make a promise and break it, it would not be his fault.

But where *had* he been?

"Where have you been?" she blurted.

"I wondered when you'd ask." He waved a hand in airy fashion as he said, "I'll tell you here and there, hither and yon and, my dear—" He cast her a whimsical look. "—I am worn to a thread with all my prancing about."

She eyed him. "Such a healthy-looking thread. You will not tell me?"

"Not just yet. And when I do, perhaps you'll have guessed.

Look," he suggested, "at those children. Are they not enjoying themselves?"

"You would change the subject?"

"I would. If you will not look at the children, tell me what you see in the clouds?"

"See?" She glanced up at the sky, frowning.

"Have you never played the game of finding pictures in the clouds? I cannot believe it."

"I have. But not since Clare and I were children."

"And have you forgotten so quickly how to go about it?" She grinned. "Well, as I recall those days, we first found a sunny meadow complete with wildflowers and lay on our backs and took turns finding a cloud shape which looked like something and then tried to make the other see what we saw."

He chuckled. "You make it sound as if you had a bit of difficulty with that last."

"We never saw the same thing. Well, never is too strong a word, but—" She pointed at a particular cloud. "—tell me what you see in that one."

"A prone man with a dog's head laid on his chest," said Marcus promptly.

"While I see the top half of one of those odd creatures with the hump on his back that are said to travel the desert and go for days and days without water."

"A camel, you mean? Hmm . . ." He shook his head. "No, I can only see my man and his dog."

They continued playing the game, complete with occasional bouts of laughter at some suggestion, until they reached the inn at which they'd stopped previously. Winifred had become quite fond of that inn. She'd thought of it often. Somehow the illicit nature of their coming to it added to its natural charm, making it a very special little inn indeed.

As a result, it was disappointing to see a light traveling carriage, trunks and band boxes strapped on roof and boot, standing near to it. "Do we dare stop if someone is staying here?" asked Winifred as Marcus pulled up.

"Of course. It is our inn, is it not?"

She smiled. "I have that odd notion in my head, it is true. Intruders should find their own inn!"

"If they disturb us we will tell them so," he said lightly as he dismounted and came to help her down. "Will you go on into the garden? I will join you soon."

She blushed as she told him she would meet him there in a moment. He smiled but did not ask where she would go first, which was good. She'd no desire to reveal the embarrassing information that she must make a necessary visit to the 'necessary' which would be found at the back of the garden! Normally she would not have needed it, but today, nervous about admitting that she'd decided to wed him . . . well, she'd not be long.

She returned to discover him already seated at the table, a bottle of wine and two filled glasses before him. He pushed one toward her and lifted the other.

"To us," he said softly and drank, watching as she did so, too.

After quickly taking the long draught demanded by the toast, Winifred held the glass out before her, frowning.

"Marcus, this tastes terrible!" She took another tiny sip. "Are you certain it is not tainted?"

"It is green, I fear, but I don't believe it tainted." He eyed her glass which was something over half empty, nodded, and took it from her. "If you do not care for it, then drink no more. You sit down and I'll see if I can get us cider or lemonade instead."

Winifred sat. An warm breeze slipped over and around her. Bees buzzed about their business. A butterfly wandered across her field of vision and was gone . . . and, gradually, without realizing it, Winifred fell asleep. She almost fell out of her chair as well, but Marcus was instantly there, lifting her. He smiled down at her, a rather sad smile, but mixed in was a touch of triumph.

He had her now!

His coach had passed over a great many of the long miles between Paris and the coast before Winifred stirred in his arms. He gazed down at her, bemused by the armful of warm woman he'd held since they'd set out. *Perhaps it's as well she's waking,* he thought, all too aware of the arm which had gone to sleep. He rather dreaded the pins and needles he'd feel as it returned to normal and, if it had been anyone other than Winifred who was the cause, he'd have shifted her long ago. But, since it *was* his love, it was worth every prick and prickle.

Winifred yawned. Her head hurt and her mouth felt dry. There was an odd taste, too. Like the time she'd had a toothache and her nurse made her drink laudanum . . .

"Laudanum!" She struggled to sit up and turned a glare on Marcus who smiled back warily. "You gave me laudanum."

"Hmm." He rubbed his arm briskly, forcing the blood to flow.

"You—"

"Blackguard? Pirate?" His smile faded. "Or simply a man in love and desperate?"

"So desperate he needs to drug and kidnap his dox—"

"His *love*. Don't put any other word there, Freddy. It was nothing but love, pure and simple, which led to your abduction. Your godmother's love. Your father's love. Even Miss Tillingford's love. And last, but certainly not least, my love."

"Lady Belemy? Clare?"

"They helped your maid pack your things. What you'll need for our journey."

"And what sort of journey is that, my lord?"

"To the coast, in the first instance. Then the packet to Dover. From Dover we'll return to your home. And, as soon as your godmother and your friend arrive, we'll be wed."

"Banns require three weeks."

"A license requires no time at all. Well, three days, but that will have passed before we reach your home. I've discussed the wedding with your vicar. Your father is seeing to a wedding breakfast and inviting guests and I stopped to see my mother and father before returning. They'll be there before us and all *we* must do is arrive." He grinned. "As you see, *I* am attending to that particular problem."

"So," she said after a moment, "when you were gone from Paris, you were in England?"

"Yes." He watched her closely. "Winifred . . . are you going to be angry with me? Because if you are, I wish you'd get on with it and get it over."

She ignored that. Or seemed to. "This is all so unnecessary," she complained.

"Remember the *masque,* my dear, and you bogged down in the same old dithering? I decided that I couldn't wait for you to realize you wished to wed me. That you *would* wed me. I've forced the issue and I know I deserve every acrimonious word you will hurl at my undefended head. I do wish you'd get on with it," he finished plaintively.

"So very unnecessary," she repeated on a sigh, and looking out her window to conceal the smile hovering around her lips.

It finally occurred to Marcus that Winifred was *not* reacting as he'd expected. "Hmm . . . perhaps you would care to explain?"

"I was so looking forward to our ride, our time at that sweet little inn . . ."

"It is a nice little inn. Perhaps someday we may return and stay a day or two?" he suggested politely.

"And I had it all planned. Exactly what I'd say. What you'd say." For half a moment she eyed him and then, in a plaintive tone, she added, "How you'd kiss me . . ."

"Kiss you?"

"Yes. It would have been quite proper, I believe." She eyed him. "Once we were engaged?"

He stared at her. Then he leaned his head back against the cushions and chuckled. The chuckles turned to laughter. Contagious laughter, and Winifred joined in.

"My dear," he said, once he'd sobered and could speak again, "You never cease to amaze me."

"Is that good?" she asked cautiously

"Very good."

"Then I will take care that, through the years, I continue to amaze you, my lord."

"Excellent." He eyed her. "Must you sit all the way over there on the other side of the carriage?" he asked, once again sounding plaintive. "If we are engaged, it should be perfectly proper for you to sit right next to me."

"There is such a great difference from way over here and the four inches which would put me next to you?"

"Come see," he suggested. When she didn't move he reached for her, sliding his arm around her waist and tugging her nearer. He turned very slightly into the corner, extending his legs across her side of the carriage, and turned her so she half lay along his chest. He tried to put his chin on her head, discovered her hat was in the way and, one-handed, pulled the pins holding it on. He tossed it and the pins to the seat across from them. Then he returned his arm around her and his chin to her hair and . . . just held her.

Gradually Winifred relaxed. He was quite correct. It was a comfortable position. And she liked the secure feeling his arms gave her. She liked the steady beating of his heart which she could both hear and feel. And she liked the kiss she sensed he dropped on her braids before nestling his chin, once again, amongst them.

"This is nice," she murmured.

"This is frustrating as the devil," he objected and held her a bit more tightly before loosening his arms to mere security.

A security she liked amazingly well. "Why?"

He smiled. She knew he smiled because she felt the change in his jaw.

"My love, that is something I wish very much to teach you, but I have sworn I'll wait until we've the right. Besides, once I've begun loving you, I won't want to stop, and I will not do more than I've already done to wreck your reputation!"

"I suppose we could wait at some inn for Lady Belemy and Clare to catch up with us, watching for them along the road. Then we could all travel together and no one could say a word."

"I suppose," he murmured, but otherwise did nothing.

Winifred squirmed. She pushed against him until he allowed her room to lift away from him. She stared at him. "I am to understand you do not care for the notion, my lord?"

"Having taken all this trouble to kidnap you," he complained, "it is quite true I cannot like the notion of giving it up."

"It?"

"This time alone with you. Without chattering friends and chaperones and people wishing us to pay attention to them and then there would be other people's plans which we must abide by and—"

"And you would rather not wait for Lady Belemy and Clare."

"Now where did you ever get a notion such as that?"

"From you, my lord," she said promptly.

He grinned, but the smile faded. "Winifred, would *you* prefer to wait for them?"

"I . . . am not certain. My lord," she said a trifle shyly, "I have never before faced the prospect of several days in the company of a man who is not my father. I find that rather disconcerting. On the other hand," she mused, "if Lady Belemy were with us I could not have your arms around me as they now are. It is amazing how much more comfortable travel can be when held thusly, my lord."

The wheels, just then, slid into a rut and bounced out again. Marcus had to make a wild grab for the strap which steadied them, along with one of his boots, which was quickly pressed against the opposite seat's cushions. Once they were going along more smoothly, he left his foot there, some protection against another such jolting surprise.

"Comfortable, you say?" he murmured, laughter not far below the surface.

"I am not in a heap on the floor, you see," she said blandly. "I think I might have been, do not you?"

"It is proof, you would say, that this is the optimal way to travel?"

"Hmm."

"Then, my lady love, I believe I shall continue with the kidnapping. I would not care for you to endure the least discomfort."

"Hmm."

"Besides, there is still that problem of admitting to the world you have changed your mind about marriage. We need never tell anyone that you did just that."

"A telling point, my lord."

"I thought you'd agree."

He snuggled her close and they remained silent until they reached an inn where they were to make a change of horses.

Winifred was replacing her hat when Lord Galveston groaned softly and, giving her no choice, removed her from the seat and deposited her, with only the mildest of thumps, on the floor. He let down the window.

"Nigel," she heard him say a moment later. "What brings you to this out-of-the-way spot?"

Lord Ramsbarrow! thought Winifred. *Oh dear.*

Sixteen

The coach door was yanked open and Lord Ramsbarrow grinned in at Lady Winifred. His eyes widened, but Winifred was almost certain he only pretended surprise.

"Ah!" he exclaimed dramatically. "An elopement!"

"Nothing of the sort," she responded crossly from her position on the floor.

"Not?"

"Not."

He scratched his head. "Not an elopement," he said, as if attempting to make it absolutely clear.

"Of course not. Any idiot can see it is a kidnapping," she responded, her nose in the air.

"Oh." His brow arched. "Then it is my duty as a gentleman, I suppose, to rescue you?"

His face was sober enough, but Winifred could hear laughter not very far below the surface. She glanced up at Marcus who sat, arms folded, scowling at his friend. "Marcus, will you please tell him to go away?"

"I will, my love, just as soon as I discover why, in the first place, he is here. Nigel, why are you here?"

"I'm on my way to a wedding," Ramsbarrow responded promptly.

"Oh, of course. What else? And may I ask who invited you?"

"Lady Belemy, of course."

It had been a rhetorical question so both Marcus and Winifred were surprised by Ramsbarrow's answer. Marcus and Winifred stared at each other.

"I should have known," said Marcus with only a hint of a sigh. "I wonder how many other people she's informed."

He'd been speaking to Winifred, but once again Ramsbarrow responded. "Only one or two, I'm sure."

"One or two should be quite sufficient to ensure the whole world is informed," said Marcus resignedly. "Nigel, go away."

"But that would not be an act of friendship," whined Nigel.

It was obvious to both that it was a made-up whine, of course.

"If you recall," he continued once he had their attention, "I promised to stand with you at your wedding. Besides, I can't go away. At least not just this moment." Nigel held out his hand to Winifred. "Would not a very temporary rescue be of interest? I've a private parlor reserved in this rather inadequate inn," he coaxed, "and the best meal they can provide should be very nearly ready."

Winifred was about to say "no" when, embarrassingly loudly, her stomach growled. She felt her cheeks heat when both men chuckled.

"Oh, all right. But only a very temporary rescue," she warned.

"You may be re-kidnapped just as soon as you've finished your meal," he promised and helped her from the carriage.

Lord Galveston crawled out after and, a hand on Winifred's shoulder, gently dusted off her bottom. "The carriage floor was rather dirty, I fear," he murmured when, shocked by the touch, she glanced up at him.

She was even more shocked when, as the three of them walked toward the inn, his hand strayed from her waist to rest very low on her hip. It wasn't that she didn't like the sensations his odd touch induced . . .

On the other hand, she wasn't certain she liked them. She'd have to think about it.

She thought about it again and much more seriously when she woke from a nap late that afternoon, snuggled into his embrace as usual, but with his hand resting, once again, where it had no business being. This time it lay, warm and heavy, against her thigh.

Thanks to a lost shoe the morning of the day they were to reach Calais, they arrived too late to catch the packet. It meant finding a hotel, which, with all the comings and goings between a Britain and a France no longer at war, would, they feared, be no easy task. At the second stop, however, the carriage door was yanked opened, as before, by Lord Ramsbarrow.

"You, my lady," he said with just a touch of exasperation, "are a very lucky lady to be rescued twice!"

"You have taken rooms for us?" she asked, hopefully.

"For the three of us and for your Lady Belemy and your cousin and, I am led to understand, one or two others as well!"

"Suffering reverses on 'change, old friend?" asked Marcus, his eyes alight with laughter.

"I have not turned courier by choice, if it is that at which you hint. I was dragooned into it by Lady Belemy, who was certain you had suffered a carriage accident or had been attacked by a roving mob of bandits or that one of you came down ill from eating bad food or—"

"But why is she fretting so?" asked Winifred. "Lady Belemy has never been one to worry over trifles."

"If you would deign to enter this poor excuse for an hotel, you may ask her yourself," said his lordship, once again, and more imperiously, holding out his hand to Winifred to help her from the carriage.

Winifred was glad to discover that here, in a very busy inn yard, Marcus still knew how to behave. He offered her his arm in a perfectly proper manner and she accepted in an equally proper fashion. It was, therefore, something she couldn't understand, the feeling of disappointment welling up from a part of her anatomy she, until very recently, had never thought about.

Lady Belemy met them at the door to the large private parlor hired for the party. "At last! I thought something terrible had happened."

"But why should you imagine anything more desperate than what did happen?"

"Well?" was the instant question, "What did happen?"

"A lost shoe, is all," said Lord Galveston, not certain whether to laugh at the situation or to feel embarrassed at how public his kidnapping plot had become. "We'd have been here much earlier if it weren't for that."

For a moment an expression which looked very like disappointment crossed Lady Belemy's features. Winifred realized her chaperone had been concerned she'd been seduced by her rakish fiancé and, with it, had worried she'd been wrong to allow the kidnapping, fearing his lordship had no intention of bringing Winifred to the altar . . . and *at the same time* was rather wistfully disappointed that a romantic seduction had *not* occurred!

"So, now I suppose I must worry myself to a thread wondering if the wind will cooperate so that the next packet leaves on time," fumed Lady Belemy. "Oh dear. There is no *time*." She glared at Lord Galveston. "If I fret myself to flinders, my lord, it will be all your fault!"

"Why? Because I finally took things into my own hands and cut the knots of our problem?"

"But you have raised so many *more* problems," wailed Lady Belemy.

Galveston's hands, which had rested lightly on Winifred's shoulders, tightened slightly. "How have I done so?"

"Don't you see? We'll barely have time for a single fitting of the gown I ordered for my goddaughter to wear at her wedding! Your insistence the marriage take place in a rush makes it impossible to plan it properly."

"Just when," asked Winifred, a dangerous note in her voice, "did you order this gown?"

Lady Belemy's brows arched in surprise. "Why, before we ever left London, of course."

"My wedding gown. Before we left London," repeated Winifred. "Long before I knew I'd meet Lord Galveston again, let alone that I'd agree to wed him?"

"But my dear," said her ladyship, her whole tone and expression indicating bewilderment, "Lady Gwenfrewi had decreed it. Of course there would be a wedding!"

Lord Galveston, behind her, laughed. Winifred felt the tension draining away from him.

"That ghost has a great deal to answer for!" she said tartly.

She was very glad that, at that particular moment, it became impossible for anyone to continue the embarrassing conversation: a hotel employee knocked peremptorily. That was followed by a parade carrying in trays of exceedingly welcome food!

The enlarged party's next stop was in Dover, where several more people awaited them. Very welcome were Lord Galveston's servants with his larger and very well-sprung traveling carriage and his best team, to say nothing of his valet and Winifred's maid, who had gone ahead to arrange for hotel rooms. Maud had, of course, gone to Calais with Lady Belemy and Clare. Lady Belemy had sent Maud across the channel to arrange for rooms, unaware that Lord Galveston's valet had also crossed, ordered to do that very task.

Not only did *they,* each unaware of the other, arrange for rooms, but so too did *Lord Somerwell,* sent there by Lord Wickingham—primarily to rid himself of his ward's moonling fiancé! Or at least, if not a moonling, then certainly mooning about because he missed his Clare. As much as Lord Wickingham, in his blustering way, loved both his daughter and his ward, he did not wish to talk about either of them at any length, and Clare was Somerwell's *only* topic of conversation.

So, when the party from Calais arrived in Dover, they were met not only by Maud and by the valet, but by Lord Somerwell, who, eyes only for Clare, managed to confuse everything to a surprising degree. The hotel's manager had to be called to the desk to straighten out the chaos before everyone else arriving on the packet was sent off told there were no more rooms to be had! But soon all were settled into their places, including Clare, who, having suffered a very bad case of *mal de mer,* had had some difficulty convincing her beloved she'd be right as rain as soon as she'd had a sleep.

"Come along Somerwell," said Galveston, bodily hauling the slighter man off to the tap room. "Your Miss Tillingford will explain everything to you once she's napped. You do not wish her to be ill, do you?"

"Ill? Clare?" Somerwell had turned under Galveston's hand and very nearly escaped him, wishing to follow Clare up the stairs.

"Only if you do not allow her to sleep," said Galveston, speaking slowly and clearly.

"But I wanted . . ." Somerwell sighed. "No, of course I do not wish her ill. But I have not seen her for ever so long." He sighed and gave Galveston one of his rueful sideways looks. "I am merely being selfish, am I not?"

"Why, if you missed her," asked a curious Galveston, "did you not follow her to Paris?"

Somerwell's ears reddened. "Swore after Waterloo I never wanted to set eyes on a frog again. Saw quite enough of them then!" He lifted his cane to his mouth and then lowered it, his whole face blushing. "Besides, truth is, I hate the sea. Get sick as a dog," he admitted, hanging his head.

"Which is exactly what happened to your Miss Tillingford. You should understand that she needs a rest now her feet are on solid ground."

"Oh. That's all?"

"That's all."

Seeing how tense Somerwell had become for a simple case of sea-sickness, Lord Galveston made a mental note to warn Lady Belemy to warn Clare that when she became *enceinte,* the new Lady Somerwell should send her husband off on an errand when the time for her lying-in arrived. If she did *not,* he would likely die of an apoplexy worrying about her!

Ramsbarrow caught up with them just then. "Do you know," he said, crossly, "that *too many* rooms were canceled? I very nearly didn't get one."

"In which case I suppose you would have to share mine, but you did, so you won't, correct?"

"I don't know about that. Our host has put me in the attics!"

"Ah. That is no place for such a prince among men. You may have half my bed if you can swear you no longer snore."

Now it was Lord Ramsbarrow's ears which turned bright red. "Marcus!"

"Ah, you cannot swear. Then I think it is the attics for you after all!"

Somerwell, looking from one to the other, suggested rather hesitantly that Nigel was welcome to the other room in his suite.

"You have a suite, Somerwell?"

"Thought maybe Lady Belemy and Miss Tillingford might have the other room. Didn't think." He hung his head.

"Well," said Nigel, clapping him on the back, "I am very glad you did not!" He went off to have his things moved to Somerwell's suite.

The augmented party reached London, where they discovered Lady Westerwood awaiting Lady Belemy in Lady Belemy's best salon. "I am very sorry to intrude," she said, "but Lord Wickingham has, hmm, *requested* that I offer you whatever aid you feel I may give."

"An excellent notion," said Lady Belemy, easing Lady Westerwood's embarrassment. They instantly put their heads together to make plans.

Winifred took one look at the schemers and grimaced. She

turned back to Lord Galveston who, lowering his voice, said he must be off. That he too had a few things to do in London before they continued on to Wickingham Castle.

He didn't truly try to gain Lady Belemy's attention when he said goodbye to her and Lady Westerwood. Therefore, he and Winifred, who wished to see him to the front door in the hopes they'd have a few moments alone, were almost out of the salon when Lady Belemy called them back.

"You, my lord, will join us for dinner tomorrow evening. Then we will, all of us, go on to the theater. I don't suppose there will be anyone there worth our notice. Not at this time of year. But you will be seen with us and it will be reported, and that will settle the tattlers into a new line of talk. That is all," she said and turned back to Lady Westerwood, dismissing his lordship very much as she'd have done her butler.

"I apologize for Lady Belemy's abrupt behavior," said Winifred once they'd left the room. "I do not understand what has gotten into her."

"Propriety?" suggested his lordship.

"Lady Belemy?"

"Oh, I'd think it likely. While we were in Paris she let down her hair and could bring herself to agree to my plot. Now we have returned to England and she's suddenly aware of all the ramifications which she could conveniently ignore while far away."

"You, however, had those ramifications in mind all along?"

"I put them in the scales when weighing up my options. I will admit I didn't, perhaps, give them quite so much weight as I might have done? After all—" Galveston's eyes twinkled and his grin was, once again, on the wolfish side. "—I too was in Paris."

"Hmm. I wonder what I should blame for my own lack of proper forethought?"

"Perhaps that you, too, were in Paris?"

She half glowered, half laughed.

"Or," he said more soberly, "perhaps you wished to have that time alone with me almost as much as I did with you?"

Instantly Winifred sobered as well. "I think we needed it, my lord. I have concluded it might be a very good thing if people who were thinking of living the whole of their lives together had some time in which they could discover . . ."

"Discover?" he asked softly when she paused.

"Oh, all sorts of things. Whether they actually had any conversation between them, for instance."

"I think we found we did," he said, thinking over the long, involved discussions of very nearly everything with which they'd passed the time.

"I was almost certain we did, but it is nice to know, is it not?"

"What else?"

"Well, my lord, you do not snore when you sleep."

"I suppose that is very important."

She grinned. "And you seem to have no little irritating habits which would gradually become big, horribly grating habits." She frowned. "Do I?"

"Not that I noticed."

"That's all right then."

"Is that all?"

"Very likely not, but Philbert is waiting to let you out." She held out her hand.

Galveston grasped it and tugged. "Philbert. Turn around." Philbert obligingly turned his back and remained that way. Finally he heard a gentle sigh and a murmured, "I must go."

"Yes."

"Philbert, you may open the door."

"Very well, my lord," said Lady Belemy's very proper butler.

The procession which set out from London a few days later was led by Lord Galveston's carriage, containing his lordship and his best friend. They were followed by Lady

Belemy's huge old traveling carriage, occupied by Lady Winifred and Miss Tillingford. The third carriage, Lady Westerwood's, carried Lady Belemy and its owner, and the fourth held Lord Somerwell. Behind his lordship two more carriages lumbered along filled with baggage and servants. All in all it was an impressive sight and drew crowds wherever it passed.

"Must we take so many days on the road?" asked Winifred when they reached the coaching inn chosen for their first night. "I really dislike spending any more time then necessary cooped up in a carriage."

"We must or I will be worth nothing when we reach the castle," scolded Lady Belemy. "As it is I don't know if I'm on my head or my heels."

"I will be very glad when this farce is over and things can settle back to some sort of routine," complained Winifred.

"Farce! It is your *wedding,* my dear. How can you suggest it is a farce?"

"It has become a circus! When I decided to allow Lord Galveston to kidnap me, I thought it the easiest thing ever. We would arrive home and, with the license he'd bought, we'd be wed. It never once occurred to me we'd become a public entertainment!"

"When you decided! My dear, what can you mean?"

Winifred remembered that no one need know she'd decided, independently, to wed him. "Oh, Lord Galveston is a gentleman," she said, airily. "He'd have brought me back to you if I'd objected strongly enough."

And with that, Winifred went into the garden where she found Marcus and spent a lovely hour strolling along the stream. Clare and Lord Somerwell disappeared out the front door. Lord Ramsbarrow, taking one look at the women remaining in the private parlor, instantly went off to see if he could find a willing maid . . . so Lady Belemy had only Lady Westerwood with whom she could bemoan, over and over, the inadequate plans the two had contrived while in London.

"Such a slipshod affair! I will never forgive myself for

allowing Lord Galveston his way. It is a disgrace that Lord Wickingham's only daughter be wed in such a skimble-scamble fashion!"

"It is, you must remember, something of a miracle she is to be wed at all!" murmured Lady Westerwood.

"Oh no. Once Lady Gwenfrewi decreed a wedding would take place, then there was no possible way it would not."

"Has she never been wrong?"

"Never. She arranged my first marriage, you know," said Lady Belemy rather shyly.

Lady Westerwood, who had hopes the castle ghost might look kindly on her own future, gave every encouragement to Lady Belemy to describe the house party at the castle where she'd met her husband.

"He died far too young," finished her ladyship dreamily, "but we were so very happy while he lived. Only eight years, but such wonderful years . . ."

Three days later Lady Gwenfrewi took her customary place among the carved angels decorating the beams in the Wickingham Village church. She was pleased all had, finally, gone as it should. She smiled to herself as she recalled how she'd actually been in despair on more than one occasion as she plotted to get Lord Galveston and her dear Lady Winifred properly together.

Or *improperly,* should one say?

That had been her original plan and she still believed that, if Lord Galveston had only seduced Lady Winifred, the whole thing would have been settled much more quickly. Lord Galveston was, after all, a very proper rake. He should have had Winifred on her knees begging him for what Winifred still didn't know was a tiny piece of heaven here on earth.

Ah, if only it were not against her principles to find a secret place in their bedroom tonight and enjoy, vicariously of course, his teaching Winifred the proper ways of loving! Or did she, wondered the ghost, mean the *improper* ways?

A rustling among the guests caught Lady Gwenfrewi's attention and she spun around until she could see the back of the church. "Ah," she murmured. "Very lovely. Beautiful, in fact."

Lady Winifred, a trembling hand on her father's arm, stood just inside the double doors. The organ wheezed into a more joyful song and, grinning broadly, a much relieved Lord Wickingham escorted his only daughter toward the altar.

Lord Galveston, turning to wait for Winifred, felt his heart rise in his throat at the sight of his bride. Her gown, ordered by the wonderfully foresighted Lady Belemy, was a pale blue and shimmered where tiny brilliants made patterns taken from the Wickingham lily and the Galveston rose. The silk flowed around her slim form as she walked toward him. A veil, made of the very finest of lace, covered her face and head and flowed down her back very nearly to her feet.

As she approached he held out his hand. When he felt how she trembled he turned to her, placing his hands high on her arms. He leaned toward her and, gently, asked if she were certain.

"Yes," she murmured and gulped.

"It will be all right, my love. After all—" He touched her lips gently. "—Lady Gwenfrewi has promised we'll be happy. Smile for me?"

She smiled. A rather weak smile, but a smile nevertheless. "Ready?"

After only the smallest fraction of a moment, Winifred nodded.

"You may begin," said Galveston to the waiting vicar, who smiled benevolently on the young couple.

Above them, Lady Gwenfrewi danced a dance of joy among the wooden angels. Oh yes. She'd chosen a very proper husband for her Winifred. How could the chit *not* be happy with such a wonderfully sensitive man?

* * *

Later that evening, after the reception and during the dance which followed, Lord Galveston disentangled his love from among the men surrounding her, half seriously threatening mayhem if they did not let her go. He led her up to the hall where they'd been, hmm, *introduced* by Lady Gwenfrewi.

"If you are here . . . ?" asked Lord Galveston softly. A brief chill passed up his spine. "Ah. You are. We just wished to say thank you. You have, my lady ghost, done us a wonderful favor and we just wished you to know we appreciated it."

"Marcus," said the new Lady Galveston softly. "Look."

Ahead of them a dancing weaving spiral of . . . *something* . . . took shape.

"You, too, are pleased, I think," continued Lord Galveston. "Now we have one more request of you."

A tinkling laugh could be heard from the swirling mass.

"You know."

A figure formed briefly. With an old-fashioned curtsy, the ghost disappeared.

"Well?" asked Lady Galveston.

"I believe, my love," said Galveston slowly, "that that was a promise she'll not join us in our bedroom."

"Thank heaven," said Winifred fervently. "I'm a nervous wreck as it is and if I knew there were a voyeur watching, I think I'd curl up and die." She chuckled, but there was truth in her words. "Even a ghostly voyeur would be too much!"

"We will, finally, be alone just as I've wished for so very long. Will you trust me, my dear? Will you come with me now to our rooms?" Marcus held his breath until, her hand shaking very nearly as much as it had at their wedding, Winifred laid it in his outstretched palm.

She might still be afraid, the look in her eyes informed him, but it also said she trusted him to the bottom of her soul. She walked steadily at his side to their bedroom.

Dear Reader,

I hope you enjoyed reading about my little Welsh ghost. Sometimes I wonder if she's half guardian angel rather than one-hundred-percent ghostly lady!

My next story, A LADY'S PROPOSAL, September 1998, doesn't have a ghost in it, but the heroine fears she may soon become one which is why Lady Helena Woodhall wishes to wed. A husband may protect her from the "accidents" she's experiencing. Accidents which, very quickly, seem less and less accidental.

Simon, the new Earl of Sanger, has unexpectedly inherited the title and a heavily mortgaged estate. He'll not ask a gently bred woman to live from hand to mouth while he pays off his debts nor does he wish to be labeled a fortune hunter, as he would be if he solved his problems by wedding one. Unwilling to wed, he is appalled when Lady Helena proposes to him.

Lady Hel isn't any too happy her proposal is turned down. Lord Sanger, who is strongly attracted to her, isn't particularly happy he must deny her, but that's nothing to his distress when, soon after, circumstances demand they instantly become engaged—or suffer scandal!

Lady Hel's engagement disturbs someone else as well. The person who wishes her dead . . . !

My novel after that, in the spring of '99, involves a heroine who travels to France accompanied by the hero. The hero thinks he's escorting her to her husband's side, and isn't best pleased when he learns the man is merely her brother. Or is he?

Cheerfully,

Jeanne Savery

P.S. Mail reaches me at P.O. Box 1771, Rochester, MI 48308. Please include a self addressed stamped envelope if you'd like a reply.

BOOK YOUR PLACE ON OUR WEBSITE AND MAKE THE READING CONNECTION!

We've created a customized website just for our very special readers, where you can get the inside scoop on everything that's going on with Zebra, Pinnacle and Kensington books.

When you come online, you'll have the exciting opportunity to:

- View covers of upcoming books
- Read sample chapters
- Learn about our future publishing schedule (listed by publication month *and author*)
- Find out when your favorite authors will be visiting a city near you
- Search for and order backlist books from our online catalog
- Check out author bios and background information
- Send e-mail to your favorite authors
- Meet the Kensington staff online
- Join us in weekly chats with authors, readers and other guests
- Get writing guidelines
- AND MUCH MORE!

Visit our website at http://www.zebrabooks.com